Courtship

Courtship

A NOVEL OF LIFE, LOVE, AND THE LAW

RL SOMMER

Cover design by Elmarie Jara/Ankerwycke.

This is a work of fiction. Names, characters, places, and events either are the product of the author's imagination or are used fictitiously. Any resemblance to actual persons, living or dead, events or locales is entirely coincidental.

Printed in the United States of America.

19 18 17 16 15   5 4 3 2 1

Library of Congress Cataloging-in-Publication Data

Sommer, R. L.
  Courtship : a novel of life, love, and the law / RL Sommer.
    pages cm
  ISBN 978-1-62722-842-8 (alk. paper)
  1. Love stories. I. Title.
  PS3619.O455C68 2015
  813'.6--dc23
                              2014038841

Discounts are available for books ordered in bulk. Special consideration is given to state bars, CLE programs, and other bar-related organizations. Inquire at Book Publishing, ABA Publishing, American Bar Association, 321 N. Clark Street, Chicago, Illinois 60654-7598.

www.ShopABA.org

Dedication

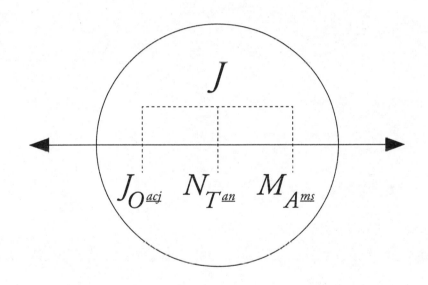

Prologue

Oh, I have been asked. By my children, by my friends. And I have thought about it, in my own private times.

First love. Late love. Of course, there are differences. Not that I'm so experienced. I wasn't one of those women of my era who had many lovers. I had only two. In 60 years, mind you.

But they were great loves. Special loves, each of them. And very different. Each came as a total surprise. Each was very different from the other. Love of youth. Love of age. Two people giving each other everything they have to give. In my case, I didn't think it could happen twice.

When my granddaughter, the novelist C. K. Van Rhym, asked me if she could write about this, I replied: "Who would want to read about an ordinary life, one with two private love affairs?" I would not have agreed to talk about my intimate life with any other writer. But she is my blood, and a professional; I loved her first book. "Deft, touching, sensitive," the critics called it. I was flattered that she wanted to novelize my life. "Just be honest, Grandmother," she said. "Don't try to edit your experiences. Trust me." And I did.

And while she worked, I got to spend all those sweet times with her, talking about the old days. We old folk love that, don't we?

I told her what happened, as best as one can filter the days of one's life. I gave her all my albums and photos to keep if she is to be our family historian. Her uncles and mother reminisced as well, of course, as did our dear friend, Cassie the elder, now tied to her home, but with time to talk. And she found so much about her grandfather's law cases, Daniel's too, in our family scrapbooks, and Micah's law firm's records, and on the Internet.

She taped our conversations, then went off to write. And then, this—this wonderful, old-fashioned love story appeared.

Initiation to Love

ONE

The Announcement

❧❦

Though neither of them lived in New York City, their names were linked that first time in a brief article in the *New York Times*. That would happen two other times in the course of their lives.

The first time their names were listed in a simple announcement, on an inside page of a 1951 midweek issue of the *Times*, reporting the annual selection of Thayer Scholars. Their names appeared under geographical groupings in the announcement, which the Thayer Scholarship committee had made public at its foundation offices in Boston. The prestigious awards have been made every April since 1940, when Bradford Thayer established a fund, the Thayer Trust, to award generous scholarships for outstanding, all-around American students to attend Cambridge University in England for two years of postgraduate studies. Their names—along with 28 others—and some spare vital statistics that barely described them were on the list of 30 predicted future stars: Micah Lehman, University of Chicago, Region 3; Anne Marbrey Strong, Sweet Briar College, Virginia, Region 4.

Anne could only vaguely remember when they first actually met five months later at the banquet in New York City for all departing Thayer

Scholars, the night before their week-long transatlantic voyage on the *Queen Elizabeth*. Their introduction was perfunctory. Each Thayer fellow was asked to stand as his or her name and a few defining facts about them were announced. The scene had been as intimate as a mass wedding. There were so many people to meet, so much anticipation and excitement, that later Anne could only recall a swirl of activity, a coming-of-age in a new place, her easy entrance into a larger world. No one person or conversation or image had stayed with her.

Anne always felt she'd belonged. And in her smaller world for the first 20 years of her life, she not only belonged but was the queen of her personal small but secure society—family, schools, friends. She had a regal look that bore the best of both her parents' finest features: her mother's social stateliness and poise, and her dark beauty; her father's quiet intelligence and strong, lean physical features. Both parents were prototypes of charm and style. Dated photographs and family albums show Anne as tall—five feet, nine inches—long legged and slim. Her hair was cut short, like Cassius in the movie *Julius Caesar*, and it encircled a chiseled, fine-featured face with marked cheekbones, a straight nose, full lips, and a natural broad smile that crinkled her eyes and brightened her surroundings. Anne projected poise and charm, a sense of belonging that flowed from her physician father's patrician New England family lineage and her mother's socially prominent Southern ties to community and church.

Theirs had been a whirlwind romance. Father from New England met Mother from South Carolina when he was recruited to join the university medical school faculty in Charleston. Mother was one of several eligible local prizes recruited for a dinner dance at the elegant yacht club at the tip of the peninsula, overlooking a distant Fort Sumter (there was no question this Yankee was entering Confederate country), to introduce the promising young candidate and hope that he would be seduced by local society. Mother was ready to settle down, chased but not caught by the local candidates, so Father—handsome, reserved, charmed by events—never had a chance. She was the second young woman the dean's wife brought to the table for an introduction and a dance; candidate one was forgotten and candidates three and four never entered the race.

Ethan Strong stayed in Charleston, and married Alicia Marbrey within a year, after a suitable period of introductions, lookings-over, and endless parties. He became a professor at the medical school and eventually the region's leading heart surgeon. They bought and renovated a stately home on Legare Street, below Broad, the best area of Charleston, with a wide and deep side porch running along the whole second floor and overlooking a prize garden that Alicia turned into one of the city's attractions at garden club tours. Dr. Strong brought the proper professional status to the family; Alicia handled all the social activity.

Anne was their first child; her brother, Philip Marbrey Strong, soon followed. Young Phil was a family problem. He was extraordinarily handsome, but dyslexia kept him in constant academic trouble. Through family connections, they were able to get him into the state university, where he partied too heartily and majored in dating fast coeds and affronting modest ones. He never finished his degree. Youthful energy not appropriately channeled led him into recurring embarrassing incidents that family connections were regularly called upon to correct. Eventually, he was sent to "find himself," working in a distant relative's bank in Columbia, South Carolina. Philip and Anne were not close or even friendly; he resented her successes, her star status in their family, and she was embarrassed by his frequent, often very public, failures.

Anne always had been the family achiever. Athletic, naturally and effortlessly bright, she rode with ease, captained the Ashley Hall field hockey and tennis teams, led her class in every category, and could have gone to college anywhere. It had been a foregone conclusion she would attend a fine woman's college. Smith tempted her, and so did Bryn Mawr. But she chose Sweet Briar because it was closer to home, she had friends there, she could board her horse, and it wasn't too far from her long-time but off-and-on childhood boyfriend, who was in college in South Carolina. She would step out of her circle, but not far. At Sweet

Briar, she was president of her class and salutatorian. Four easy and happy years passed quickly and easily at the peaceful, verdant Virginia hillside college that protected, prized, and prepared the pick of Southern womanhood. The year before graduation, Anne was chosen to lead the procession at the Charleston Cotillion, held each year by the St. Cecilia society at the temple-like Hibernian Hall. In the best sense of the term, she was an eligible Southern belle.

Anne dated every attractive young man at the Porter-Gaud School in Charleston, every jock star from the Citadel, and every potential president of the Charleston Bank, but she never lost her heart or self-control. From grade school on, off and on, she dated Wiley "Red" Carter. Everyone in her social circle viewed them as the perfect couple, including their parents, who were sure that eventually they'd be in-laws. Wiley's father headed the biggest engineering firm in South Carolina and was plugged in to the political and social scene, and Red, his only son, was at Clemson preparing to join the firm as heir apparent. The Carters and Strongs loved the others' children and were friends themselves.

Anne held private reservations about this presumed libretto; never sure why, she refused Red's fraternity ring when she left for college. They wrote and dated at college weekend events, so family expectations were encouraged. Anne dated others while she was at Sweet Briar. She knew she wanted something more and different, but she didn't know what, or who. She was facile in the ways young women were socially active, but protective of their virtue and reputation in those days. Anne and Red Carter were cautiously intimate, but Anne was always in control. Red was patient; in those days young men waited for their wife, but cavorted with "faster" coeds. Eventually Anne gave away her virginity to an older fellow, at a weekend fraternity party at the University of Virginia (locals referred to it as "the University") during her freshman year. It was an act of independence due less to love or even infatuation than simply because she thought it was time. She was curious. The episode was so unrewarding she didn't have a repeat performance (many tried; none succeeded) throughout her matriculation at Sweet Briar.

At college Anne's grades were excellent. She was the extracurricular campus queen, popular with students and faculty, a good athlete and a good student. Her mentor, an award-winning poet-in-residence, urged her to aspire to be the school's first Thayer awardee. It was the second year women were eligible for the award. The first year's crop was all from large Ivy League schools. When Anne was chosen by the Thayer Committee, it was the delight and talk of everyone at the small college. It seemed especially apt for the star of a small, sheltered women's college to be one of the first awardees to bear the title of the misogynist benefactor of the prize. Brad Thayer had served as an advisor to the Allies in England in World War I. After the war, he made a fortune there and in the United States in aircraft manufacture, and wished to become a patron of "men of excellence" in the Anglo-American world. Changing social mores eventually forced participating schools to seek to amend the gender-based application of his grant, and the trustees reluctantly agreed.

Anne was accustomed to gliding easily through life; she didn't have a fixed goal. She had begun to contemplate taking science courses at Cambridge aimed toward a future in medical school, despite her father's urging that she use her two years simply to read widely and travel the continent, leaving the region's health care to him. She ignored her mother's lectures that she finish "rounding out" her schooling and come back to Charleston to be the prize flower in her well-cultivated social garden.

Micah told her later that he did recall the first time he saw her. It was at the Thayer embarkation party. Not that bells went off and thunder struck, the sort of scenes that happen in romantic movies. He was too anxious about his place at this event, too awed by what was happening to him. He felt out of place socially. He'd come far, fast—jumped hundreds of years in a generation, his older sister Ada had said in conversation over a family dinner that summer. From his grandfather's remote village in Poland to his family's modest but comfortable apartment in Chicago, in one generational leap, and now a scholarship to Cambridge, England; how remarkably different his life and options were from his father's and grandfather's.

The Lehman family—Micah's grandparents—had arrived at Ellis Island at the turn of the century from Bransk, a Polish shtetl. They settled in Chicago (émigrés sought comparable climates and geography, and any personal contact) with a distant cousin whose name and address was all they knew about anyone in America. As was the custom, Cousin Avram, now Abe, offered them a place to stay for a week and his help finding them a job and an apartment of their own. Micah's father, Shmuel, soon Americanized to Sam, had left school and gone to work at the ripe old age of 13. He found menial jobs with landsmen selling wares on the bustling streets of Chicago. Like others in his milieu, a combination of energy, aspiration, and fear of the consequences of failure moved Sam Limonovsky (the full name was soon cleaned up, Anglicized by the ear and preference of his new society) from menial job to job. As soon as he could afford it, he married his teenage sweetheart, Lida, whose family had come from an adjoining village in Poland. Good fortune and his ferocious industry in the Depression years led Sam to a partnership with two other immigrants who took over a modest dry goods store in a neighborhood that grew from cheap and dangerous to bustling and gentrified by an influx of people like the Lehmans. Eventually, the store became his (one partner died, and Sam borrowed money and bought out the other) and he was able to slowly move his family into the middle class—but barely.

Like the offspring of other families from this time and place, Ada the first child and Micah the second and last were doted on, prodded to excel in the local public schools, and sheltered by their social and economic circumstances. Both won scholarships to the University of Chicago; Micah's academic scholarship meant his tennis team scholarship could be paid to him in other, cashable ways. By commuting from home and working six days a week at part-time jobs along with study and team practice, he had barely looked up for four years, but he thrived. He knew little of the world outside Chicago. He and his sister worked after school and summers (at first in local stores, later at college-generated jobs), and they lived contented if confined lives. They liked and respected each other but were distant, preoccupied, more dutiful than engaged with each other. Ada continued on to medical school—rare at the time for young women—and was preparing to become a pediatrician. Micah wanted to be a professor of English literature. He'd won a prestigious fellowship for promising literary lights at the University of Chicago and was being encouraged to write and teach by his mentors there. But the family pushed him to follow in Ada's footsteps and to enter a revered, financially rewarding profession. The words "to be a doctor," in those days and in his world, suggested certain financial success and social acceptance. The consequence was that during the Thayer years, he'd planned, reluctantly, to pursue a combination of courses in science to bolster his faulty pre-med background, along with an advanced reading and writing program that he would audit for the joy of it. His real goal was to attend Trinity College and study under Lloyd Jameson, the internationally respected critic and literary scholar.

Micah was striking looking, though not handsome by the conventional, high school, American standards that governed taste in his young world at that time. He was tall, six feet, two inches. His mother called him skinny, though in more elegant circles *lanky* would have been the descriptive word of choice. He shambled a bit when he walked, the mark of someone who was big in size but not athletic in gait. His features were swarthy, his head large and hairy, his beard heavy and dark. But what shone through his uncertain mien was an overall kindliness; he had a sweet smile, a warm and modest charm that made him popular with his elders, and that touched girls especially.

Micah never really thought of himself as sexy or even socially attractive. There simply hadn't been enough time or opportunity for him to develop those skills. Even so, he'd been invited to all the sweet-16 parties by the Jewish girls in his circle, and he was the first choice at spin-the-bottle parties and Sadie Hawkins dances by every Rebecca, Rachel, and Shirley in the neighborhood. Once, the "hot tamale" in his crowd, Debbie Tannenbaum, touched him down there provocatively while they necked on her family couch, but he wasn't sure what to do about that or even how to enjoy it. More to his surprise than as a manly conquest, he was seduced in a deserted office at the college by Laura Molino, an older bohemian graduate student from New Jersey who worked with him one semester at the university in Chicago. She taught him new insights into James Joyce's avant-garde literary style, as well as the possibilities available to boys and girls their age if one were to lose oneself in uninhibited, untutored, unembarrassed passion—emotional conditions that had neither been discussed nor experienced before in Micah Lehman's small world.

At the Thayer farewell party, there were comments by sophisticated, world-traveled veterans of the program, promising the members of the new class that they were about to have the time of their lives. Packages of informational materials were distributed to the 30 lucky students describing the final arrangements for their journey and matriculation. Micah recalled noticing Anne, and thinking she was lovely, but he felt her style was foreign to him and outside all his experiences. She seemed unlike anyone he'd socialized with. He would not have thought to approach her. The formal dinner service included more spoons and wineglasses, placed and replaced by more hands, than Micah had ever encountered at one meal. The hand-inscribed bilingual menu promised a dinner with countless courses punctuated by endless speeches. Later, there was dancing, but Micah stayed at his table chatting with some of his new classmates. He only danced once, with a quiet girl, a budding but boring future mathematician from Stanford, a Chinese-American whom he noticed sitting alone at her table. When the slow fox-trot ended and the bouncy lindy began, he walked her back to her table and returned to his. Anne danced each dance with a different handsome Thayer alum or fellow traveler, and each young man at her table. When Micah glanced in her direction, she was always engaged in animated conversation, lively dancing, and much head-jogging loud laughter.

Anne and Micah didn't really meet until the first night aboard ship.

TWO

The Introductions

Anne's parents reserved several suites at the Yale Club on Vanderbilt Place, "the best buy in the city during summer weekends," for the two days before departure. They dined well, long luncheons at the Algonquin, dinner at the Edwardian Room at The Plaza, a late-night indulgence at Luchows. They shopped at Abercrombie and Fitch, Saks, and Rogers Peet and saw an overrated, overpriced Broadway play. Three of Anne's best friends came to see her off, tearfully, as did the Strongs' closest Charleston friends, the Savages, who had been Anne's godparents, along with one of Dr. Strong's medical school roommates, Eli Milling, who was now teaching at Albert Einstein Medical Center in New York City. Her long-time beau, Red Carter, surprised her (though not her parents, who had arranged the surprise), arriving at dinner the night before she sailed.

Anne's was one of many bon voyage parties in the staterooms of departing tourists on the bright end-of-summer day the *Queen* sailed. Her room was bustling with Anne's and her cabin mates' friends and families. People crowded into the passageway holding their champagne glasses and tiny sandwiches while they air-kissed cheeks and toasted to Anne's imminent adventure. When, at noon, a startling blast of the vessel's foghorn and a broadcast announcement from the captain signaled departure time, Anne's admirers gave her final hugs and friendly instructions.

Micah's farewell party had been held several days earlier, at his family's apartment in Illinois. He described it to her after they met on their week-long, life-changing voyage. The rooms overflowed with all the local people who were close to Micah. There had been an article about his award in the Chicago newspapers (and a picture), and he was a local celebrity, a source of great pride in his modest community. Longtime friends from high school, a few newer ones from the university English department, including his favorite professor, some aunts and uncles and their children, even their garrulous if uninspiring young rabbi toasted Micah with seltzer, wine, and slivovitz and ate from platters overflowing with rich food, including his mother's specialties, stuffed cabbage and noodle pudding. The guests gave the departing scholar presents that embarrassed him, but whose contents generated much laughter and hugging. A homemade "Bon Voyage" poster hung across the entrance to the crowded living room. After a serious prayer, the rabbi teased, "So, Micah, you're the first member of our synagogue to go to Trinity College. Some alma mater for a Jewish boy." His father beamed, silently; his mother cried.

He arrived in New York City by train the night before sailing to attend the embarkation Thayer party. Next morning, after a restless night in a nearby inexpensive hotel, he came aboard the *Queen*, early and alone. Micah dropped his bags in his assigned room; then he went outside to the deck railing to watch the cargo loading and the people arriving and departing up and down the gangplank. Eventually, he could feel the ship and his life slide slowly away from its guarded mooring and into the open-endedness of the Hudson River. Micah had a lump in his throat as he watched the Statue of Liberty and Ellis Island float by— they could have been metaphors of his brief life—as the grand *Queen Elizabeth* started its slow entry to the Atlantic. Micah wondered why he wasn't overwhelmed with joy as were the revelers he passed in the corridors around the staterooms. Why the sense of—guilt? He'd earned this wonderful adventure; years of hard work had gotten him here. He wished he felt more excited, more celebratory. But he did not.

Micah was deep in thought when he was startled by the greeting of a young man he recognized from the Thayer party the night before. Portly, excessively verbal, Falstaffian in presence, Roy Garfield was a Columbia graduate who was studying Japanese literature. He spoke four languages, which he used casually to speckle his conversation, and dressed a bit foppishly—a wrinkly cord suit with a vest (with a drooping gold watch chain and attached Phi Beta Kappa key) and a blowsy bowtie, in the summer? Micah thought Roy probably was the height of urban fashion, especially in comparison to his own Midwest, Ichabod Crane, off-the-racks garb.

"Deep in thought, my new friend and colleague," Roy's words, delivered in a stentorian tone, snapped Micah out of his daydream.

"Yes, I guess. Didn't we meet last night? I'm Micah Lehman." He stuck out a hand and flashed his mate an earnest look.

"Roy Garfield. First trip abroad?"

"Yes, yes, I'm from Chicago and this is my second time in New York, let alone Europe."

"Well, my dear boy, I've been abroad before, but never to Chicago. So there. Always wanted to come with my book of Carl Sandburg to witness 'the hog butcher of the world,' but haven't made it yet. Perhaps you'll show it to me someday. Today, we should toast your good fortune, and my own. Come to my suite and partake of some of my savory bubbly." His new friend took Micah by the arm and directed him toward the stairs down to the staterooms. Roy's family was not there, nor was anyone else to see him off. Micah wondered why, but didn't ask. As Micah looked back one last time at the scene behind him, the New Jersey coastline was disappearing from the starboard view, as was the tip of Manhattan Island on the port side, and the great liner was entering an abstract world of sky and water.

"Where am I going?" Micah wondered to himself.

"Lead on," he implored Roy.

Roy was show-offy but appeared to be worldly—the kind of character Micah never had associated with before. But there was something he liked about him nonetheless; perhaps that he had sought out Micah, led him confidently into a social scene that was new to Micah, and made it unnecessary for Micah to initiate the contacts that were necessary if he was to participate in his new world. From his rush of conversation it was clear Roy knew about boat schedules and planned events, about the planned Thayer meetings and shipboard social occasions, and Micah found following Roy's pushy leads easier than asserting himself.

Roy had a more expensive cabin, with only one roommate, an uncommunicative fellow who was not in the Thayer group and would spend all his time alone in the cabin, reading and avoiding all social contact. Roy and Micah shared some of Roy's "bubbly"; he didn't like the champagne and presumed it was his uncultivated tastes. They exchanged introductory niceties, then separated. At Roy's urging, they arranged to meet for drinks before dinner—not a regular practice in Micah's life.

Micah was in a four-person cabin, but in a different part of the ship, along with three other young men from the Thayer group—a fey but friendly fellow from Greenville, Mississippi, who planned to write the great American novel; a soulful, crew-cut aspiring Methodist minister from Wilkes-Barre, Pennsylvania; and a fallen—and effeminate—theology student from Portland, Oregon, who was planning to shift his focus to theater. After introductions, the mediation accompanying the assignment of berths, and some perfunctory unpacking, the four roommates agreed to meet for dinner. Micah took a long walk around the ship, exploring all the alcoves, peeking into the public rooms, reading shipboard information on bulletin boards, observing the movements of passing shipmates.

Later, when Micah arrived at the salon, he saw Roy at a table with two young people, one of whom he recognized from the farewell party the night before. All three were dressed more formally than he and were animated and loud in their conversation. Roy waved to Micah, motioning him to join them.

"What will you have, chap?" Roy bellowed, lifting an arm toward the bartender.

Micah was hungry and preferred to go directly for dinner. He wasn't accustomed to cocktail hours, but he thought he should be sociable and join the group for a drink. Roy was drinking a Pimm's Cup, which Micah had never heard of. The other fellow, James Ordway, another New Yorker, a friend of Roy's and the other Thayer fellow from Columbia University, was sipping something colorless, "juice of the juniper berry," he claimed, from a long-stemmed cocktail glass. And the young lady, a raucous and pretentious blond from California whom Ordway had just met at the bar, was drinking a ghastly looking green fluid that she informed Micah was Chartreuse. She pronounced it with laughable, guttural accents, "shar–trúce," as she set it down like a cowboy would a shot of whiskey at a Western bar. Micah asked the waiter for a beer.

"Boddington all right, sir?" the bar waiter asked.

"Sure." Micah didn't know a Boddington from a Pimm's Cup, but went along with the waiter. He never had been much of a drinker, and that was usually a longneck Budweiser with tennis buddies after a hot match, or a rye and ginger ale on prom night.

The conversation he joined was stilted and Micah was uncomfortable. The young woman, Mauney White, was describing a prior trip to Switzerland. "Geneva," she recalled, was such a sophisticated city, but *so* expensive. "It was, you know of course, where Stendhal lived when he wrote *The Red and the Black*," she informed her small audience. In fact, as Micah recalled from his studies, but did not bother to add to his companion's superficial commentary, Stendhal was a Geneva journalist, but he wrote his famous novel based on an actual murder that had occurred in a small cathedral in a tiny village in the east of France, named Brangue. Micah was not interested either in showing off his superior information or pointing out his table mate's superficial knowledge. He was quiet, uncomfortably out of place.

As the others bandied about strained anecdotes and shared inside jokes, Micah's mind wandered. He hoped this new adventure would improve. So far, he felt foreign and out of sorts. To his relief, his group of cabin mates soon appeared, urging Micah that they go to dinner together. The three at the table with Micah were invited to join them, but only Roy accepted. James and Mauney preferred to dine later, after a more sophisticated cocktail hour. Mauney thought dining late was worldly; James was investing in the prospect of a week-long assignation.

When the five young men arrived at the dining room, a maître d' greeted them, looked over a seating chart, then led them across the vast, slightly tilting room toward a table set for four, but which was soon expanded to seat five. At surrounding tables in this large tourist-class dining room, six other groups of Thayer colleagues were at various stages of ordering, dining, and conversing. Anne was at one table that seated the largest group. The people there were involved in several simultaneous and very ebullient conversations.

Micah enjoyed the company and light conversation of his new coterie. Dinner was served in high style, and consumed with gusto and easy camaraderie. Roy was an engaging conversationalist and an entertaining storyteller. The budding novelist from Mississippi, Jackson Dunlap, was too, and Micah liked him more than the others. Two hours later, he and his dinner partners left the dining room, strolled along the corridors, and peeked into the various social rooms. His three roommates lingered in a small, almost empty lounge where there was a piano. Jack Dunlap played while the others sat, smoked, and daydreamed in cozy armchairs. Micah liked the music Jack played—Cole Porter, Gershwin, Ellington. It was elegant and cosmopolitan and classy, qualities Micah felt he lacked in comparison to his travel mates. He would have stayed and listened longer, but Roy eventually took him by the arm and led him away, to the ballroom, where dance music was playing.

"Come, my good man," Roy remarked, acting the worldly socialite, "let us join the swing and sway of the entertainment, and assess the lovely maidens yonder."

The bar and the tables around it in the large ballroom were crowded.

At one long table, a group of the Thayer fellows sat in a haze of smoke, clutter, and conversation. Led by Roy and waved over by one of the familiar fellows at the table, the two new friends joined the eight others, as people snuggled closer and chairs were pulled up to make room. Easy introductions and handshakes across the table were extended. Later, Ann remembered that first meeting, when she reached out and shook Micah's hand and made room for him to slide in next to her on the banquette. She remembered the rush of conversation that followed and her first impressions of Micah.

"Where y'all from, Mike?" she asked as he sat beside her.

"Chicago. It's Micah. People always call me Mike, but it's Micah," he corrected in a smiling, easy way.

"Oh, I adore all the prophets' names. Obadiah, Zechariah, Malachi," Anne turned toward Micah. Her direct eye contact made all others in their crowd fade from his consciousness. "How good your parents gave you a name with character and history. It's a woman's name, too, you know? Solomon's daughter. But I like it best on a man." She was informed and exuded honest enthusiasm; her genuine intensity made Micah warm to their conversation, as he had not to others since he'd begun this new journey.

"You know your Bible," he smiled at her.

"It goes with my territory," she drawled. "Sunday School. In the South, we're serious about religion, don't you know." She smiled back.

"It goes with mine, too," Micah replied. "And *very* serious and quite personal," he added.

"Anne is such a plain and uninteresting name," she complained to her now-rapt companion.

"I don't agree," Micah replied. "It's precise, smart, straight-forward. Very New Testament to my Old."

"True, so true," Anne answered. Her eyes glanced into space and she seemed to be thinking about his characterization.

"Where are you from? I can guess the region, but not the interesting details," Micah brought her back to their conversation.

"Charleston. Beautiful, languid, otherworldly Charleston," Anne replied, in an exaggerated, singsong way. "Ever been there?" She had a lilt more than an accent and a distinctly different dialect than Micah had heard in the voices of other Southerners he'd come across. He liked it. It was warm, and engaging, and surprisingly intelligent.

"Almost went once to the Music Festival. A friend of mine, a musician, performed there, and he could bring a guest. But I couldn't get away from work."

"Too bad. You must come when we get back. What kind of work would keep you from a free festival?"

"Several kinds. I needed a war chest to go along with the Thayer stipend. I gave tennis lessons at a day camp and worked the night shift at the school library. Had that job for three years while I was at the university."

"You must be good, then. We must play!" Anne said enthusiastically. "I've had lessons for as long as I can remember, and play a good woman's game. Three point five. *You* must be very good."

"4.0, but not a lot of style. I was never trained early, but I played a lot on the public courts in a park near our house. Great courts, pink clay."

"If you gave lessons, you must have been good. You're too modest, Micah." Anne had a way of conversing that made Micah feel as if he was the only person in the room. And that they were old friends. She was easy to talk to, and so attractive that Micah grew more alive and relaxed in his own conversation.

"Not really," he moved closer and leaned in toward Anne. "You should have seen who I taught at the tennis camps. But I had a good coach in high school, played a lot, and since the University of Chicago had a weak team, I played singles and doubles, mostly against better players. Learned a lot. Lost a lot," he said smiling. "But, yes, let's play in Cambridge. Have you played on grass?"

"Yes, and I hated it," Anne answered. "Very slippery, freaky bounces, easy to twist your ankle. I love clay, so you had it best on your park courts." Anne was clearly from another world, Micah thought, but she had a friendly way of seeing his in the best light.

Their conversation moved from the past they were leaving to the future they were approaching. Anne would be living at Sidney Sussex College, a 400-year-old former Franciscan monastery whose most renowned alumnus was Oliver Cromwell. His remains were secreted there. She had read about the college and knew more about it than Micah knew about his more prestigious new home, Trinity College. "Sussex is the only college to accept women, but I confess I was most curious about Trinity," Anne said.

"I'm excited about Cambridge. And Trinity," Micah replied. "I read a lot of books by Trinity authors my professors suggested—and I can't wait to get there. It should be like entering a page of history."

Anne responded, "I hope you have rooms at New Court so I can come see where Keynes, E. M. Forster, and Lytton Strachey and that whole group lived—what were they called?"

"The Apostles."

"Yes, they lived in Trinity, and began their careers in Cambridge at the turn of the century. And their story explains the source of the Bloomsbury Circle."

Anne could tell that Micah was really impressed. He would tell her later that his preconceived notions about her had been quickly replaced by a surprised but immediate attraction. This girl, who had picked her college so she could bring her horse and who seemed at first like the typical Southern homecoming queen, knew the Old Testament and had read widely about early twentieth-century Cambridge.

"I guess you're going to be part of literary Cambridge, and I'm to be in political Cambridge," Anne remarked.

Anne and Micah never stopped talking or rejoined the table chatter surrounding them. Their companions noticed Anne and Micah seemed to be in a personal zone and gradually left them to their private conversation. One bit of introductory small talk led easily into another. They both loved jazz, particularly Dixieland; Ann loved Pee Wee Russell. Micah's favorite was Wild Bill Davidson. They compared music stories.

They both followed baseball: she teased Micah about his passion for the hapless Cubs; he wondered about Anne's devotion to the feisty Brooklyn Dodgers. Anne knew her baseball as well as her Bible. Micah was enchanted by her energy and the variety of her interests. Their conversation became more animated as each new subject came under discussion. They both were critical—in hushed voices—of some of their Ivy League companions. They thought that they were haughty, not their type.

Micah's boyish frankness and his self-deprecating manner impressed Anne more than the bragging and posturing of the young men she'd dated. They both planned to travel during their Cambridge stays: Anne couldn't wait to visit the museums and gardens in Paris; Micah wanted to walk the English pathways and read the famous writers' works in the places where they were written. Each thought the other's plans were more interesting and asked questions about them.

They became entranced by each other's personality: Anne's warmth and engaging way made her listener open up and feel as if she hung on his every word; Micah's easy, relaxed way made Anne feel that he cared about what she said, and his measured way of talking seemed to reflect a wise earnestness. Anne's boyfriends weren't interested in talking about ideas, least of all hers. She knew that she was thought of as a catch by the boys, but they weren't interested in her in the way Micah appeared to be.

They discovered that while they were at nearby colleges at Cambridge, they were on reverse courses. His family was pushing him to pursue science and medicine, but he preferred literature. Anne's dilemma was just the opposite. Her family wanted her to come home and live a conventional "woman's" life, which in Charleston meant marrying, having children, and joining clubs. Anne wasn't interested. They discussed careers for a long time, and their imagined goals. Anne wasn't sure where she was headed. Everything came so easily, she just assumed she would follow her father's career, but she had no real passion about it, she admitted. Her reason for competing for the Thayer prize was to get away from her scripted life in South Carolina. "I like the idea of helping people, but I'm not drawn to any special kinds of medical practice." She hoped the Cambridge interlude might make her goal clearer.

Micah told Anne that while solicitous of his family's plans for him, he imagined teaching American literature at a picture postcard small college like Amherst or Haverford. He'd write a serious but popular book that would establish his reputation. He had a theory that twentieth-century American literature was entering a new phase at mid-century, and he planned to be the first to chart its evolution. They discussed their favorite authors and books, and their reasons for their choices. They found themselves talking more than they ever had in comparable social situations, more thoughtfully and earnestly; each was impressed with the other's ideas and knowledge and their genuine interest in what they were saying. In a noisy sea of small talk, their conversation connected two people who were surprised and delighted by their own level of interest in their companion, and intrigued by the obvious fact that their interests in each other were mutual.

When Micah learned that Anne's favorite professor, and her mentor at Sweet Briar, was Marie Graynor, their conversation became intense. He adored Graynor's work, and quoted many of her lines. Anne agreed, and recited a few of her favorites. After quoting and commenting about her naturalistic poems, Micah asked if Anne knew Graynor's poem *For The Dead*, and she said, quietly, "Yes, I do," and suddenly her eyes seemed to fill! Micah wondered how this quintessential southern WASP could feel such personal emotion over a powerful and sentimental poem that dealt with the Holocaust. He'd discussed it with Jewish scholars, intellectually, but she was reacting emotionally. It may have been the moment Micah lost his heart to Anne. At least, it was the moment when their superficial differences disappeared and their kindred spirits joined and locked.

Years later, in private moments, they discussed how they felt that night, how the floor beneath their feet seemed to collapse as they fell into a new place in their lives, together.

For both Anne and Micah, the attraction they felt so strongly and so fast contrasted with all their prior experiences. Neither had known, certainly never dated, anyone like the other. Each had had a stereotypical image of the other's lives that was shattered by their surprising feelings about the reality of each other. It wasn't that each thought the other exotic because they were so different. Rather, each had feelings of delight in their sense that they were attractive to the other for reasons of their own individuality. They were infatuated, unsure of the source of their own feelings, but overwhelmed by a desire to know more about their new friend.

"Does she think I'm some exotic guy she's being kind to?" Micah wondered.

"Wouldn't Mother be surprised if I brought this fellow home to dinner," Anne mused.

Long after the others had left the table, wandering off to bar or bed, the newest friends talked alone until early in the morning. They were the last people in the room. Neither wanted the evening to end. At a lull in their conversation, after a few minutes of pleasant silence, Micah spoke. "You must be tired. Can I walk you to your room?" Anne looked worn; her lipstick was blotted away, and the long day had taken a toll on her freshness, but not at all on her beauty. She looked especially attractive to Micah, who couldn't think of anything or anyone else at that moment.

"I'd like to go on deck and see the sky, feel the fresh air," Anne replied. Micah rose and helped her slide away from the banquette, past the table strewn with full ashtrays and empty glasses.

"Me, too. Where shall we go?"

"I want a sweater," Anne said. "Walk me past my cabin, then let's go as close as we can to the very tip of the ship so we can feel the motion and sense the water."

They walked to Anne's cabin. Unconsciously, Micah's arm was around Anne's shoulder; Anne's arm responded lightly, holding Micah around his waist. At her stateroom, Anne retrieved her sweater, noticing that her roommates were asleep. They left the stateroom area and climbed the narrow stairs to the tourist-class deck. The sky was vast and inky black, filled with a billion stars. The air was breezy, but balmy.

Anne took Micah's arm and they walked to a railing at the farthest point forward they could reach. Micah was delighted to be taken along by Anne; she was delighted to be with this tender, receptive admirer. Anne had always loved looking at the sky; she remembered it clear and sparkling on her walks in the Virginia countryside surrounding Sweet Briar, and magical looking across the Cooper and Ashley Rivers when she sat on the public pier with friends at home in Charleston. They truly came from different worlds. Micah was not sure when he ever looked at the sky in his years growing up in Chicago. He had been too busy stepping along in his busy city life to look up.

"I never see the sky, really," Micah remarked. "Chicago has lots of pavement and cement and energy, but I never see the sky. I love it when I do." No girl had held Micah by the arm in the way Anne did. It made him feel needed, cared about, personally close to his special escort. For the first time, Micah felt that he was an important man: this beautiful woman who could chose all her company and controlled all her social action seemed to be choosing him. She was more soulful than girls he had known, and was not the spoiled young lady he might have expected.

Micah was more attentive to Anne's views and interested in her plans than were the young men she had dated. He had a charm and honesty about him she'd not witnessed in the eligible boys who had filled her life up to this time.

"Here," Anne stopped. "Let's sit here a while and listen to the sea sounds and just drink in the sky." They dropped to a spot on the deck where they could lean back on a railing and share an unobstructed view of the sea and sky. They were silent for a long time. The air was fresh and salty, and the young couple was reviving after too many hours sitting in smoky rooms. Micah had never sat in silence with anyone, certainly not with a woman. As wide and vast and open as the atmosphere was around them, Micah felt intimacy with Anne, an intimacy he couldn't understand, and couldn't resist. They'd known each other for about five hours, but she already seemed like an old and familiar friend.

In an impulsive moment, uncharacteristic of Micah, he turned and moved his head down toward Anne. She was looking at the sky, her head leaning back against the support. "What?" she remembered asking, as she noticed Micah looking at her. "What are you thinking?"

Micah didn't answer, but he leaned toward Anne. She moved, barely perceptively in his direction, looking directly into his eyes. Each felt an emotion that was strange to them, a deep desire they had not experienced before. Micah moved closer again and touched Anne's lips with his. It was not a kiss, at first, simply a coming together, softly and incredibly personal. Then, it was a kiss as passionate as either had ever experienced.

For a long time they held the position, each feeling the other's pulsing reaction, discovering the other's soft scent and taste. They then moved closer, silently, holding each other, never disengaging, and for a long time they remained together that way, enveloped, lost together, aware only of each other's feel and presence, sensing the constant motion of the ship slithering along mounting and descending waves, until their minds and bodies were lost and they entered a place they'd never known.

THREE

The Journey

﷽

Anne and Micah were never apart during the week they crossed the Atlantic and traversed their personal Rubicons of intimacy and involvement. They joined the other members of their group occasionally, more out of obligation than to be sociable. They were self-conscious that they had noticeably become loners, lost in each other's company. To those they were traveling with, they seemed almost like brother and sister, or old best friends; they seemed so respectful and close. They were intent and interested in everything the other said. They seemed as compatible as an old married couple, and this after a mere week's time. Others in the Thayer group were dating and socializing among themselves and with others on shipboard. But people sensed that what was going on with Anne and Micah was different.

This least likely couple had been a subject of speculation and Thayer group gossip. "Now there's a surprise couple," one of their group commented.

"Having fun, stranger? I never see you, but I understand why," Roy quipped when they saw each other one evening in the dining room.

For Anne and Micah, theirs was the most personal relationship either had ever experienced. It was overwhelmingly romantic; their private intimacy was a result of a mutual and growing admiration. They were completely absorbed in each other. They couldn't understand it, or resist it. They couldn't leave each other. Periodically, exhaustion forced them to return to their cabins for rest. The crowded quarters precluded their retiring to sleep together, a reality they never discussed, however natural it would have seemed. Their classmates gossiped and presumed they were lovers, they realized. "You two ever apart?" one classmate inquired. But their feelings were at a different level than outsiders presumed, or than they had ever known. Their passion exceeded anything either had experienced. Their frustration was less over the lack of opportunity to consummate their intimacy than the inability to be completely alone all the time. They found it impossible to separate from each other, even after staying together all night on deck, watching the sun rise.

Early in the mornings, before the dining room opened for breakfast and their shipmates arose, succumbing to overwhelming hunger, they would walk past the ship's bakery, where the day's loaves and pastries were being prepared. Aromas of fresh-baked bread lured the tired lovers. One of the white-suited bakers befriended them, smiling, and offering a hot loaf just out of the oven. Anne and Micah tore it apart and gobbled chunks of the bread, washing it down with cold milk they slurped from the bottle, laughing, wiping each other's lips and chins, enjoying a simple physical indulgence they would always remember. Sometimes they'd return to their separate cabins at daybreak to be there in bed when their cabin mates awoke. At first, they forced themselves to meet with others in their group for meals, but even that resolution eventually faded. They would freshen up, change clothes, and find themselves together again for a friendly breakfast with their travel mates. "Here come the lovers," their Thayer mates would snicker when they would arrive at scheduled meetings or join in group events. Mostly, they were alone, in a world of their own making.

In an alcove adjacent to the bar, Jack Dunlap found a piano. Every evening, at the same time, he'd be there playing—at first alone, but inevitably surrounded by a growing crowd. When Micah and

Anne approached his piano, Jack changed what he had been playing, mid-chord, and switched to "People Will Say We're in Love" as others turned, smiling, to greet Anne and Micah.

"May we join in?" gathering travelers would ask, some from the Thayer group, but many from all ranks of shipboard passengers. Jack would smile and nod "of course," and people would cluster around the piano, eventually singing along with Jack's playing. Drinks were bought for Jack, who would nod his thanks and sip his whiskey between songs. The gathered ensemble would call out requests, most of which Jack would oblige. Singers would chime in on songs. Some were very accomplished vocalists. This serendipitous event continued every night, with regulars showing up with newcomers. Some late-night gatherings would continue until early morning hours, until Jack was exhausted and rose, exclaiming, "If I don't stop and get me some sleep, I'm going to faint away." Then the crowd would drift away, chattering as if they were old friends leaving a friend's home.

Anne and Micah found themselves there every night when dinner was done. They wanted to be sociable before they needed to be alone. They liked Jack, as everyone did—how could you not admire and be attracted to such an entertaining man? Jack seemed friendly to everyone, though he didn't seem to have a close relationship to any one person—no girlfriend, no special chum. All the girls and women aboard the ship related to Jack, but he seemed to be either in the center of a crowd or alone. Everyone in the tight Thayer group knew Jack. All, like Ann and Micah, were his friends; none his confidant. The magic of Jack's music was a personal branch on which all the Thayers clung in what would become their community of friends after they reached Cambridge.

Mostly, though, Anne and Micah were alone, and time sped by. They walked endlessly around the decks, explored the boat, usually ending up settling to rest in a small, little-used alcove they discovered adjacent to one of the social rooms. They appropriated it as their private nest. They jogged around the deck and swam laps in the small pool because they both felt the need for exercise. There were more meals served daily than either of them had ever eaten, and they were restless, not used to sedentary days.

They talked, continuously, about every subject under the sun, usually cuddled on the window seat in their special alcove, where Anne would lean across Micah's chest, holding hands, her long legs stretched across the bay.

"I love this place; I feel all alone in the world with only you, and I love the way this feels," Micah whispered.

"Mm," Anne murmured. "Did you ever feel this way with other girls? Truth, now."

"Never," Micah answered. "Except with Diane and Barbara. Yes, also I guess with . . ." he teased. Anne turned and pinched him, and they giggled and cuddled closer.

As they never had before, they learned the personal intimacies of the other: how Micah smelled a particular, personal scent that came from him and not his shave lotion, a smell that Anne loved. Micah would never forget discovering how Anne tasted, how the warm wet of her mouth had a sense of its own that he adored. Anne was fascinated by the intensity of Micah's eyes when he talked about something that was serious, and how his forehead furrowed when that happened. Anne's smile touched Micah inside as no other woman's look had ever done to him before. Micah noticed physical details about Anne, her long slim fingers, her lithe legs, the fuzz that showed faintly on her top lip and in a line down her cheek from her ear. Anne was infatuated with a dark spot above Micah's upper lip; she would touch it, kiss it, and she couldn't imagine why she did this, any more than she could comprehend why she loved to watch him when he shaved, how he stretched his mouth and pulled his cheeks to allow his razor to slice the cream away from his face. Little intimacies. Personal engagements.

They noticed and teased about each other's eccentricities in dress. Anne always wore black; all her dresses and combined outfits were black. As a teenager, it was her bohemian excuse for not shopping or conforming, and it became a habit she never changed. There was subtle variety in the materials, combinations, styles—but it was always black. She would add a scarf over her shoulders, or a belt or hair band of some striking color set off against her black outfit. Anne could have worn anything, any color, and been beautiful. It was as if she subconsciously decided to take away all distraction of costume from her appearance in order to show off the striking person.

Micah paid no attention to clothes; he suffered from a low budget and an even lower concern about them. But his random combinations had a simple and eccentric charm that Anne found endearing. All her beaus had dressed from the same official preppy clothing manuals, so no one looked different from anyone else. Micah's unstudied look was distinctive in its plain way. Anne loved straightening his tie, wearing his shaggy old sweaters, putting her stylish slick silk dress up against his rough corduroy jacket that didn't quite match his slacks. Each of them loved the way the other looked, and were surprised to find themselves even thinking about such things for the first time. Each wore the items the other remarked about, his favorite of her dresses, her favorite of his sweaters, conscious of the effect of their appearance on the other. It was the joy of discovery, of being noticed, and of being adored for the right reasons.

They told each other long stories about the different worlds they'd come from, realizing that they'd left those worlds forever, with each other, without conversation, doubt, or hesitation. They wondered whether they would be together forever. Anne saw in Micah a special kindness she had not sensed in other young men; he exuded a respect for her on a genuine personal level that touched her. Micah was awed that this elegant and beautiful woman was seriously interested in him, in his ideas and his plans and his speculations about life. Neither of them had ever opened up to another person or shared their innermost thoughts, fears, dreams with another.

"Is this some passing shipboard infatuation, do you think darlin'?" Anne asked Micah one night while they were on deck, looking at the stars.

"Why do you ask? Do you think that?"

"Well, here we are, the first time we leave our old life, and boom! I can't remember where I came from, or what I was thinking or doing before all this. It's as if I was waiting for this. For you."

"I know," Micah responded. "I feel like everything before we met was a warm-up. But I never dreamed it would lead to this. I pinch myself. Could a woman like you love me?"

Anne looked at Micah, said nothing, deep in thought about them, and the meaning of all this.

The first time they made love was touching and natural and pleasurable, and it was not calculated, or what either had expected of sex. It was the afternoon of the next-to-the-last day aboard ship. The morning after next they would reach Southampton and be met by special buses and driven to Cambridge. They sensed an interfering reality closing in on them, intruding on their privacy and exclusivity. Micah had walked Anne to her cabin late in the afternoon. She was weary from their blur of days and nights that merged. She said she needed a nap and shower before dinner. The all-nighters on the deck were tiring her, but she did not want to miss the last two times they'd have on deck under the stars in their private reverie before the end of their journey. When they arrived at Anne's cabin, her roommates were gone. The room was messy, with clothes and cosmetic apparatuses strewn on every surface. They smiled at the scene.

Anne turned to kiss Micah, and the kiss never stopped. The door was closed. No one said anything, no questions, no hesitancy. One thing simply, naturally, led to another. The kisses became more passionate, the touching more intimate. Eventually, Anne stepped away from Micah, her eyes never leaving his. She opened her blouse. He stepped toward her and they embraced, long and tenderly, but with a growing physical passion. Then they were together on Anne's bed, touching, kissing, sighing, crying into each other's cheeks and shoulder, wrapping each other's bodies, until they were totally together. Excruciating pleasure overwhelmed both of them until their coming together was complete.

A moan from Anne. A gasp from inside Micah. A tear drifted down the side of Anne's face. Micah kissed it. She smiled up at him. They fell asleep exhausted, locked together.

An hour later, they were jarred from their brief private dreams when the door opened and two young women barged in. "Oops, sorry!" one exclaimed, and they quickly departed, giggling down the hallway. The lovers smiled at each other, knowingly, embarrassed. Micah hurriedly dressed. Then he stopped and looked at Anne. She had not moved, and was staring at him.

"I love you so much, Anne," Micah said, leaning over her and kissing her warm, salty lips.

"I love you, Micah." Anne realized she had never said those words to anyone before. She knew she meant them. She had always wanted it to be that way.

Micah turned and quickly returned to his own cabin.

There was a party for everyone the last night aboard ship. The Thayers' tables were moved together so they had their own private party within a party. Everyone dressed in their best, most fashionable outfits. Micah wore his new and only suit; Anne wore a long, tight-fitting black silk dress. There were long tables instead of the twos, fours, and eights that had filled the dining room at other times. The dance band performed in the dining room (it had played in the salon all the other nights) and the ambience was loud, cheerful, celebratory.

Micah and Anne arrived separately but sat together; no one had said anything, but there was an implicit understanding that this was a serious couple, and the others made way for them to sit together. Micah went out of his way to include Roy and Jack near him at the table; Anne sought out her roommates. Anne and Micah had resolved to be more sociable with the clique they would be part of for two years, so they danced with everyone else at their table before they danced the last set together, silently, serenely. The band played old favorites: "Polka Dots and Moonbeams," "Those Little White Lies," "You Belong To Me," classics that had been sung for years by crooning balladeers, Sinatra,

Dick Haymes, Jo Stafford. They held each other tightly, swayed to the music, nuzzled each other's head and neck and shoulder—in a world of their own.

Their last night alone was planned carefully. After everyone left for sleep, carousing, whatever everyone else did, usually after midnight, they would change into comfortable, warm clothes, bring blankets, and sleep these last dark hours together on the deck. Then they would return to their cabins to pack, have breakfast with their cabin mates, and meet with the whole Thayer group at an assigned social room to complete arrangements for their disembarking in Southampton and their ride to Cambridge.

Their last night on deck was a reverie: loving; precious, because they both knew that a special time in their lives had happened; sad, because it was about to end. They were hopeful but uncertain that later chapters could be as sweet. Neither Anne nor Micah had ever had so close a friend as they had become with each other that week at sea, so different from all the friends each had made during their separate lives.

As they lay huddled together that last night on the deck, feeling the subtle motion of the ship and sea, feeling profoundly the warm, very personal presence of each other, they wondered where this journey would really lead. In silence, Anne and Micah thought of their families, their homes, their cities, their friends, how surprised all their previous world would be to know how quickly their prodigals had fallen in love, and more questioningly, with whom. For the first time each of the lovers returned in thought to the people they had been and what they and all who knew them previously thought that the future was likely to present to them. In that context, the person lying close in their arms seemed for the first time so foreign, so different from everything and everyone in their past. But their feelings were so strong they could feel their hearts, as if that part of them had never existed before and was awakened and probing, pushing at them.

These thoughts, along with the night air and their otherwise exhausted state, chilled them. As if each sensed the other's fears, they instinctively nestled closer, without speaking. Neither slept.

"You know what, darlin'?" Anne said, out of the blue.

"What?" Micah asked.

"You know why I adore you? What the difference is about this, this, whatever it is that's happening to us?"

"Tell me!" Micah asked, smiling.

"It's how you say you love me," Anne explained.

"I do love you," Micah replied, "and I'd probably love you more if I understood what you are saying."

"Every other fellow I ever went out with before you," she said, "when he wanted to—get close—you know what I mean. He would say, 'I *love* you.' You say, 'I love *you.*' Understand?"

Micah finally did get it. He adored Anne and he understood in some deep and private way that he did love *her* as a person, and he wasn't infatuated with being in love, or trying to bed her for a little loving; he just loved *her.* And she understood this. He put his arms around Anne, and they were silent; at that moment they understood in the deepest, most permanent way what had happened to them.

As the first rays of light illuminated part of the sky and the moon hovered but began to disappear from view, as if embarrassed and suddenly retiring, Anne whispered to Micah.

"I want this to last, my darlin'. Why does it have to end?"

"It won't end, ever," Micah whispered into space, not looking at Anne, but tightening his arm around her shoulder.

"Won't it?" she murmured, snuggling down closer under the blanket they shared like hikers on a mountainside. "Promise me it won't, Mr. Lehman; promise me this isn't a sweet but evanescent shipboard romance."

"A week ago, I didn't know you, didn't imagine I could feel anything like the feelings I have, didn't know why I was here or what I wanted. A week ago, all I did was worry about the rest of my life."

Micah was barely audible; his stream-of-consciousness monologue might have been said to no one present, or to an imaginary spiritual or psychological listener. It was said to Anne but was a rumination to

Micah himself, as he analyzed his new consciousness. "I worried whether I'd succeed by my parents' standards, by my teachers' standards, by my image of what I was supposed to be and do. Now, I don't care—for the first time, I really don't care what anyone thinks about me, except you." Anne pushed her head closer into Micah's shoulder, but she was silent. She thought of nothing, listened only to his words. "You are my world now and I don't know where we will be or what we will do, I only care that it is with you. You know that, don't you?"

"I do," Anne whispered. "I do and I will be with you, my love."

Time disappeared as the grand *Queen* sliced silently across the ocean. Life aboard ship departed not only from distant shores but also from familiar references—place, pace, people, all were changed for these two passengers. The vastness of the sea, the sky, the very air around them dissolved. The past slipped away without suggesting a future. There was only the present. A new personal allegiance formed. Time became liquid. For Anne and Micah, the week was a passage of the most deep and personal kind.

FOUR

Cambridge

Anne and Micah agreed that they'd stay with their group when daytime overtook their dreamy private world aboard ship. During their ocean crossing, they seemed to have traveled metaphorically from a personal old world to a new and shared one, though in fact they'd come from the new world of America to the old one of England.

The morning the *Queen* returned to harbor in England, there was chaos and movement and confusion as the boatload of people poured from their cabins, crew members bustled with chores, and cargo and suitcases were unloaded.

"Darlin'," Anne instructed Micah as they left each other for the last-minute arrangements required for their departure, "if we're not on the same bus, come to Sidney Sussex as soon as you get settled. I want to be with you for our first night in Cambridge." Micah looked after Anne as she hurried down the passageway, suddenly feeling estranged from his surroundings, lost without Anne as his anchor.

"Yes, yes, I'll see you there." It touched him that she wanted to be with him at every special time, just as he thought about her.

The Thayer group of 30 was met at the customs kiosk by a smiling group of three staffers from Thayer House, the stately old mansion in Cambridge that was headquarters for the Thayer program and the site of its organized meetings and social events. They were directed to three waiting minibuses—each destined for different colleges—that would carry them and their luggage on the four-hour drive to Cambridge. By assignment, Micah and Anne went with their college mates-to-be onto separate buses, agreeing to find each other that night after the scheduled indoctrination session at Thayer House. Being separated for the first time on the first day of the rest of their lives left them feeling strangely empty and disoriented.

On the bus ride north, the cheery Thayer representatives described points of interest along the way and passed out information packets for each of the students describing their schedules, meetings, and quarters. Anne's bus was filled mostly with the other few young women and a few men who were assigned to their same college, Sidney Sussex. Micah's was an exclusively male busload, also assigned by Thayer housing standards, mostly to Trinity and King's College. Everyone was provided a box lunch, so the long ride stopped only once for gas, visits to the toilets, and a respite at picnic tables set along a patch of field across the road from the gas station. When Micah's bus reached the point of respite, Anne's group was already there and engaged in conversation. Micah walked by Anne's table and touched her shoulder, and she smiled up at him. But her group was preoccupied in conversation, so he moved along to his table of travel mates, feeling lonely and distracted.

The buses arrived in Cambridge in the late afternoon and slowly moved over the small bridge spanning the Cam River, then wended their way down narrow cobbled streets, stopping often to allow a few small cars and a mass of students on bicycles to pass. Micah's bus stopped at the end of an alley across from the ancient and ornately designed circular library building near Trinity College. Baggage from those passengers who were assigned to Trinity was emptied on the street and quickly carried to the college entrance by formally dressed porters who appeared as soon as the bus arrived. The Thayer representative walked the students to their respective colleges as bus mates called greetings and waved from the windows. At the entryway to each college, several elderly porters stood in an enclosed room perusing papers that indicated names and room assignments. Formal greetings were issued by the black-clad porters, who accompanied new residents individually to their rooms.

Inside the entryway there was a wide grass courtyard, encircled by a walkway with entrances to the buildings that contained the housing units. Micah was at once thrilled by the charm and historic feel of the classic old building that was to be his new home, but he felt estranged in a place that seemed so foreign to all his experiences. His room was spare but spacious. There were window boxes at the leaded glass windows and old but usable plain furniture in his room. Perfunctorily, he unpacked and examined his sparse new environment.

After unpacking, there was a meeting in the common room of all new students with the rest of the undergraduates who were housed at Trinity. They were introduced to members of the administrative staff, tutors in residence, representatives of student organizations. The formal meeting was followed by champagne served outside on the encircled green, where the students all met and chatted, then separated into smaller groups when dinner eventually was announced. Micah, who arrived late as his bus had come late, had no time to walk to Anne's rooms to see her. The scheduled group meeting at Thayer House was postponed until later that week. He attempted to phone Anne, but each time he began to return to his room another friendly person walked up to him with words of welcome and introduction. Micah moved from cluster to cluster, slightly anxious, very weary, and lonesome for Anne's company.

Micah and his Thayer colleagues at Trinity entered the long hall and were assigned to seats at two long wooden tables arranged perpendicular to the main table and facing each other. Behind them were huge oil paintings of prior masters, who had presided over Trinity for centuries. The tables were candlelit. The students wore gowns, as they would at all the evenings they dined in the hall that first year. The dinner was introduced by formal prayers, erudite and witty toasts, and welcoming commentaries. Lovely as the room and the scene in it was, the seats were hard and uncomfortable, so the four-hour-long dinner presented the weary travelers with a painful, if impressive indoctrination.

When the evening dinner finally ended, Micah was whisked away along with the others in his group by friendly proctors who insisted on showing the Thayer arrivals the favored local pub. Not wanting to appear rude to his new colleagues, Micah went along with them, accompanied by his shipboard friend, Jack Dunlap, the other Thayer member assigned to Trinity. He tried to call Anne, hoping she'd be able to join them at the pub. He could not reach her, nor could he leave his group of revelers until the pub closed. When it did, he separated from his new friends and raced through winding empty streets to Sidney Sussex College. Micah learned where Anne's room was and, finding no one there when he knocked, slipped a note under her door telling her the location of his college rooms and asking her to come to him whenever she returned. "I miss you madly. Wake me whenever you get in, Micah. Portal 9, room 1."

Anne liked Sidney Sussex; it was newer than Trinity by about 200 years, and smaller, but it had its own cachet. The bones of Oliver Cromwell were hidden there, she was told by her college master, and by custom only he knew the location. She, too, participated in a long dinner, complemented by a series of fine wines from the renowned Sidney Sussex collection, and a post-dinner gathering over port at the master's rooms. She returned to her room late, weary, woozy from the various wines, and hoping to find Micah, or a message from him.

She was told by the desk porter she had no messages. She did not notice Micah's note in her doorway. Anne perfunctorily finished unpacking, hoping Micah would come soon, but finally, exhausted, she fell asleep fully dressed across her bed, presuming he would come eventually.

She awoke early the next morning, chilled by the night air and lack of bedclothes, and submerged herself in a hot bath. Micah awoke in his room, disconsolate and lonely, and raced immediately to Anne's room. She didn't hear him knock because she was running her bath water. By the time she left for breakfast, Micah was on his way to meet his tutor. Their schedules the first day took them to different places, so they didn't meet until dinner. To them both, their day apart from each other, however engaging, seemed an eternity. Micah came to Anne's room again, and when she answered, he stepped in and they fell into an embrace of joy and longing. Like newlyweds who had known each other for years and returned from a long separation, they were almost in tears to be together, embracing.

"Where were you darlin'? I thought you'd forgotten me," Anne gushed as they kissed. Micah was almost in a frenzy.

"I couldn't find you," between kisses. "I was going crazy last night, trying to reach you," between more kisses. "I couldn't wait to get through this day, and to find you," he gasped.

"Darlin', darlin'," Anne whispered amidst their zealous embraces.

That night they dined together in a small Indian restaurant they discovered on a quiet street near the colleges. They decided to avoid all distractions, however intriguing their new environs were, and explore Cambridge alone, together. They wandered the narrow cobbled lanes around the colleges, browsed the shops and old bookstores in town, and eventually discovered, outside the center of town, a pub called the Plough and Barrow.

They stopped abruptly under its sign: "That's where the Apostle authors met," each remembered. It seemed destined to be their place. "When you become a literary celebrity at your college, Professor Lehman," Anne teased, "you can tell your students you and the famous Trinity authors met here."

"Your lips to God's ears—or to some search committee's," Micah responded, a faraway smile on his face. They entered, looked around in joyous discovery, and sat in a corner booth. They drank the warm local ale, held hands, and told each other of their experiences while they were apart. All the closeness and special interest in each other returned as they slipped quickly into their partnership of intimacy.

Anne was tired, so they walked back to her college around midnight. They kissed and embraced for a long time in Anne's room, and then

Micah helped her to bed, stroking her head as her eyes fell shut, tucked an extra blanket around her, and slipped away.

Anne and Micah quickly fell into the routine they would follow for most of the time they spent at Cambridge. Each of them threw themselves into the specific Trinity and Sidney Sussex, Thayer, and the broader Cambridge communities. They had a circle of separate and mutual friends, and each of them developed a new close personal friendship.

Anne's particular friend, who would become a lifelong soul mate, was Cassandra Fleming, an English graduate student whose life had been an Anglo reflection of Anne's American social background. Anne rode horses with Cassie across the wide fields and along the country lanes beside the Cam, aside the winding river, around the outskirts of Cambridge. Cassie's family retreat in Ashton Hill, a small picturesque village in the Cotswolds, became Anne's and Micah's, but especially Anne's, home away from home. Weekends and holidays and times when real privacy was required, Anne spent there, at Washbrook Farm, sometimes with the Fleming family, who adopted her and whom she came to love, often with Cassie and Micah and other Cambridge class- mates and friends of Cassie. The Flemings' capacious London apartment in Belgravia was always open to Cassie and her friends for their forays to the theater or a lecture or concert or party, but their wonderful country home was the place Anne loved to visit most; it became the symbol of what her time in England meant to her. The Strongs offered to enter- tain the Flemings on their visit to England to see Anne, and Cassie was invited to come to Charleston with Anne when she returned midway in her Thayer years to attend an event honoring her mother's closest friend and her godmother, Celia Savage.

Micah remained friendly with Jack Dunlop and with Roy Garfield and other Thayer fellows who lived at other colleges, but his special friend at Cambridge was the person who fortuitously changed his professional life. When he first met Daniel Barth after a debate at the Cambridge Union, he thought Daniel was arrogant, though he was awed by his brilliance and self-confidence. Daniel debated a visiting black

South African professor from Oxford, Percy Nkondo. The subject of the debate was the black Holocaust, the question whether the Holocaust was a uniquely Jewish phenomenon or one that applied to other ethnic catastrophes, particularly the enslavement of blacks. The Oxford professor was a celebrity; he'd been a political leader in his country, had written a book on race relations that was hailed internationally, and had become a vocal and visible commentator in the press and on radio talk shows.

Percy Nkondo had the more popular argument to make; Daniel Barth's position seemed parochial and based on self-interest. To make the moment of debate more dramatic, Professor Nkondo was a tall, extraordinarily handsome, almost regal man with an orotund voice that sounded theatrical and professionally trained. Barth—handsome too, but less imposing physically—not only held his own in the debate but carefully, craftily made a strong case using wit, flashes of brilliance, and an encyclopedic knowledge of historical details to make an argument to which the audience, prepared to swoon to Professor Nkondo's presentation, responded with resounding cheers of "Hear! Hear!"

"No person, Jewish or non-Jewish, even Holocaust survivors themselves, has the exclusive right to appropriate the message, the meaning, the idea, the lessons, of that awful event. Alas, if it is to have a universal, indeed generic moral meaning, it has to be an experience—intellectual, moral experience—of *all* people. Indeed, one could argue that if the lesson of the Holocaust is to be memorialized permanently, uniformly, the real test is that it reaches non-Jews, and affects world values," Nkondo had argued.

"True," Daniel responded, "as far as it goes. But certain subjects pertain particularly to special groups of people." Then Daniel turned the table on his opponent using a risky device. "The world should condemn apartheid, my distinguished opponent surely would argue; but would not whites appear patronizing, possibly hypocritical, by appropriating the term defining that unjust policy for other examples of systematic oppression of racial groups? Wouldn't that be an offensive comparison to Africans, emotionally loaded and historically inaccurate?"

Professor Nkondo snapped back: "The Jews, no less so than others, I should expect, should understand that the horrors cast upon them in the past world war were human horrors of inhumanity. The Jews have no monopoly on injustice, even class discrimination." He continued, "I invite my learned debating opponent to come to South Africa today if he needs proof of the globalization of class exploitation and state murder."

Back and forth they parried.

"Analogies to the Holocaust cannot be legitimately made," Daniel Barth countered. "Degrees of difference become differences of kind. One may sympathize with the likeness of apartheid to the early days of Nazism, but when the organized death camps killed *millions*"—Daniel emphasized the number with tone and pause—"the state policies of Nazi Germany and their end result in what we have come to call the Holocaust transcended comparable evil regimes."

Micah was upset by the haughty manner in which Professor Nkondo seemed to make commonplace the unique suffering of Jews in a way no one ever had in all his prior discussions among like-minded people. He was all the more upset when the professor spoke with disdain in an aside about America's history of racism. "The United States," Nkondo threw off in an aside, "holds itself out as the moral savior of the world, but it eradicated its own native population in the name of economic expansionism and developed its early economy on the back of a slave-based agrarian society."

Micah was outraged, but impressed with Daniel's poised and balanced responses. Micah wondered if he could have been so controlled. Back and forth the debaters parried until their time had expired. At the conclusion of the debate, the audience rose, cheering the debaters, who shook hands with each other, Professor Nkondo embracing Daniel while the debate organizers summed up the evening's presentation.

After the debate, Micah stood with a group of students who had lined up to congratulate Professor Nkondo and Daniel as they stood at the speakers' table. Micah had studied the Holocaust and thought he knew the subject and that Daniel had made a brilliant and correct case. Micah's immediate family had survived the disaster in Eastern Europe, and members of the family he never met but knew about had perished. The subject was discussed often by their family, and of course it was studied during his religious training. Micah eventually shook Daniel's hand and enthusiastically remarked, meaning to compliment the debater, that he had clearly and fortunately dismissed a false and widely held misconception and done so against a daunting forensic opponent. To his amazement, Daniel replied: "My good man, the arguments I advanced I did as a debater, and one who had been assigned an indefensible position. A human slaughter is a slaughter, after all. If you were to compliment my forensic skills alone, I'd consider your remark as correct as it was generous. However, if you believe, as you indicated, that my opponent's position is based on false premises, you really do not fully appreciate the issue" (he pronounced it "appresiate the issyou").

Micah was nonplussed and stepped away; he left the hall believing he'd met an obnoxious intellectual snob. He told Anne about the incident later that evening when they had their end-of-day walk and settled in for a drink at their favorite pub. To his surprise, shortly before the closing hour, a group arrived at the pub, including Daniel, his debate opponent, and several others whom Micah recognized as the leaders of the debate society. Daniel noticed Micah and approached the table to greet him and Anne. After a brief introduction to Anne, toward whom he was courtly, Daniel said to Micah: "You seemed surprised and hurt by my comments after the debate. Perhaps we should talk more about the subject. A good debater, you see, must be prepared to argue well on both sides of any controversial point, and so I did. It trains me well for my future career as a barrister, you see." Micah was confused. He'd just told Anne how off-putting this fellow had seemed, and now he was charming, friendly, and logical.

"Yes, indeed, I'd like to talk to you more," Micah replied.

"Will you be my guest for lunch at my club, Justinian?" Daniel asked.

"I'd love to, yes."

"Monday next, then, all right? At 1:00 p.m. The porter there will direct you to my table." With that, Daniel smiled in courtly fashion at Anne and presented Micah with his engraved card and departed, returning to his table and colleagues. Micah shook his head, smiling.

"I like him, darlin'," Anne said.

When Micah and Daniel did meet, several days later, they talked over a long and liquid lunch that lasted late into the afternoon. The conversation continued past the lunch, into the library, then at the pub, and long into the evening. Micah had called Anne at dinnertime to tell her they were at the pub and to suggest she join them. She arrived after her dinner at the college, and the three of them remained at the pub until closing time. Micah summoned every fact and argument he could to convince Daniel that the word *Holocaust* was essentially and fundamentally a term that should be confined to the one central moral collapse of the twentieth century, and not a generalizable description of every example of ethnic cleansing. What happened to the Armenians during the Nazi era, even what happened to black African slaves centuries before, were truly cruel and inhuman, as Professor Nkondo had argued, Micah claimed passionately, but they were not examples of the same phenomenon, and could not be appropriated by other historical situations, even if they shared comparable features.

The word *Holocaust*, Daniel argued, derives from a Greek word, *Holokauston*, predating World War II and Adolf Hitler's bestial final solution.

"Not so," Micah replied. "The word comes from Jewish antiquity. There may be other examples of genocide, but there was only one Holocaust."

Anne offered a different point of view: if other mass murders were fundamentally different from the Nazi plan to eradicate a whole race— she agreed with Micah that there was a difference—what about the American Indians? Weren't they annihilated—or wasn't there an attempt to do so—in that case, by American governmental policy?

"It may have been a real result of Western expansionism gone amok, but it wasn't United States government policy to kill all Indians," Micah replied.

"But isn't it important to universalize the lessons of the Holocaust?" Anne continued to press Micah. "The world's guilt goes along with the greater guilt of the Nazis. If Christians refused to collaborate with Nazi horrors, they couldn't have continued. And if the world, other than Jews, doesn't remember and make the commitment never to repeat that event elsewhere—anywhere—what will we have learned?"

"Forgive me, Anne," Micah interrupted, harshly. "What 'we' may have learned, as you put it, is just very different from what 'we' Jews learned, which, forgive me again, is that there is no 'we' in the world when it comes to Jews."

Anne was silent. She looked at Micah, startled, and her eyes filled with tears. For the first time, there was a distance between them. Daniel sensed the strain of the moment and shifted the conversation away from the subject that divided Anne and Micah, back to the one that separated Micah's views from his.

Back and forth the argument continued, with Daniel speaking calmly and dispassionately, but forcefully, and Micah becoming more and more emotional. By the time their conversation concluded that evening, both Micah and Daniel were left with private reservations about their previously held intellectual positions, but with a deep personal attraction to each other as human beings. Daniel admired Micah's passion; Micah was impressed by Daniel's ability to use cool logic to attack hot subjects. Anne and Micah walked Daniel back to his apartment, and after refusing his offer of a nightcap but making a date for the three of them to meet again, Anne and Micah returned to her room, where they talked continuously about his all-day conversation. Dramatically different as the two young men were, they each were attracted to the other. Anne told Micah she believed he had won the point, but as never before, as long as she had known him, he had lost his composure, which weakened his case. He agreed. And he understood that as much as they had had an earnest debate, Daniel had taught him a lesson. By demonstration, Daniel had made his point about the effective arguing of issues, a point Micah would not forget.

When Micah apologized for his put-down of Anne earlier in the evening, she said nothing. As they fell asleep on Anne's bed, Micah was replaying in his mind his debate with Daniel. Anne was wondering about Micah's angry retort to her. Each had been aware of the chasmic separation between their religious backgrounds and simply assumed their extraordinary feelings of love bridged that separation. For the first time, Anne wondered.

Micah was unaware that his haughtiness, appropriating the subject of victimization, had an impact on Anne. It was his first insensitivity toward her. The differences in their religions were insignificant in their insular private world. They shared an ecumenical interest in each other's religion by attending chorales at Trinity's church and a school-sponsored Seder. But their real religion had been a personal one—their total immersion in each other. Orthodoxies, ceremonies, rituals played no part in their current lives together. Neither missed what had been their prior practices.

Daniel and Micah became permanent friends. Indeed, it was after another late-night conversation one weekend at the Barth's family home outside London, over the scotch Micah had developed a taste for in England, that Micah realized he was going to be neither a professor of literature nor a doctor. He would be a trial lawyer, too. When he told her, Anne said she was not surprised; he was too heartful to be a scientist and too avid about social issues to be happy grading dissertations about dead novelists, she had thought. "It was always in your stars, darlin'," she told Micah, who was surprised that she so readily agreed with and supported his decision. "Remember Micah the prophet, your namesake, fought for social justice, deplored the expropriation of the poor and the unjust enrichment of the rich and ruling class," she calmly commented. "It was your fate, darlin'—do justly, love mercy, walk humbly with thy God. You just had to find it in your own time." It surprised and delighted Micah that Anne was so insightful and supportive. It completed his resolve.

Micah soon began to study jurisprudence under J. A. Heavens, the noted legal scholar at Cambridge. Daniel had completed his third-year bachelor of laws degree and was assisting Professor Heavens's work on his book while deciding whether to pursue a graduate degree before formally clerking for a London barrister at one of the Inns of Court. Daniel became Micah's mentor as well as his friend, opening the professional door to what was to become the rest of his working life.

Micah and Anne never went a day without being with each other. They had busy schedules, but even on the busiest days, they always rendezvoused late at night at their favorite pub. They slept with each other many nights, not always, but invariably with a passion that did not diminish and a tender affection that grew deeper and more profound. They played tennis and biked around Cambridge. They went to Oxford when their friends debated. They competed in intramural and intercollegiate tennis matches, there and elsewhere. They took sojourns to visit the Flemings and occasionally the Barths with their friends, and occasionally without them as they became part of their chums' extended families.

On weekends and vacation periods, they took frugal trips together to Scotland and Wales, where they read Bobby Burns' poem about *Tintern Abbey* on site; to Stratford to see Shakespeare performed; to Ireland, where they visited Yeats's tower and explored Joycean environs; and to the glorious English countryside, where they walked and bicycled. Although they were happy to be alone together, they made friends easily; they were attractive, and open, and fit in readily. At the village pubs they visited, they learned to throw darts, and the locals welcomed them and included them in raucous competitions. Anne was a natural and the patrons adopted her; she and Micah competed for long mugs of the local ales over darts in every smoky pub in every village they visited. They traveled abroad when time and budget allowed. They visited a glacier park in the northernmost part of Norway and ferried to France for obligatory lovers' jaunts walking the streets of Paris.

Anne had always lived her life with crowds, and for the first time she was content to be with one person. Micah, too, had done everything with others—study, work, family: all were many-peopled events—and he was usually at a loss as a loner. Now, he was happiest with Anne, alone. The times they did things with others were easier because she was present, but it was the time with just Anne that made him happiest.

The week Anne had to return to Charleston to attend her godmother's 50th birthday party upset both of them. Anne had rejected family urgings to return for a visit on several prior occasions, but this time, because she was close to her godmother, she could not refuse. Her mother had sent her nonreimbursable plane tickets, and Celia Savage had called personally to say how touched she was that Anne was coming. How could she not go? Anne realized, as she envisioned returning to her life before Micah, how very committed her life now was to Micah, how little everything and everyone else mattered. Micah's limited budget ruled out her inviting him to join her, and Cassie's schedule at school precluded her joining Anne as they had planned. Anne was not ready to deal with her family's expectations about her future and what she was sure would be their disappointing reaction to her relationship with Micah.

For the two days before she left, she and Micah were both distracted, depressed, unable to focus on anything except her departure. First, there were the hours of long-distance plans. They were followed by a day of confused arrangements necessary to get her away from the college and to Heathrow Airport, and then picked up by her family in South Carolina. With time changes and connection problems in the United States and a deadline imposed by social obligations, both of them did little else but cope with Anne's travel arrangements for those days. But the notion of separation after over a year depressed them both. Micah insisted on accompanying Anne to the airport and seeing her off; Anne promised to call him at appointed hours late each night, and he promised to wait at his phone for her calls. He was silent as they embraced before she left; she held on to him for a long time and he could feel tears on her cheek. They each felt a longing over their impending separation.

The week Anne was away seemed like a year to Micah. He tried to lose himself in endless chores and catch-up reading and study. He had no interest in the social entreaties of his solicitous friends. The one night Anne did not call, he went to the pub and for the first time in his life got drunk. Fortunately, Daniel had come looking for him and brought him home just as Anne's call came; she had not been able to call earlier for reasons she'd explain. She was whispering and sounded troubled, which worried Micah. He promised to pick her up at Heathrow with a rented car the following Sunday and spent the rest of the week wondering what it was that he detected was troubling Anne.

Anne looked wan when he met her at the airport receiving room outside customs. Not long into their drive back to the college, after her cursory description of a week of family commitments, he asked, "What's wrong, Anne? You seem anxious, love, what's wrong?"

"Nothing." But there was something, Micah sensed. After a brief silence, "Can we stop for a bite on the way, darlin'? I'm starving. I couldn't eat the airplane food. And I'm not ready to be back at the college."

"Sure, should we go to the pub?"

"No, I want to be alone someplace." Anne quickly added, "With you." Micah had a foreboding. What he picked up from telephonic vibrations several days earlier when she called late that night was real. "How about The Anglers' Inn? Nobody we know will be there on a Sunday night."

"That'd be fine." They didn't speak, except perfunctorily, for the next half hour until they pulled into the parking area at the inn. Micah helped Anne out of the car, locked the doors, and they walked in. The inn was empty, but the bartender said he could bring them some supper. They snuggled into a table near the fireplace, sipped their pints of local ale, and eventually Anne told Micah what had been troubling her.

"Well, Mother made a bad time worse." She talked elliptically for a while, and a curious Micah remained silent, listening to learn what the real problem was. Soon, Anne got to it. "First of all, instead of Mother and Father meeting me at the airport, as I expected, Red Carter was there. All smiles and a huge bouquet. That was awkward, to say the least. My family was hosting a cocktail party for Celia at the club, and he had been delegated to pick me up and bring me there. That should have been the first clue, but naïve little old me didn't catch on. After the party, which was as nice as these things can be—I truly love Celia Savage and her family, and she was genuinely touched that I'd come so far—but it was *so* clear to me how distant this world had become, how supercilious that life appeared to me, how much I missed you . . ." Micah squeezed her hand at this. "After the party, Mother informed me that she'd invited people to our house for a nightcap and her car was full. She asked Red to bring me home. Red said of course he would. But on the way, he drove to one of our old favorite places—forgive me, darlin', we used to go there in high school to neck, but now the only one I want to 'neck' with is you, my love. Red asked when I planned to come home. He wanted to plan our engagement. He seemed pathetic at first when I told him—as kindly and clearly as I could—that it never was going to happen. I'd said it before, not certain I meant it, and he probably thought it was only a question of time. God knows how my family encouraged him to make this pitch. Without details, 'cause it was none of his business, I alluded to someone I'd met and fallen in love with. When he realized I truly meant it, he got ugly for the first time ever with me. He groped, and wouldn't be put off. He'd drunk too much at the party. He smelled from liquor, and was acting crazier than I'd ever seen him act. I thought I was going to be raped."

Anne was crying. Micah stood and came around the table to sit next to her. He put his arm around her, listening quietly to the rest of her story. "It was so sordid and ugly, darlin', I was angry and frightened. I'm a big girl, but Red is bigger and very strong, and very drunk, I realized. Finally, I screamed and reached out and pressed steadily on the horn. He had my dress up and was hurting me—not *that* yet—but hurting me. Thank God, another car happened to come by and stopped near us— there were times when no one ever comes to that spot. But Red stopped, pushed me away, started the car, and raced home. I was frightened. I thought he was going to wreck the car and kill us. He didn't say a word. I was crying all the way home. I hated him. Mother. Charleston. I wanted you to be there." Anne dropped her head onto Micah's shoulder. She paused for a while before finishing her story.

"When we got to my house, he leaned across me, opened my door, and blurted, 'Good-bye, Anne.' I ran from the car. There was a crowd at our house. I believe Mother had thought she had engineered a spontaneous engagement party. I was in tears, disheveled, and ran upstairs while everyone stood around, glasses in hand, silently looking at me."

Anne continued her saga, and Micah listened quietly, holding her close. There was nothing to say now. Anne didn't want conversation. At her own pace and time, she would finish telling him this story. "Mother and Father followed me to my room. I told them what had happened. Mother refused to believe me. 'No, Red wouldn't do that,' was her response. Father was silent, though he sat next to me and put his arm around my shoulder. I began to tell them I'd met someone I loved and that they'd meet him soon. Mother made me feel as if *I'd* done *her* a wrong. She couldn't be interested in you, us. 'Have a bath, Anne, and get some rest. You've had a terribly long day and night, travel and all.'

"I don't remember what happened the rest of that night. I couldn't sleep, thinking about what happened. And about you. That's when I called you from the kitchen, middle of the night, just to hear your voice. Next day I walked through the motions of being sociable. Nothing more was said about my ordeal. But on the way to the airport the day I left, Mother began to needle me."

Imitating her mother, she intoned: "'So tell us, Anne, who *is* this young man who is obviously a subject of your fas-sin-a-shun? Michael, is it?' As if she didn't know your name. 'All those Jewish boys' names sound so famil-yuh!'"

Now Micah knew what was up. Curiously, he and Anne had never discussed the subject because it seemed so irrelevant in their private world at sea and school. How naïve!

"Does she object to me because I'm Jewish?" Micah asked.

"Oh, no! Ladies, Southern ladies, Southern ladies of Mother's stature, would never *object*," Anne blurted forth. With an angry intensity Micah had never seen in her, she finished the story.

"Dad let Mother go on. Before I got on the plane," he said, "Anne, dear, Mother and I are thinking of coming to London on one those tax law–inspired, medical meeting boondoggles. Could you—you two, of course—join us in London for a few days?"

"What a coincidence, eh? Guess who's coming here in two months? Maybe you were right when you told me that night in the pub that 'we' Christians would always be different from you. I hate thinking you might be right, and my own family would be the proof of it." Anne looked at Micah and took his hand.

Micah kissed her fingers and looked long at her, trying not to show hurt or concern, and replied: "Anne, I was wrong on a lot of levels that night. Most, for making you think that you and I inhabit two worlds. You were right. We are in the same world, and we have to make it work better, for both our sakes. I don't want to be in any world that doesn't have you. As far as your parents, I look forward to meeting them."

"Well, I don't, darlin'." She looked down. "I hated Mother, not for some bigotry I'd wish she was smooth if not smart enough not to show, but for tryin' to control my life, for spoiling for me what I presumed—silly me— would be a happy announcement, whenever we wished to make it. I had this romantic scene in mind out of a corny movie that both our parents would be in London at some point to see us and I'd make you propose to me before we saw them, or I'd propose to you, but we'd come to dinner beaming and they'd all guess and hug us and each other, and we'd be a big happy family.

"Problem is," Anne mused, "Mother imagined me as the quintessential Southern matron like herself. Educated for manners, not trained. Married to the cute quarterback whose daddy had the business waiting for him. While he sowed his oats, I rode, learned French and flower arranging, and was queen of the cotillion."

"Not much different from a nice Jewish boy from Chicago," Micah interrupted, half seriously. "I was supposed to work hard in school, marry a nice girl from a good family—some money wouldn't hurt. 'It's just as easy to fall in love with a wealthy girl, Micah, as a poor one.' But the pressures were the same, to fit into their well-meant but ultimately stultifying world."

"I suppose," Anne more wondered aloud than agreed, "I guess we both are disappointments for our personal successes, darlin'."

Anne was crying when the dinner finally arrived, and she stood and left the table for the ladies' room, leaving a fresh trout to cool and a sad lover to ruminate.

Neither of them ate much that night. They picked at their food. Over coffee they talked about their imminent encounter with Anne's family for a long time and only left when the owner signaled it was closing time. Neither of them wanted to go back to their rooms or to see anyone.

"Let's go to the Flemings' farm tonight, love; I just want to be with you," Anne suggested. The Flemings had offered them the use of their place anytime, and they'd never taken up the offer without at least Cassie and usually the whole family being there. Cassie had the key. Anne called Cassie from the inn and asked if they could use it.

"Something the matter, hon?" she asked when they arrived at her room to get the key.

"Yes, but I'll talk to you about it when I can. Thanks, Cassie. We just need to be there alone for a day or so." Anne hugged Cassie and left.

"Call me if you need me, sweet one, promise."

They drove in silence to Ashton Hill and arrived there shortly before midnight. They let themselves in, dropped their things in the guest room, and Micah built and lit a fire in the big stone fireplace. Anne dressed in an old bathrobe hanging in the bathroom, brought a blanket to the couch facing the fireplace. In that outfit, in her exhausted state, anyone else would have looked like a bag lady; Anne looked beautiful, tired but adorable.

The young lovers cuddled together, said nothing, holding each other as if their closeness could keep away the world's intrusions. After a quiet while, Anne slid away from Micah. He looked up at her, wondering why she had moved away and broken their embrace. Anne stood near him, looking directly to his eyes, and slowly took off her bathrobe. She was naked. She had never acted so brazenly, so hungry for love. She slid under the blanket, close to Micah. Soon they pulled off his clothes and the two of them, silently, but with more passion than ever before, made love again, and again. When the fire in the fireplace finally burned out early in the morning, the two lovers were asleep on the couch wrapped in each other's arms.

FIVE

And the Walls Came Tumbling Down

❧❧

Anne and Micah returned to Cambridge the next day. What Micah feared might augur the sad end of their love affair instead had sealed their commitments to each other and led them to a new level in their relationship. Anne told Cassie about her trip home. Micah told Daniel that he and Anne were going to marry, but might be facing troubles along their path to matrimony. Micah realized that his parents, too, were likely to object to his marrying a *shiksa*. Would they carry on? Would they spoil their future with their son, as they surely would if they hurt Anne? He'd never considered the subject because he'd never imagined being in this predicament. But his parents were parochial and likely to be as small-minded from their perspective as the Strongs were from theirs. Anne and Micah were sure of each other, and were prepared to be disinherited and abashed.

"Religion can pose sticky issues," Daniel counseled Micah when they were alone, discussing the future. "Have you and Anne discussed the life questions that arise after the passions subside, kids come, and society imposes itself on your private world? It is more involved than whether you'll have a Christmas tree or a Seder, old chap."

"A bit," Micah responded. "Mostly we're going on faith, reason, and love."

"Not a bad place to start," Daniel responded.

"It worries me, Daniel. This is the kind of problem that happens to other people—not me."

"Don't jump to that conclusion, Micah. You may be pleasantly surprised. From all you've told me about your family, I expect they'll do the decent thing—whatever their private reservations may be."

Micah wasn't sure. After all, he'd been crass to Anne himself that night he drew a line between Christians and Jews on Holocaust questions. If he felt a difference, how could his parents not?

Micah and Anne continued their good life together in Cambridge. They poured themselves into their studies and extracurricular activities for four busy days each week, then went off together for sojourns, mostly walking the meadows and drumlins and pathways that covered the bucolic English countryside. When they were together, the rest of the world was someplace else, and they thought little about it. They talked endlessly about the miracle of their finding each other, and the magic of their time together. They talked about where they might live, what they might do, what their children would be like, when they would go public with their plans. On one of their walking trips, to Cornwall and Devon, heavy rains kept them at a small inn near the sea where they were staying. Over a very late breakfast, they decided the time had come to communicate with their families about their plans. They brought their pots of tea to small tables near the broad stone fireplace, and each wrote the letter they knew they had to write but had postponed.

Micah's letter to his mother and father began with telling them of his decision to switch his studies to the law. "I may not be a doctor as you'd like," he teased, but becoming a lawyer was not so bad, they'd have to admit. He told them of his enthusiasm about becoming a trial lawyer, championing great causes, like a fledgling Clarence Darrow. His advisor had recommended he attend law school at Harvard, but he thought he would go to Yale, if he could get a scholarship. It was smaller, less intense but equally renowned. And he had read the jurisprudential writings of one irreverent professor at Yale whose disciple he was ready to become. Professor Heavens would help. Micah described some of the trips he and Anne had taken. His letter was enthusiastic and colorful, detailed and upbeat.

Then, he turned to his serious message. He hoped they'd be happy to know he'd met and fallen in love with a wonderful woman. They planned to be married when they returned home next year. Though they come from very different worlds—social, economic, religious—they really were soul mates. He'd never felt this way before about any woman and hoped they'd share his joy. They planned to seek counseling from clergy at the school to work out a way to have a marriage that combined the best of each of their backgrounds. Anne was well schooled in religious studies, well informed about his religion, and open to finding a comfortable place for them to live their lives respectful of their past and committed to their future together.

Micah finished his letter with a subtle editorial pitch. Anne's mother had grievously hurt her daughter by reacting insensitively, and that would only damage their relationship without changing Anne's resolve. He was sure his parents would be welcoming to the woman he loved, despite whatever their misgivings might be about their cultural differences. He hoped they'd share this news with his sister, Ada. He knew she would be as happy for him as he was when he learned she was in love and engaged.

Anne's letter was not so diplomatic, nor as optimistic. She sent it to her father, knowing he would have to share the news with her mother. But this formality permitted her a distance to say indirectly to her mother what would be too awkward to say to her directly.

"Dear Daddy—I've not been able to forget the terrible way my visit home ended last month. The incident with Red was bad enough. Far worse was the way my parents—especially Mother—dealt with it, with me. We never discussed my life as a life, ever. We talked about what school I'd attend, what coaching I needed, what summer plan seemed best, what I should study. But I see now that those chapters were part of a script you and Mother had in mind and presumed I'd follow. I know now that it isn't a script I choose to follow. I never realized there was a script for me: you made life so easy and pleasant for me that having a plan of my own, it didn't seem necessary. But when I left for England, I felt at once the need to make a responsible choice, a life's plan during my two years away. By the most extraordinary, fortuitous, wonderful twist of fate, that choice came at once when I met and fell in love with Micah. If you knew him, you'd know why I feel this way; and if you loved me as I'd hope, you would be happy for me. That awful evening before I left, after Celia's party, Mother made me feel that I'd disappointed you both, that my failing to follow the choice you'd made for me was more sorrowful to you than the happy fact that I'd made an important one for myself. That you deserted me after my ugly experience with Red, I don't think I can ever forget or forgive.

"That evening drove me away from you, and I'm sad and sorry for that. I don't know if or how to make things right. Perhaps when you come to London, after you and Mother have had time to think about what I've written—of course, I will too—we can make sense of all this. For now, I can only thank you for helping me come to this point in my life—you've always given me all your love—and hope you can find a way to be part of the next chapter of it. You'll have to deal with this fact: that chapter is called Micah. Love, Anne."

Anne and Micah bundled up in their wet-weather clothes, walked to the village post office, and ceremoniously mailed their letters. They smiled to each other as they performed this symbolic act, an announcement and an emancipation for both of them. Then they walked back to the inn, went to their rooms, and made love, never leaving their bed until the dinner hour. The room was cool and damp. They huddled together under the down quilt. They talked, and touched, and slept, and wakened, and aroused each other. As the day ended and the room darkened, they reeked of their lovemaking and were exhausted from their day-long reverie. They bathed together, dressed, and returned to the quiet dining room below with prodigious appetites and a glow of satisfaction.

When they entered the small, cramped dining room, Anne and Micah noticed that the elderly couples at the three other tables looked long at them and smiled to each other, whispering. They sensed they were the subject of everyone's conversation, and had no idea why.

"What's with them?" Micah wondered aloud to Anne.

"I think I know," Anne answered with a shy smile and a downward glance.

"What?"

"Remember our 'nap' this afternoon?"

Micah's face reddened. They had made love three times, and the last time their ecstasies were very loud, and he realized that the thin walls allowed their inn mates to share their ecstasy. They smiled at each other and held hands. Their dinner was subdued, and they eventually escaped the small dining room quietly. They sat together on a stuffed couch in front of a fireplace holding hands, mesmerized by the crackling fire, each daydreaming their separate dreams about their unknown future.

❧❦❧

About a month later, the Strongs arrived in London on a Monday morning after an all-night flight. Dr. Strong had meetings all week, so family events were reserved for the weekend. Anne pleaded disingenuously that exams kept her from a visit with her mother before Friday, so they arranged to spend that day in neutral and preoccupying situations touring and shopping. Mrs. Fleming took Mrs. Strong to all the right shops and museums, an act of grace to Mrs. Strong and one of diplomacy on behalf of Anne. Micah would join them Friday evening when Dr. Strong's medical sessions concluded. The Flemings had insisted on taking them all, with Cassie, to their private club Friday evening, so any offensive encounter was postponed to Saturday, when Anne and Micah had suggested taking the Strongs to Kew Gardens to walk around the extraordinary grounds. Mrs. Strong would love the rare flowers, Micah suggested.

Friday night was light and frivolous. The Strongs knew the Flemings had been surrogate parents to Anne, and they were their charming best. They insisted that Cassie join Anne on her next trip home, as if Anne could imagine one soon without Micah. The Flemings' hospitality was heartfelt, and the Strongs insisted on reciprocating Saturday evening. John Fleming must choose the place for dinner, but they all would be guests of the Strongs. Micah instinctively liked Dr. Strong, who was courtly, but pleasant to him all evening. In fact, Micah would have liked Mrs. Strong, except for what he knew was brewing at her instigation. He also could sense that Anne's afternoon with her mother had not gone well, though the two of them had no opportunity to be alone to discuss stressful details. Her parents had implored Anne to stay with them at their suite at the hotel, and the Flemings solicitously invited Micah to stay at their apartment with them and Cassie so the Strongs could catch up with their daughter. It all seemed simple and reasonable.

The next day, Cassie joined Micah when he picked up the Strongs at their hotel, and they took the tube to Kew Gardens. They walked around the expansive grounds all day, with a brief stop for lunch at a café near one of the glass greenhouses. In the casual switch of walking partners, when Micah found himself alone with Mrs. Strong, the conversation was impersonal and pleasant, if superficial. Mrs. Strong knew about flowers and horticulture, and Micah was a good audience. He and Anne spoke only with eye contact, and Micah could tell she was unhappy. Anne changed for dinner at the hotel; Micah changed at the Flemings. Dinner at Mr. Fleming's suggested restaurant, Green's wood-paneled dining room, was long and laugh-filled, and for Anne and Micah diversionary. They ate well—Dover sole, the house specialty—and drank much, as Dr. Strong, who was feeling relieved of the week's responsibilities and anxious to reciprocate the Flemings' generosity of the night before, ordered many fine wines and an after-dinner digestif. They separated late, promising to meet the next morning at the hotel for brunch before the Strongs had to pack and leave for the airport. Cassie questioned Micah about Anne and her mother that night when they returned to the

Flemings' apartment. Neither had had the chance to find out from Anne what was up.

The following morning everyone partook of a grand English breakfast at the Strongs' hotel, fitting for a day's ration. Then there were hugs, invitations, and good-byes, and at last Anne and Micah were together and alone. Cassie was joining her parents to attend a family social engagement; Micah and Anne were invited to join them but declined. They took the afternoon train from London to Cambridge. Micah didn't ask Anne what had transpired between her and her mother, waiting for her to get around to it in her own time. After they had left the city and settled in for the two-hour trip, Anne recounted her conversations over the past few days.

"Mother's not a Nazi, darlin', that would make my life easier. There were no directives or gauche accusations. It's all more subtle than that," she began. Mimicking her mother's voice, she continued: "'Michael seems like a very nice young man, deah.'

"'It's Micah, Mother.'

"'Micah, yes. He seems very nice, and bright, I'm sure. Your father and I discussed your letter, of course. We only ask that before you get any final ideas, Anne, that you consider some facts of life. He's switching careers, he comes from Chicago, and really, the religion thing can't be sloughed, Anne. I'm a liberal . . .'

"Sure she is!" Anne interrupted her own imitation of her mother's conversation.

" . . . 'I'm a liberal and know and enjoy some of Charleston's Jewish people. You know Mrs. Jacobs on the theater committee? I enjoy her very much. But, Anne, how would you and he fit in, what would you do about the church, the country club . . .'

"As if that's what's really on my mind," Anne ad libbed.

"'We are tolerant people, Anne, you know that.' It's that word, *tolerant*, a giveaway word of superiority. As if we gentiles have some right to grant Jewish people some formal approval—to exist," Anne blurted out.

"We've never talked about any of those things," Micah added, charmed by Anne's remark. "Are we missing something?"

"Darlin', I never dreamed we'd be living in Charleston *or* Chicago. I don't care about where I go to church. When have you and I gone to chapel, except to hear the choral singing at Christ Church? And I can live without country clubs. It's about control, and about my living the life she planned for me. My brother Philip was a disappointment to them both, and Mother saw me as her project, her successful social activity. While I was following the path she viewed as appropriate and successful, everything was perfect. But that's when I was her creation. Why can't she accept what I want to do on my own, where I want to go, and with whom? Dammit, why is she spoiling our love affair?"

"Don't let her. She can't spoil it for me, unless she hurts you," Micah reached out and took Anne's hand. "What did your father say about all this?"

"Not a thing. Daddy's not part of these conversations. He would never raise these questions with me. But no doubt they've talked about my letter, and he knows she's telling me these things. He either agrees with her, or is too meek—no, he's not that, really . . ." Anne trailed off.

"Maybe you should talk to him," Micah suggested.

"Maybe," Anne pondered. "I'll just have to ask him whether he knows about Mother's not-so-subtle interference and find out if she speaks for him. 'Frankly, I don't give a damn,' to quote Rhett Butler," she drawled, keeping some sense of humor about their otherwise unpleasant situation.

After a while, Micah spoke. "I wonder what my folks will think. All they know is that I've met a wonderful person who I am seriously in love with. So far, no comment. Though my parents are not big letter writers."

"Have you told your sister?" Anne asked.

"Kind of; not any deep or detailed information. Just that I'm in love with a beautiful, wonderful South Carolina WASP."

"Darlin'," Anne spoke looking off into space, "you know what makes me feel the worst about all this?" It was a rhetorical question. Micah knew it was and listened, not answering. "I feel some of her in me. And I hate it. I don't want to be like that. Like her."

"You're not anything like her. Not in that sense," Micah responded.

"Yes. Yes. Some of it is there," Anne continued, plaintively. "Ah member," her voice slipped into a more pronounced accent, unconsciously. "Ah member once, I was in New York with my boardin' school class, going to the planetarium and the Museum of National History and the Statue of Liberty, an' all the sites, you know. An' we were on the subway and my girlfriends and I were being giddy and loud, laughin' and all. An' there was this cute boy sittin' up the aisle from where we were standin' holdin' on to the straps, you know." Anne was looking into space as she spoke, seeing that scene in her mind's eye, describing it as if she were someone else, watching from the sidelines, reporting. "We all saw him and whispered about how cute he was. And one of my friends, it was Loti, said, 'Go on, Anne, go sit near him. There's a seat empty next to him.' He was readin' some folded-up newspaper, not payin' any attention to me, of course."

Anne continued. "So brazen I walked over to him. I don't know what in the world I would have done. But I suppose I was goin' to flirt, captivate him there in public where it would be safe. And then we'd all talk about it forever after, I guess. So I walked over to where he was sittin', you know. And he was real cute, tall and informal and comfortable lookin'—like you, really, darlin'; I guess I like your style." Micah smiled.

"And as I reached the place where he was sitting, he noticed me, he smiled, and stood up so I could pass in front and get to the seat next to where he was." Anne spoke slowly now. "As he stood up, I noticed he had on this . . . headpiece clipped to the top of his head."

"A yarmulke," Micah added.

"Yes. And I was so, so shocked by it, I turned away and dashed back to my friends, who were watching and giggling. I suppose they thought I had cold feet. But that really wasn't it, I know. It was the foreign, exotic thing on his head that set him apart from what I was. I'm embarrassed to say this now. But it was there, Micah, it was there . . ." Anne's commentary trailed off.

"So what does that mean now?" Micah asked. "If I saw an Amish woman in her outfit—say she was beautiful, but I was not attracted to her because she came from another world, what would that mean? That I'm some sort of racist or prejudiced person? Of course not." He answered his own question. "It only means we all are distanced from people whose outfits bespeak a different time or place. We're uncomfortable with our differentness as much as theirs."

"It means we are culturally prejudiced," Anne interrupted. "And I don't think it's everyone who feels that way."

"So you're some kind of closet Klanner? Is that what you are confessing to?" Micah kidded.

"No, darlin'. Don't you see? It's her. She's part of me, and that's why I hate what I see in her, about all this!"

"Anne," Micah took her hand and brought his face close to hers. "There comes a time in every kid's life—often when we're not kids anymore. There comes a time when we look at our parents, those people who we thought were models of what adults, people, we were supposed to be. We look at them and see something we censure and are embarrassed by. And we think, who are they? They aren't me! I don't want any part of what they are or do. That's what you're seeing now in your mother's handling of your stepping out into a world that isn't hers. And she's small. All of a sudden, small. And imperfect. She may have been your model when you were young and without other models. But she is not your choice. That's the key. You can't fault yourself because you are so close to her. Because you once held her up to yourself as the model of you. A model that's not your model now. That's natural, for everyone. And if you remember some, some, thought you once had, or some faux pas you once made, or some social sin you ever imagined, don't make the false presumption and say that shadow of someone else is you.

"And remember this, Anne," Micah added. "You *are* a product of her, and I love you, so there has to be some good in her."

Micah and Anne sat silently as the train continued its monotonous journey. Anne's eyes welled with tears. "Ah do so love you, darlin'; I love you so much."

Anne snuggled closer to Micah, put her head on his shoulder, and they silently daydreamed during the rest of the train ride to Cambridge.

There, they went to Anne's room and eventually to sleep, wrapped in each other's arms. Nothing more was said about this problem. What could be said? Each was moving away from the momentum of their lives and was unable to even imagine the specifics of their future. They only knew that it would be together. That was enough.

The lovers' troubles were not over, nor were they confined to Anne's parents' social pretensions. In the aftermath of the Strongs' visit to London, Micah and Anne threw themselves more than ever into the Cambridge life. Micah immersed himself in his studies, becoming more and more absorbed by the law. Anne and he were a sought-after tennis couple. Because their game was good, they often were invited to play in private clubs as mixed-doubles partners. Because they were such an attractive couple and played so mannered and competent a game, they were sought after for social gatherings. Anne was persuaded to audition for a serious play and won a role. She was enjoying something she'd never done before, and showed—she was told—real talent. Weeks sped by. Their time together was precious. They were completely absorbed in their everyday life, and completely in love with each other.

It was too good to be true. Two months after the Strongs' visit, Micah was awakened in the middle of the night by the porter on late duty. There was a call for him from the United States. Micah was not fully awake when he arrived at the gate office, picked up the phone, and heard his sister's voice.

"Micah, I have very sad news: Daddy died today. He had a heart attack driving home from work . . . ." Micah only heard words thereafter, as an unthinkable reality sunk in. His father was only 64, hardy, not sickly. He couldn't imagine his vulnerability, much less his mortality.

He called and woke Anne, who rushed to his room. They embraced. Micah was stunned and confused, and said little. Anne just hugged him and whispered in his ear, "Micah, darlin', I'm so sorry. Now I'll never meet your daddy. I'm so sorry for you. I love you."

Somehow, he and Anne arranged for him to get home within 24 hours so he could be there for the funeral, which under Jewish practice must be within 48 hours after death. Anne called Cassie and asked to borrow her car. Micah packed hastily. They drove to Heathrow to be there when operations opened. Under emergency procedures, he was able to get a seat on a morning flight, but there were endless hours of rushed arrangements. He functioned in a haze of stunned semi-consciousness; Anne helped manage all the calls and money movement and arrangements that were beyond Micah's capacity to cope with.

Micah moved through the next days in a half stupor. He stared out the window, not eating or conversing throughout the endless plane ride. He arrived in Chicago and went directly to his family's home. There, relatives hovered, friends arrived with platters of food. He found his mother in her room looking older than he ever remembered seeing her. She cried when Micah arrived. They embraced. His sister was there with them, and they told Micah the little that could be told to explain a sudden, unpredictable fatal heart attack. They were about to have their regular Friday night Sabbath dinner. Dad was sitting in his car at a red light, and slumped over, dead. That fast. That unpredictable. So final. Ada was coming to dinner that night with her boyfriend, a medical school classmate whom Micah hadn't yet met. The whole scene seemed to him like a chapter in an unfamiliar book, someone else's life.

Micah's letter was not discussed. The week's numbing events precluded Micah ever mentioning his wonderful life in Cambridge; it would have seemed a gratuitous boast to his sad family. To open the issue of his love life and its social implications then was out of the question. His sister privately congratulated him, with little of the enthusiasm or curiosity he would have expected over his news. She hinted that his letter had troubled his parents and that the family was unsure how to react to it.

They reminisced about their father. He was from another world; he'd made their lives possible by pledging his own. He worked hard, lived modestly and privately, and rarely spoke with his children about anything beyond the day's demands. He never looked up, never connected with them. There was respect, duty, obligation, but no personal involvement. They respected him, and regretted they did not know or feel more, especially at this time.

Micah was wracked with guilt. He moved through the motions of attending to family business. His father had prudently provided for his mother. Mortgage insurance meant she owned the house free and clear of financial obligations. His business had an insurance policy that paid the widow an annuity and continued her medical insurance, so she had no worries about managing her modest lifestyle. That was what husbands did for wives in those days, in those social circles. His sister Ada and her fiancé would soon be practicing medicine as a husband-and-wife team in gynecology and pediatrics in Chicago, so they would be there to look after his mother. Micah felt so apart from his family in emotional and intellectual ways that his guilt was consuming.

By the end of two weeks, in a burst of manic activity, he had taken care of the necessary details regarding the family's mundane affairs. Legal papers were recorded. The will submitted for probate. Tax reports made. Funeral arrangements handled. Micah could relent to protestations that he should return to his life in Cambridge. Now, he would do that. He spoke to Anne each evening, and on their last call he told her he'd be on the first flight arriving at Heathrow the morning after next. His anticipation of being back in his new world with Anne preoccupied his thoughts the last few days at home. He was overly attentive to his mother and her affairs, assuaging his guilt about leaving. But after two weeks, the shock of his father's departure from everyone's life in the family had worn off and life began to go on in its changed form for his mother. Micah had implored her to come to London, where she would meet Anne and they would take her for a tour of England. It would be therapeutic for her. Everyone in the family and their circle of close friends encouraged her to agree, and eventually she acquiesced. They planned that she would come soon, when she thought she could travel. Micah thought that plan made his leaving graceful, and the visit would provide the perfect situation for introducing Anne to his mother.

The last night in Chicago, Micah had dinner alone with his mother. It was the only time they talked about Anne and his change of plans at Cambridge.

"Your father would have been proud to have a son a lawyer and a daughter a doctor," she said, wistfully, apropos of nothing they had been discussing. "Do you go to law school there?" she asked.

"No, my advisor there thinks I can get a scholarship to a good school in the States. I'll start applying soon, and come back before September, when classes start."

"And what will happen with Anne?" She asked next, directly and with no hint of her own thoughts on the subject. "She's going to be a lawyer, too?"

"No, no, Anne's father is a physician in South Carolina, and she was thinking of medical school. But she's not sure. You will love her, Mama. She is warm and beautiful and bright. She's special. I never felt this way about anyone before. She's very anxious to meet you. When you come, we'll show you Cambridge, and take you to our friends' farm in the Cotswolds. You'll enjoy the change of scenery. And we want to share our love affair with England with you."

Micah's mother said nothing. Showed no emotion. Betrayed no judgment. Her diffidence could as well have been the result of her state of bereavement, or her retiring nature, or her unwillingness to make an issue of Micah's love affair. Micah was certain Anne's winning way would assure his mother's affection. It wouldn't be long before they were a family.

Anne didn't answer his call the night before he left, but their plans had been set and he would soon see her at Heathrow. When he walked into the terminal after his all-night flight, past immigration, he saw Cassie, but not Anne. He assumed she was in the car outside. Cassie seemed subdued when they greeted. She asked how his mother was as they exited the terminal with Micah's luggage slung over his shoulder, but said nothing of Anne. When they got to her car and Micah saw that Anne wasn't there, he stopped, looked at Cassie, and asked: "Where's Anne? Is something wrong?"

"Get in the car and I'll tell you," Cassie responded. When they both were seated, Cassie turned to Micah: "I don't know a good way to tell you; it's so unfair that you've had nothing but bad news."

"Tell me, Cassie, what's happened?"

"Anne's been injured. She and I were riding together yesterday in the field where we usually ride. Her horse suddenly bolted when a swan, of all things, flapped its wings and darted across its path. Anne was flung from her saddle and struck her head. She's had a serious concussion and is in the special care ward of the university hospital." Now Cassie was in tears.

Micah was in shock, depressed, and panicked. "Let's go there right away," he ordered.

"I'll take you, love, but you won't be able to talk to her. She's in intensive care and can't have visitors. Even her father, who's on his way here, couldn't talk to her. Her mother's coming, too, later this evening. Mother and Dad are fetching them." Cassie started the car and began their trip to Cambridge.

"Is she conscious? What do her doctors say?" Micah asked as they began their drive.

"That she's in serious condition. That she's young and could come out of it completely." She hesitated then; she clearly wasn't saying everything, and Micah could see that was the case.

"What does that mean? 'Could come out of it completely.' Might she not?" Micah was hurt by the mere words he'd asked, and what they implied.

"The doctors are very good, and she's getting the best care. And Dr. Strong is consulting with a neurosurgeon in London who is supposed to be top drawer, and he's on the case, too."

The rest of the drive was quiet, gloomy, endless. Cassie gave Micah time to digest the bad news and gather his composure. They were good pals, and she was the best person to be with Micah at this time. She reached over and took Micah's hand, steering with the other. "Anne's going to be okay, luv, have faith."

SIX

The End of the Journey

When Dr. Strong heard about Anne's accident, he and his wife were thunderstruck, and guilt-ridden. Mrs. Strong made arrangements to fly to London, where the Flemings would meet them, and closed their house in Charleston. Dr. Strong located the leading neurosurgeon in England. Sir Owyn Samuels's work at London's Queen's Square Hospital Neurological Institute was world-renowned. Having been approached by mutual colleagues in the United States on behalf of Dr. Strong, Sir Samuels had spoken with Anne's attending physicians at Cambridge and was prepared to take charge of Anne's treatment. He spoke to Dr. Strong over the phone and advised him of the status of her situation.

"I'm sorry, Dr. Strong, to meet you under these difficult circumstances," he began. "Let me get straight to the heart of the matter, as I know you must be terribly concerned, and decisions must be made immediately."

"Your reputation is well known to me, Dr. Samuels," Dr. Strong said, "I'm grateful that you are available and relieved to have your advice and participation. Tell me about Anne."

"Yes, indeed. Anne has suffered a severe blow to the head resulting in a traumatic brain injury. She's in a coma, in intensive care at the hospital in Cambridge. I've ordered her put on to a ventilator as she may have suffered subdural hematoma and diffuse brain edema. She's at high risk for brain herniation. She's had a global brain injury, and we can't know now if it will be reversible. But as you know, time is of the essence. Anne needs immediate neurological evaluation and should be brought here immediately. I'm sure you'll understand."

"Yes, yes, of course. Has she had a pneumoencephalogram and an EEG, Dr. Samuels?"

"Please, it's Owyn. We'll do that immediately when she arrives. My team will be waiting. We should do this tonight, with your permission. Time is precious."

"Yes, of course. We should be there—my wife and I—in the morning and will come straight to your hospital."

Anne had been removed from Cambridge and was on her way to London in an ambulance before Micah arrived at the hospital with Cassie. Things were moving fast, and Cassie hadn't heard from her parents, who by that time had been called by the Strongs. Anne was strapped to a stretcher, her neck immobilized, her head shaved; intravenous lines were inserted into her arms and a naso-gastric tube was placed through her nose and down into her stomach. Attendants with her were well trained for emergency transport of head and spinal injury patients. Queen's Square in London was well known to everyone at the Cambridge Hospital, and Sir Samuels's interposition had added even more priority to their already high state of attention.

When Micah came running into the Cambridge emergency room with Cassie, she asked for the physician she knew had been in charge of Anne's treatment. When they learned Anne was not there, Micah was beside himself in agitation and worry. For 40 minutes he paced the halls until the physician could be found and brought to them. Cassie introduced them: "Micah, this is Anne's doctor, John Steadman. John, Micah is Anne's dearest friend."

"Yes, of course. I'm sorry, Micah. Let me tell you where things are at the moment."

"Yes, please. Where is Anne? Will she be OK? What's happening?"

Patiently, Dr. Steadman explained. "Anne's had a severe head injury. She's in a coma. We're concerned she's suffered a subdural hematoma, which is a blood clot that has formed and is pushing on her brain. It *must* be removed, or she could die."

"Oh my God," Micah turned around in excited concern. "My God."

Dr. Steadman continued, calmly, carefully. "Anne has the best person in England taking charge of her case. Queen's Square is the leading center for this kind of operation. Right now, the blood clot is sitting on top of her brain and causing massive brain compression. The Strong family has consented to neurosurgery by Sir Samuels if it is necessary. His operation should take about two hours, and if you go there directly, it should be done by the time you arrive."

Micah sank with exhaustion and the weight of the news he couldn't comprehend, process, cope with. Cassie spoke. "Micah, why don't I take you to your dorm? You should get some rest; you've been up all day and night. You'll be under more stress when we get to London. As soon as we hear Anne is out of the operation, I'll drive you there. You can stay with me at Mother and Dad's apartment."

"No, no, I need to get there, Cassie. But I'll take you up on your offer to get me there. I'm in no shape to do much except pack and leave. I want to be with Anne."

That is what they did. Micah returned to his rooms. He deposited one set of clothes and replaced it with another, contacted his proctor to explain his prolonged absence, and within an hour was back in Cassie's car retracing their earlier route and on their way back to London. Micah was in a netherworld between shock and exhaustion. His life was crashing around him, it seemed, out of control.

When they arrived at the Queen's Square Hospital in London and found out where Anne's room would be, they rushed to it. Anne had just been brought there for post-op recovery and two of her doctors were there, along with her parents and Sir Samuels. Anne was in bed and unconscious. Her head was bandaged. Unable to breathe on her own, her body was attached to an artificial breathing machine by a series of tubes and hoses. A tube ran from her bandaged head, draining a bloody liquid into a bottle. Intravenous tubes ran into both her arms. Her eyes were closed. After a quick introduction, Micah picked up the conversation going on, as Sir Samuels explained to the Strongs what the operation had accomplished.

". . . the surgery resulted in the evacuation of a large subdural hematoma, which should diffuse the brain compression. She needs to be fully supported until she wakes up. We'll keep her on the ventilator, feed her with a naso-gastric tube, and provide fluids through IV. So far, she's unresponsive."

At that, Dr. Samuels did a neurological examination to demonstrate Anne's condition. "Anne," he shouted, "squeeze my hand." No response. "Open your eyes." No response. "Tell me your name." No response. He pressed the nails on two of her fingers. No response. He gently poked a small pin into her leg. No response. Anne lay still, motionless, the only sign of life being the slow, steady rise and fall of her breast as the ventilator forced her breathing. Mrs. Strong cried out. "Oh, no, Anne, my baby!" Micah looked on in silence. He felt his life leaving him. All he wanted was to be with Anne, and he might never be able to again.

For the next week, there was little change in Anne's condition. Micah and the Strongs maintained polite society, relieved by the Flemings' caring presence. Evenings, Micah and Cassie split off from the two older couples, walked the city streets, and talked about Anne. Micah couldn't even imagine the rest of his life. After four days, Anne's eyes opened periodically, but she did not respond to the doctor's tests. She was awake, but without any sense of recognition, as if in a deep sleep.

One morning, during the second week after the operation, as Micah stared from Anne's window, deep in thought and deadening rumination about what awaited him and Anne, something inexplicable made him turn toward Anne. She looked at him, head cocked in his direction, with a look of terror in her eyes.

Softly she said her first word: "Mi–cah."

He came to her bedside, took her hand, tears welling in his eyes. "Yes, Anne. Anne. You're back! It's me! Oh, God, I'm so happy to hear you." But then her eyes shut and they lost contact. Micah ran into the hall and waved and called for the attending nurse. She came running, just as the Strongs arrived. Micah told them what had happened. Soon, one of Anne's doctors arrived. He explained: "This is a defining moment." Anne's brief recognition of Micah meant that Anne had turned a corner and was on her way toward some level of recovery. The doctor performed a neurological exam as he talked, but again Anne did not respond. "That's okay," he told them. "She should become reactive slowly, over time, but that *will* happen."

It would be a long way to that recovery.

The group didn't quite know what to make of this news, but that evening they all did have a subdued celebration. All six went to the Flemings' club and toasted Anne. Micah was part of the group, but he felt apart from the Strongs and at the same time closer to the Flemings. The Strongs had to realize the depth of Anne's feelings about Micah from that day's event. That night, back at their hotel room, Dr. Strong told his wife firmly that like it or not, if only for Anne's recovery chances, she had better treat Micah as more than an interloper in their family. He clearly was a deep and important memory to Anne.

During the next week, Anne's third postoperative week at Queen's Square, she showed further modest signs of responsiveness. She struggled to speak, showed signs of understanding. But the family had its next shock one morning, when Dr. Samuels, after his rounds, called them all together. They presumed he might be suggesting a transfer of Anne's case management from neurosurgery to rehabilitation, but that was not why he called them together.

"I have some news that may be a surprise," he began.

As the Strongs and Micah looked at him intently, he continued. "We did routine postoperative blood tests on Anne. Were you aware that she's pregnant?"

The Strongs and Micah could not have been more startled. "Did you know this?" Mrs. Strong said accusingly to Micah.

"No. No, I did not," he shot back. "I had no idea."

"Micah, please tell us what you know," Dr. Strong interjected.

"I'm totally surprised," Micah added. "I love Anne. Surely you know that. But she never said a word. But, now I—" he stopped.

"What?" Mrs. Strong demanded.

"Well, when she came back from Charleston two months ago, she was *very* upset about her conversations with you—no disrespect meant, Mrs. Strong," Micah explained. "I was surprised at the depth of her anger. She said she thought you were spoiling our love affair." Micah surprised himself with his bluntness and candor. Dr. Strong shot a glance at his wife.

Dr. Samuels looked down. Nothing more was said for a moment, then he added, "Best we can tell, she's in the early stage of her second trimester. Abortion would be out of the question, I should think. I presume if anyone else should be advised, you will see to it," he subtly concluded.

"Will this hurt her recovery?" Micah asked.

"No," both doctors responded together. "It's too early to really tell, but if she continues to make a good recovery, the pregnancy should not pose a problem. It might even be good therapy if Anne knew," Dr. Samuels added.

"Oh my God," Mrs. Strong sighed, covering her eyes and looking away.

Later, Dr. Strong walked around the hospital corridors with Micah while Mrs. Strong sat in Anne's room. "Micah, this is awkward to ask. But is Anne's pregnancy a total surprise to you? Forgive me for asking. But I'm only trying to gauge what Anne's reaction might be."

"Dr. Strong, I love your daughter more than life itself," Micah's earnestness was disarming. "We loved each other, presumed we'd eventually marry, took precautions, but not always, not rigorously . . ." he trailed off, looking away.

Dr. Strong put his arm around Micah. "You should tell Anne, then, at the appropriate time." That was all that was said. After another week of bedside vigil and Anne's barely perceptible progress, Dr. Strong returned home to attend to his practice. Mrs. Strong called him with daily reports and remained at the hotel and hospital. Gradually, her relationship with Micah went from chilly and hostile to civil, with occasional flashes of awkward chumminess. Sometimes they ate together at a small tea shop in the neighborhood. Micah always accompanied her to her hotel at the end of their day at the hospital.

They never spoke about Anne's pregnancy or about Anne and Micah's future. By the fourth week post-op, Anne began to move slightly and to attempt speech. The doctors informed Micah and the Strongs that Anne had a suffered a stroke to the left side of her brain, partially paralyzing her right arm and leg, slurring her speech. She had what was called expressive aphasia, a language problem that meant Anne could comprehend others but was unable to speak normally, stuttering her words in broken and choppy sentences. It would be frustrating to her, but with patience and arduous rehabilitative therapy, Dr. Samuels felt her condition would improve and she could get back most of her normal skills. "She is young and in very strong physical condition," Dr. Samuels told Micah. Long therapy would cure most of these symptoms. The best brain injury rehabilitation center was in the United States, at UCLA's medical facility. It was time to plan her departure from Queen's Square. Dr. Samuels and Dr. Strong had talked; they were able to arrange such a move in two more weeks.

The minute he learned that Anne might be going to UCLA for prolonged treatment, Micah's plans became clear. His mentor at Cambridge, Professor Heavens, had been urging Micah to go to Harvard Law School, where he taught intermittently, or to Yale, in whose educational environment he thought Micah would thrive. Micah made an appointment to see Professor Heavens the next day and took the train to Cambridge. He told Heavens about Anne's situation, saying he wanted to go to UCLA Law School the next semester, if possible. Heavens knew the dean at UCLA and was happy to intervene on Micah's behalf. With Micah's background and Heavens's intervention, there should be no problem. Within a week, Micah had received word that he would be given a scholarship to UCLA Law School, details to be arranged when he got there. Micah told Anne the good news that night when they were alone in her room. She beamed, sensing, Micah hoped, that their life together was returning.

Several days later, a strange event occurred. It was Anne's birthday, and Cassie had brought a birthday cake to her room. Some of the nurses and doctors were in the room with Anne when Cassie, Micah, and the cake arrived. Anne smiled at the sight of them, beaming her special warm, you're-the-only-person-in-the-world smile. All the attendees sang "Happy Birthday." Midway in their performance, Anne began to sing with them, ". . . birthday to you." The onlookers exchanged startled glances back and forth, and when the song was completed, Micah took one of the doctors aside and asked incredulously: "She can barely talk. How can she sing? What's happening?"

The stunned young doctor explained, "The left side of the brain controls spoken language. The right side controls musical language. Anne's injury was to her left brain, which is why her right arm and leg are paralyzed and she can barely speak. But the brain works in magical, mysterious ways, and the right side controls singing. That's why she can sing but not speak." The mysteries of Anne's mind and body would continue; it would be a lifelong exploration for her and Micah. But the road back to normalcy had begun.

When Anne was strong enough, two weeks later, she was told that soon she would be going to California to begin her long rehabilitation. Dr. Strong had seen to the arrangements. Micah and Anne had talked, in their evolving new method of communication. One night when they were alone, Micah told Anne they were having a child and he begged her to marry him. "I love you, Anne. I want my child to have you for its mother." Tears streamed from her eyes and she softly squeezed his hand. "Besides," Micah said smiling, "it'd kill your mother to have a bastard Jewish grandchild."

Haltingly, Anne told Micah she wanted him to arrange for a private ceremony; no one else was to be present. Micah persuaded her she had to invite her parents, along with the Flemings, Cassie, and Daniel. They would have a bedside ceremony. The chaplain of the hospital had been visiting Anne routinely; he would do a simple civil ceremony. They would time it so his mother and sister would be on an open phone line and could be part of the event, however far away. He exaggerated her parents' kindnesses to him, and Anne went along. She had no strength to resist, and on reflection, she wanted her friends to be there, so she could not exclude her mother and father.

Two days later, the selected guests arrived at Anne's room. The Flemings had sent bouquets of flowers that filled every surface of the room. The Strongs and Flemings, and all of Anne's doctors, including Sir Samuels and Anne's therapists, were there. Cassie had bought Anne a lacy white gown from Harrod's. The nurses had given her a white turban to cover her surgical scar. Her mother gave her a family heirloom, an antique pin in the shape of a heart with garnets along its circumference, a memento she'd had from her mother. Micah's mother had sent Micah her wedding ring with a note, saying, "I hope you and your bride have the happiness your father and I had." Anne cried when Micah told her of this and called her mother-in-law-to-be to say so.

Anne looked gloriously beautiful; she shone with a glow of happiness and peace. Few mortals as battered as she could dominate a room with such beauty. Each man there thought how fortunate Micah was; no one felt sadness or sympathy. Anne was the lovely centerpiece in the cramped hospital room.

Micah arrived last, with a golden-haired puppy on a leash. He'd gotten special permission to do so. "My present for my wife," he announced. "To reflect her past history and to start our new family, I think we should name her Charleston." As he said so, the pup leaped onto Anne's bed and started licking her radiant, tearful face.

As arranged, the ceremony was brief and ecumenical. Cassie was maid of honor, Daniel best man. Micah's mother was on the phone along with his sister, as prearranged with the hospital switchboard. Dr. Strong popped open bottles of champagne, and Daniel and Cassie made adoring toasts. Micah sat beside Anne at the edge of her bed that had been raised so she could sit up, his arm around Anne's shoulder. In his toast, Daniel described his dear friends as "bruised, battered, and betrothed, and the envy of all who aspire to true love." Cassie read from Shakespeare's Sonnet 116, which seemed to combine the pair's message of love with the politics of their unusual situation. ". . . love . . . an ever-fixed mark that looks on tempests and is never shaken . . . Love alters not . . . nor no man ever loved." When she finished, few eyes were without tears.

After the ceremony, Anne said, "Thank you er–body. Pease. May Mic and I be lone." Each of them kissed Anne, hugged Micah, and left. Anne beamed at Micah. He snuggled next to her on the bed. Charleston perched between them, nuzzling Anne. Eventually, all three members of the newest Anglo-American family fell asleep on the bed. That was their honeymoon: the wounded patient, her young beloved, and their dog, alone in bed in a London hospital.

Ever socially conscious, Mrs. Strong had handled one final family matter on her own. She'd managed to arrange a carefully worded notice of the wedding in several U.S. newspapers. In fact, it was the second time Anne's and Micah's names appeared together in the *New York Times*. This time it was on the Sunday social page, under a photograph of Anne taken when she was in college.

Dr. and Mrs. Ethan Strong of Charleston, South Carolina, recently announced the betrothal of their daughter, Anne Marbrey Strong, to Micah Lehman, son of Mrs. Lida Lehman and the late Samuel Lehman, who was an entrepreneur in the merchandising business in Chicago. Dr. Strong is head of cardiology and dean at the University of South Carolina Hospital in Charleston. The bride and groom met when they were Thayer Scholars studying at Cambridge University, England. The bride graduated salutatorian from Sweet Briar College in Virginia; the groom graduated magna cum laude from the University of Chicago. The couple will reside in California.

It would be a long road back to their independent life together, but Anne and Micah had begun. It would take every bit of their energy and good fortune to get there.

SEVEN

A New Start

In the early days of sound movies, the beautiful song and dance star Elaine Morrison and the rugged cowboy hero Bud Pomeroy were among the most popular young stars at the Warner Brothers Studio. They had been in a terrible car crash returning from a tryst in Palm Desert. They survived, but their careers were over. Photos of their badly burned and mangled bodies were etched in the public's mind. There had been magazine cover stories and graphic descriptions in news and tabloid papers. One result was that Warners founded, and other studios and adoring fans contributed to, a rehabilitative department in the stars' names at UCLA's medical facility. The specialty was new, and as a result of its visibility and remarkable funding the Morrison-Pomeroy Rehab Wing gained wide attention. Later, when Ronald Reagan, who was close to the movie community, became governor, state funds for research were committed, which attracted excellent staff. With the top professionals came an international reputation. Years later, it had become the leading facility in the world for comprehensive physical therapy and rehabilitation.

Dr. Strong arranged for Anne's treatment at Morrison-Pomeroy Rehab when she could safely leave Queen's Square in London. When the day came for Anne to leave, the staff all came to Anne's room to bid her farewell and wish her well. Even Sir Samuels dropped by, and petted Charleston, who had become a pet of the ward. The three Flemings and Daniel were in tears; they embraced Anne and Micah, who told them they would always be a special part of their lives, and promised that they would be back—someday.

To Micah and Anne, the voyage home on the same *Queen Elizabeth* on which their journey had begun, it seemed a lifetime ago, was the start of a new chapter in their lives. This chapter was theirs together. Now they had a room of their own (shared with Charleston). The shipboard doctor had been briefed about Anne's condition, and examined her each morning in her cabin to be sure no problems would arise during the weeklong ocean journey. Because of a partial paralysis of her right side, Anne could not get around without Micah's constant assistance; he lifted her from bed to wheelchair to dining chair. Micah pushed Anne around the deck in her wheelchair each day so they could spend time outdoors sunning themselves before resting in deck chairs wrapped in blankets and reading. Anne wore her old white baseball cap with the orange V from the University of Virginia to cover her shaved and scarred head. Shipmates thought she looked adorable, and many of them stopped to chat with her and Micah in the dining room where they sat alone.

One morning, as Micah and Anne sat on deck chairs, sunning themselves, holding hands, daydreaming, Anne spoke softly, still haltingly: "Don't you won–er when we made our baby, darlin'? You've never ask."

Micah startled, stammered: "I don't . . . it doesn't matter when. I'm just happy . . . ."

Anne interrupted: "Boys are funny. So dumb. So dear."

"What do you mean? Why am I dumb?" Micah asked.

"It was all I wonered bout, in my haze, after you and Doc Samuels told me. You were so excited; it never 'curred to you to won–er when this 'portant thing in our life happen?"

"You mean, no stork," Micah kidded. "I was so happy; it really doesn't matter, does it?"

"I'm not crit–sizin'," Anne's language still was choppy, "just, I wanted to know the moment, if I could recall it, then I did . . . ." Anne's conversation faded, and she looked off into the distance.

"Well, you can't leave me wondering, if you know," Micah finally interrupted her long pause. "Tell me. When?"

". . . 'member months ago, when I came back from my visit to Charlton, and we met and went to the Flemin' country house . . . ." Anne was looking into the distance, speaking brokenly, as if she was watching a reenactment of their night in front of the fireplace at Ashton Hall.

"I do remember." Micah squeezed Anne's hand as his recollection of their passionate night together returned. "I thought about that when the doctor first told me and your parents at the hospital. I guessed that. But how can you know?"

"I knew then . . . I just knew . . . somehow . . . I think I wished it to be . . . that night . . . I was so raw from my visit home . . . then . . . when I was with you again . . . I just meant . . . to be part of you, and for you to be in *me* . . . and for us to be so in–nately together . . . I'd not felt that way ever before . . . I wanted your baby—my baby . . . our baby . . . I think I *knew* that night . . . and then I forgot about it when we got back to Ca bridge. I had hints in the next months, and I finally just knew. I was going to tell you when you came back after your father passed . . . but . . . then I couldn't. . . ." A tear slid down Anne's face. She stopped talking.

Micah sat up and moved onto the edge of Anne's deck chair. He put his arm around her. "I'll never forget that night, Anne. Now it is even more special."

"I was going to tell you we should name our baby Sam, for your father. But when I was . . . hurt . . . I thought maybe I'd killed our baby . . . I didn't know, Micah; I thought . . . ." Tears streamed down Anne's face, and Micah encircled her with his arms, and they rocked together. Anne whispered, wetly, into Micah's ear, "Micah, I'm worry that you're stuck with a broken woman."

"Beautiful, not broken. You'll always be beautiful, and soon you won't be broken."

"Oh, Micah, I worry for you . . . for our baby. I hope . . . haven't hurt you both. I love you . . . much," she whispered.

"Anne. Don't. Don't. Our baby is fine. The doctors say so. It will keep alive my father's memory. You've done a wonderful thing." Soon Micah was weeping too.

After a while, Anne continued. "Micah, when that thing happen in Char'ton, with Red Carter, all I worried 'bout was being dirtied and hurting you. I knew then, that all my boys before you were . . . different. It was never love, and that's why I always resisted any serious commitments. Until you, my darlin'. Ours—you—were different. And I couldn't wait to come back to you, and *know* real love."

"Oh, Anne. My dear, dear Anne," was all Micah could reply.

Suddenly the moment changed from the sublime to the mundane. Standing next to them, as they were wrapped together in their special private moment of intimacy, a ship's steward inquired, "Some consommé?"

Micah and Anne smiled at each other, unwrapped themselves from their embrace, and Micah said: "Yes, thank you. That sounds very nice. Very nice."

One calm and bright night, toward the end of their voyage west, Anne insisted they go on deck at night to see the sky as they had done on their earlier crossing. With Micah's help, they moved her wheelchair to an open deck where they could lean on the railing. They talked about their child and their marriage.

"We can never tell our children who proposed," Micah smiled at Anne and continued. "I was going to propose to you when I came back to Cambridge from Chicago. I knew then my old life was over, and you were my new life."

"I was going to, too," Anne answered. "I wanted to elope and be married at the Flemins' farm." They stared into the sea as their ship and their past slid by silently.

"They'll think we had a shotgun wedding," Micah kidded.

"Let them think, darlin'. I'm just happy we're together. And I want to be well for you and our baby."

Micah held Anne in his arms, really alone for the first time in months. He looked at her for a long time and said, "I'm so happy to live my life with you, I couldn't wish for one thing more."

"Mic, love you," Anne said as they kissed, and lost themselves in a reverie, wondering where they would be and what they would be doing after Anne's recovery.

❧ ❧

When they arrived in New York, Anne and Micah were tan and rested from their week's voyage. All the privacy, fresh air, rest, and good food had refreshed the young lovers. The Strongs had arranged to greet them on arrival and to spend two days in New York City with them. There wasn't much activity Anne could join in, and her stiff relationship with her mother created a tense environment. The Strongs had been helpful in making many of the arrangements for Anne's treatment in California, so much of the conversation was limited to that business. Anne and Micah were grateful for their help, but happy to leave on the next leg of their journey.

They took a train to Chicago to meet Micah's family for the first time. His sister Ada and her husband, Les, met them and brought them to their house, where Micah's mother was waiting. She and Anne hugged and spoke warmly of Anne's joining their family. They hugged again— and cried together—when Anne showed her the wedding ring. There was a celebratory family dinner, then Anne retired early, exhausted by the travel and emotions of the prior days. The next day, Mrs. Lehman had arranged a party to introduce the couple to all their Chicago friends and family. Again, the reception was warm and welcoming. Everyone brought presents that Anne opened to group oohs and aahs; it was like a shower she and Micah had never had.

Whatever distance had resulted from Micah's elopement and unorthodox marriage quickly closed because Anne was so warm and charming and lovely, and because she reached out so embracingly to them all. By the time everyone left, there were hugs and toasts and promises to visit again as soon as possible. Each guest whispered to Mrs. Lehman how lovely a girl Micah had married. Ada and Les talked long into the night with Micah about the family's life in Chicago, and Micah and Anne's prospective life in California. Anne was tired and had to go to sleep early or risk losing ground in her recovery. They knew of one young doctor at UCLA Hospital whom they called to introduce to Micah and Anne. They promised to visit Micah and Anne when Anne was better. In all, it was a warm reception, quite a contrast from the strained days with the Strongs.

Several days later—Micah and Anne had been in the United States a week now, and were anxious to get on with their travels and settle down in their new life—they arrived by overnight train in Los Angeles. The Morrison-Pomeroy Rehabilitation Center sent a van to bring Anne to its facility. When she was settled in and introductions and paperwork were completed, Micah embraced Anne. "I'm on your shoulder every minute, my love, watching you and rooting for you. I'll be here every day. You get better soon so we can get on the mixed-doubles tennis circuit and show our stuff."

"Bye, darlin'," Anne whispered, wondering what awaited her, but anxious to get on with whatever it took to become well and return to a normal life with Micah, whatever that might be.

❧ ❧

The law school had made a married student apartment available to Micah, and he moved his few possessions into it immediately. Anne would live indefinitely in the Brain Injury Unit at Morrison-Pomeroy. She could walk haltingly, with assistance. Slowly, painstakingly, she would be retrained to talk, walk, eat, dress herself, and manage all the daily chores of normal independent living. Her days were exhausting, and Micah could only see her briefly in the mornings on his way to school, and evenings in her room after his classes and study, on his way back to his apartment. Her progress was incremental, barely perceptible on a daily basis, and grueling. But Anne's athleticism and determination to be able to take care of her new baby and to live independently with Micah provided a strong motivation. She admired the therapists, who saw in her a model patient. After a while, Anne even worked with several of the other, more seriously injured patients, particularly a young girl who looked up to her and whose adoration of Anne provided her with a psychological lift.

Micah used his free time to throw himself into his studies. He had a full scholarship and a job at the law library that paid for their university apartment. Anne's family paid for her treatment. Dr. Strong's insurance and professional courtesies meant that Anne and Micah wouldn't be deep in debt from medical bills when they started their life together. Micah lived very frugally. He loved law school and quickly established himself as the star of his class. Paul Lee, an Asian American, also a scholarship student who worked in the library, became Micah's only real friend. Micah had many friendly acquaintances in his class, but there was no time for social friendships to take seed and flower. He and Paul played ping-pong in the student lounge after eating their brown-bag lunches, worked together in the library, and studied together for exams. Paul was very short, muscular, and had a constant and infectious smile. Micah had become very thin and was shabbily clothed, a product of his hard work and ascetic lifestyle. The two friends were known around the law school as Mutt and Jeff, a moniker that followed them for years. They both excelled and competed for the first place in the class ranking each year. They decided to practice law together; it would be Lehman and Lee or Lee and Lehman, depending on who came in first at the end of their courses. Micah kidded that it had to be his way or people would think it was a one-man firm, Lee N. Lehman. Micah did become valedictorian, beating his friendly competitor for the top spot in their class by a fraction of a point.

Anne's rehabilitation progressed well, and she was not only the favorite patient of the staff, but was also becoming interested in their work. She was good with other patients. Her athleticism as well as her outgoing, warm personality motivated her therapy mates. She was smart and upbeat. Anne began to think this might be work she would enjoy in the future. The therapists encouraged her to consider working there after her rehabilitation was complete. Already she could walk and talk, carefully and slowly.

Micah and Anne had few personal pleasures during this period, except the hours they had together. They were counseled about Anne's prospective delivery; Micah planned to be with her. In their few free hours, they would lie on her bed, listening to music, playing with Charleston. Eventually they could listen to and watch their baby's movements in Anne's expanding belly. Their love of each other grew, and occasionally they could make love—precisely, delicately, but with a pure passion that brought them closer than ever.

Micah and Anne never spoke about sex; they just did it. Anne thought that was strange; Micah did not think about the subject. Their relationship was tender and satisfying and natural and respectful—but Anne thought it was an act that called for some personal commentary, but none came. That absent part of their intimacy puzzled Anne, and she was unsure what to do about it. When she asked Micah if he loved her, he replied, perplexed: "Of course." He could not understand how she could have such a question.

Once Anne attempted to discuss their physical relationship, using humor, but Micah missed her point.

Anne giggled coquettishly once after they made love, as she lay in Micah's arms.

"What?" Micah asked. "Why are you smiling?"

"It's like an acorn, darlin'; I never noticed, but it's like a pink little acorn," Anne whispered.

"What are you talking about, dizzy? What acorn?" Micah asked.

"Your, your, thing, darlin'; it's really like a warm little acorn. I'd never seen but a few pictures, you know, David in Florence, and a few men, and they were Christian boys. They're different. Yours is nicer." Anne smiled and cuddled close into Micah's arms.

Micah was tongue-tied. He'd never heard candid talk about such personal things from girls, and was uncomfortable hearing it. He was prudish, naïve, and inept at talk about personal subjects like this. "I certainly hope you haven't seen many men's private parts," he responded eventually. "And I'm glad you like mine. You're stuck with it now."

"Was that a pun?" Anne teased. Micah said nothing, so Anne dropped the subject, wondering about Micah's reticence, while pleased—if a bit uncertain—that she had a man whose sexual experience would be hers alone.

Micah was in school the afternoon Anne went into early labor. She was in therapy working on upper body strength exercises on the parallel bars, straining, sweating, when she suddenly felt soaking wet in her midsection. She called out and fell to the mat. Her trainers saw that her pants were blackened with more than the expected water that was broken. She was hemorrhaging.

Anne was rushed to the OB ward for an emergency delivery. The other patients in the exercise room called out "good luck" to her as she was hurriedly wheeled away. She wasn't prepared to deliver when it happened because there was an indefinite due date. She thought she was a month away from delivery. She could not have a Cesarean delivery because undergoing anesthesia still would have been a risk to her and to her baby. Anne was in good physical condition, aside from the lingering problems from her head injury, so the delivery went well. But at the time the baby actually was delivered, Anne detected through her haze of pain and drugs that nurses were gathering quickly and activity around her was increasing. In fact, she was hemorrhaging because, as she later learned, an abnormally formed placenta had ruptured. Anne was in strong physical condition from her rehab exercise, and the professional staff were well prepared and took every care.

That wasn't enough. The baby suffocated on the way out of its mother's body. Despite heroic resuscitation efforts, the baby—Anne and Micah's son—died as it was born.

When Micah arrived for his regular evening visit, Anne wasn't in her room. When he learned she was in labor, he raced to the OB ward. The nurse in charge informed Micah, bluntly: "Your wife is healthy, but your child died at birth." The baby boy was named Sam after Micah's recently deceased father, following a Jewish custom. Anne wanted to do this; when she learned of Anne's gesture, Micah's mother was forlorn but deeply touched. The doctors told Anne and Micah that the freak accident at birth might have been caused by Anne's prior accident, but they couldn't be sure. There was no reason why they could not have other children through normal births.

Anne went into shock, and later depression. She was emotionally devastated and physically spent. She had invested so much of her energy into preparing for recovery and motherhood; that event had become her very raison d'être. She spiraled into depression, stopped her rigorous therapy, spoke very little, wept herself to sleep. She did not want to see anyone; her parents came but left after a few frustrating days in which Anne barely spoke. Micah spent as much time as he could with Anne, holding her in his arms, reading to her, reading his law books when she fell asleep. Often waking early in the morning on Anne's bed, he would return to his apartment, shower, dress, and go to law school, stopping on the way there to sit with Anne while she sipped at her tea and nibbled at her toast.

It was little Roberta Sailor who got Anne back on track. Roberta was a ten-year-old black girl who had been horribly burned in an apartment fire that was caused by violations of several city housing codes. Though her family had no money to afford the Morrison-Pomeroy Rehab Center, the public news of her calamity had prompted the creation of a fund to be used for Roberta's treatment. She was in terrible physical condition after numerous skin graft operations and worse psychological condition because she had lost her mother and two sisters in the blaze. It was a miracle firefighters had saved Roberta, but when Anne first met her on the ward, no one had been able to get through to her.

Micah kept Charleston in his apartment, but the Rehab Center had given Anne permission to walk Charleston daily on the grounds and along the halls with Micah. Anne had heard about Roberta and once, out of the blue, asked her therapists if she could try talking to her, and bring Charleston. When they entered Roberta's room, Charleston stood and put two feet on her bed and started nosing her hand. Roberta looked down and a wide grin crossed her face. Anne and she talked—mostly Anne—and they became friends. Anne enlisted Roberta to walk with her and Charleston on Micah's daily visits. Having a friend seemed to bring Roberta out of her shell, and their friendship flowered. Anne was told by the staff that she was a natural in dealing with damaged people, as well a model in the therapy sessions. Anne continued to think this indeed might be a career she would enjoy.

After her child died, Anne hadn't seen Roberta for a week. One day, her door opened and Roberta hobbled in supported by a walker. Charleston raced to her side and jumped at her in greeting. It was the first time Roberta had ventured out of her room on her own; the nurses allowed it, thinking it would be good for Roberta as well as for Anne. The visit seemed to awaken Anne and prompted her to move out of her own depression. If this child's pitiable condition didn't stop her, how could Anne continue to wallow in her depression? Anne and Charleston walked Roberta back to her room, and that day Anne returned on her own to the therapy room.

When she told Micah about the incident that night as they ate together in her room, Anne had her last self-pitying cry. The next day she was back at so vigorous a pace of therapy that the attendants had to tell her to slow down.

Six months later, when Anne was ready to leave the inpatient rehabilitation section of the hospital and live with Micah in their apartment (she returned to the hospital for treatment daily), her speech had improved remarkably, she could walk alone, and she had only traces of her disability. Anne was told she could work as a part-time volunteer at the therapy center. Being useful and having even a token job had a therapeutic effect on Anne. She should not become pregnant for a few years, but she could start having as normal a life as possible. That meant breakfast and dinner each day at the apartment with Micah—a ceremony they would follow throughout their lives—increasingly longer walks on weekends, daily swimming and exercise, and therapy every day at the center. Micah hovered over Anne during this period, fatherly as well as husbandly, doting on her and actively making their decisions and being solicitously protective of her.

She and Micah began planning the rest of their life. They would have a child when Micah's practice was earning them a living. She'd work more and more as a volunteer at the center, and take the courses that would permit her to make this work her career. She had a good head start, having taken physiology and anatomy in college, some of the basic courses in pre-med that would be required in her new career, and having been through the rigorous rehab process as a consumer of this treatment.

Anne and Micah had new careers in clear view and were on the path toward a new life together. On weekends, they drove around the different neighborhoods in a used car Micah's mother had given him, looking for a dream home to settle in—someday. Their world was far different than either of them would have dreamed of when they first met, but they were thoroughly committed to it and to each other, like an old married couple, and happier than they ever had been to finally be free to pursue their new life together.

The Life of a Lawyer

EIGHT

In Law, Practice Makes Perfect

❧ ❧

The years after Anne's daily therapy and Micah's law school matriculation ended were the first years of real married life for them. Up to that time they were overwhelmed with their long days of work, and exhausted when they finally finished and could come home together. Through a connection of Paul Lee, they were able to rent a modest house in Sawtelle, a residential area between Los Angeles and the ocean, populated mostly by Japanese Americans. It was a clean and safe and cordial neighborhood, and their small bungalow-style house had a yard for a garden where Anne could plant and harvest flowers and vegetables and Charleston could bury bones and rest in patches of sun.

After dinner they made a fire in their small fireplace, lay together on their old hulky couch, talked and read to each other until one of them fell asleep. Sometimes they would wake up early in the morning in their clothes with an open book sprawled across one of their chests. They were each other's peace and pleasure, and they neither needed nor sought more from the world. Sometimes, they would invite a friend of Anne's from the rehabilitation center or of Micah's from school to a simple dinner Anne had cooked, but mostly they were each other's social life.

Anne grew stronger physically and more enthusiastic about her work at the center. She took on more responsibilities there and was very popular with the staff and the patients. Eventually, her part-time job became full time. She took courses at the school and eventually was accredited as a therapist. Anne mastered the traditional skills of physical therapy quickly, and she developed an interest in innovative techniques to complement orthodox treatment. She read voraciously about the use of music and drawing in certain kinds of treatment, and of acupuncture and massage and psychological counseling in appropriate situations. All these modalities of treatment were new, and as the country's leading center, Morrison-Pomeroy was the natural place to try out evolving ideas. Anne became the person there to coordinate new treatment trials, and eventually she would open and manage Morrison-Pomeroy's Alternative Treatment Center. Her career blossomed.

When Micah completed law school and embarked on his new career, he had no notion what that career would be, what he would do, where his work would take him. He had no experiences, nor models to guide him, no connections to bring clients or provide financial wherewithal. He knew he didn't want to join a traditional law firm, so he didn't respond to recruiters. Making money for rich people, laboring on a treadmill up a ladder at a firm never entered his mind as an option. The idea of teaching, not literature but law, did appeal to him, but the economics of the academic world were discouraging, and hc and Anne were close to impoverished after their first years of marriage and treatment and schooling. He knew no one in the world of law in Los Angeles, Chicago, or anywhere. With no roadmap, he would cut his own path, toward he knew not what.

His friend Paul Lee was, except in his competitive scholarship at law school with Micah, Micah's opposite and an unlikely partner. Paul was active in various organizations in school and community—church, fraternities, ethnic groups, political and social clubs—and as a result he had many personal contacts in the city he thought he could count on in developing a practice. And he wanted to do it with Micah. With no other options nor plans, Micah and Paul started a law firm, an act of total blind optimism. They rented a small suite of inexpensive offices because Paul had a family contact in the real estate community who gave them a rental break in return for some prospective legal assistance Paul promised to provide. Lehman & Lee had an open house that was attended by hundreds of people the Lee family knew, a handful of professors who knew them both, and a few professors who had mentored Micah hoping he'd join them in the academic world when he got this adventure out of his system. Anne invited people from the UCLA rehab community, made invitations, and decorated the spare offices with used furniture from local shops. The grand opening was warm and crowded, but it was not grand. From novices to professionals, it was—at the start—a rough and uncertain crossing.

In the early days of Lehman & Lee, a few friends referred clients to the fledgling law firm. Paul joined professional, social, and political organizations and solicited most of the firm's business. Micah worked hard on cases, but did not go after business. In all his spare time, he wrote on subjects that interested him. He wondered if he should have accepted the full-time teaching position his alma mater had offered, being more interested in the ideas of the law than the business of it. He promised himself someday he'd do that, but only after he and Anne were financially provided for.

Micah had worked very intently at school. He loved the law. During his summer breaks he had interned at a large law firm that paid the best salaries in the region. There, he had a sense of what big-time legal practice was like. He didn't like it, and decided, after long talks about it with Anne, who agreed wholeheartedly, that he should not join any of these firms. He would make the most money if he did, but he did not want to simply sell his skills and good mind to any bidder for any price. He didn't like the drudgery. He was accustomed to hard work, but not on behalf of people or issues he didn't care about, and under slavish, impersonal conditions.

He wasn't sure how he would make a living on his own, having no business or social connections, but he would try. A few of his professors (they uniformly respected Micah) thought they might be able to steer some clients his way. Fortunately, Paul's family and circle of friends was vast. With few Asian American attorneys practicing in the area, Paul was a well-known success in his community, and its members supported him. From the day he and Micah opened the doors of their modest offices, they were busy. Poor, but busy.

If one case elevated Micah Lehman's public reputation as a legal tactician and formidable courtroom advocate, it was the Valdez case. Micah was a young man, early in his practice, when unpredictable events thrust him into a very public legal and political battle that lasted for over a year. His advocacy made both news and law and led to massive legislative reforms of the country's labor laws.

A young, charismatic labor leader, Cesar Chavez, had attended a meeting of California policy makers on the future of agricultural reform in the United States. In attendance was a UCLA law professor, John Koretz, who spoke on labor reform. Chavez approached him after the formal proceedings, challenging him to match the promise of his academic words with meaningful social action. Koretz offered to help, and invited Chavez to the law school for a meeting with some of the professors on the school's faculty, along with student leaders and influential alums. Micah was there; he had recently graduated and had just started his firm. Micah was touched by Chavez's passion and commitment and offered to help. Several days later, Chavez came to Micah's office with a group he'd just formed of farm workers and representatives of his new union's officials. They met all day, and later Micah went to their modest headquarters. He listened to their stories of hardship, to their troubling grievances. They invited him to visit worker sites, union halls, and Chavez's retreat in La Paz, outside Bakersfield. Micah listened, observed, and wondered what he could do about their problems.

He and Anne talked about them and brainstormed about what he could do that might help. Writing something to plead their case would do no good. There already was impressive journalism, press exposés of farm worker problems, and popular literature like John Steinbeck's classic book, *The Grapes of Wrath*. How to bring about change? "What good is the law if it can't help people out of predicaments as extreme as these?" Micah pleaded to Anne.

Anne actually had the idea that sparked Micah's historic course of action. "Aren't most of these horrible conditions violations of the law, darlin'? I can't believe this is all legal. Is the question how to enforce the existing laws, or the need for new laws?"

Anne's commonsense remark helped Micah see through the miasma of details that crowded his mind. "Of course, that's it," he said, standing and pacing across the candlelit screened porch where he Anne often sat after dinner late into the evenings. Anne smiled to herself. After watching Micah pace, sit, pace some more, deep in thought, Anne blew out the candles. "Micah, you've had your epiphany, darlin'. Now take this steamy wife to bed and love her to death." Micah's body followed, but his mind was elsewhere.

Micah left for his office early the next morning, his mind racing with questions, ideas, half-formed theories. He talked to his partner, seeking a fresh approach. He called Chavez and asked him question after question about life in the farm workers' fields. He called faculty friends at UCLA to try out evolving ideas. He recruited help from law school friends who worked for state legislators who were interested in relevant fields of regulation. Within weeks, Micah and his advisors and law school intern assistants had developed the outline for his strategy. He brought home the emerging game plan each night to explain it to Anne and hear her reactions. He was energized by the intellectual stimulation of problem solving for a good cause. Several weeks later, he sat in his conference room with a crowd of helpful cohorts: labor leaders from Chavez's corps, students in the law school's clinical program who had volunteered to work on fact gathering, faculty experts on regulatory legislation, and his partner, who led the research effort and when needed would assist him in court.

Months later, their two-stage strategy was complete. There would be a lawsuit in the federal court and hearings before a state, and later, a federal congressional committee. Micah had screened worker candidates brought to his office by a Chavez aide. The key named plaintiff would be a symbol and had to be perfect for his role as a noble and attractive representative victim of an inhumane system. Jesus Valdez was the man. A fourth-generation farm worker with a large family of his own (six children), his life was typical of those his work came to symbolize. He was tall and handsome in a rough-cut way, but he had a gentle demeanor and a naturally beatific smile. His name provided the perfect coincidence for his role.

With the help of his own aides and Chavez's staff, Micah prepared a large checkerboard illustration of farm worker hardships. On it, he had marked black squares noting laws designed to aid farm workers, such as the minimum wage law and health, safety, and housing regulations. The intermittently marked white squares listed horrible conditions farm workers endured without protection: exposure to pesticides, lack of enforcement of employment placement regulations, inadequate schooling for migrant children, and absence of even minimal medical care. Micah would later use comparable charts and illustrations throughout his career to make points to juries and media with great effect, and this chart was his best. Micah framed and kept the original checkerboard chart as a permanent memento on his office wall. It would become the symbol of farm workers' rights on insignia and flags.

Micah filed his case in California six months after his team's preparations began. Judge Everett Marks, a conservative Republican who was a former prosecutor, was a hard-nosed, nondoctrinaire, fair-minded judge with an excellent reputation (years later, he would be elevated by President Reagan to the U.S. Supreme Court), but he was not known as a bleeding heart. If Micah could persuade him, his chance of having his judgment upheld on appeal would be excellent. In his papers, Micah asked the court to classify the lawsuit as a class action and presented abundant proof that this case was appropriate for such action. His students and paralegals had found representative workers up and down the Western migrant streams in Washington, Oregon, Colorado, California, and

Arizona. Micah told the court that with time and resources he could demonstrate that the conditions in question existed throughout the other migrant streams in the United States, not only from California to Washington State in the West, but up and down the East Coast from Florida to Maine and in the Midwest from Michigan down to Arkansas and Texas. It was a shameful national scandal that he would bring to the court's attention, if permitted.

After a long hearing, enriched by the data and statistics–loaded Brandeis brief that Micah, with Paul's help, had developed, Judge Marks allowed the class action and gave Micah three months to prepare his now-national case. With help from the union's offices around the country and a growing staff of assistants whose work was modestly funded by an interested foundation, Micah organized a dramatic case. He worked around the clock, while his law practice and the rest of his life all but disappeared. Except for Anne. She worked evenings with the coordinating administrators of the burgeoning case in an office adjoining Micah's, and occasionally brought in picnic dinners for everyone, but always for her and Micah. There were few hours Micah allowed himself any respite.

His judicial team (called the blacks, using the checkerboard metaphor) worked on preparing witnesses, documents, photos, and legal memoranda establishing the systemic legal violations for the court case. Paul managed the legislative researchers on his team, the whites, who prepared proposed laws to cover areas requiring legislation where none existed. Micah coordinated all their efforts, and worked with friendly legislators in California and later in Washington, D.C., who would prepare hearings to highlight the problems on national television. He would propose a new set of laws called the Agricultural Workers Bill of Rights. Occasionally, they had an office softball game pitting staff members of the blacks against the whites, but as the case developed, games became fewer and fewer. Micah's office looked like a war games room. The hours were demanding, consuming, but the esprit de corps was intense.

The lawsuit began on a sunny Monday morning in the federal court in downtown Los Angeles. Micah called Jesus Valdez as his first witness. There would be 99 others; he arbitrarily decided to use 100 witnesses. Valdez was simply eloquent and personally stately. In a straightforward and patently honest presentation, he described a typical day in a farm worker's life. As Valdez spoke, Micah showed photographic slides of the scenes throughout farms in the Imperial Valley and north in worksites in Oregon and Washington State. Micah's photographers had catalogued vivid illustrations of these telling scenes in farm worker camps, agricultural fields, and labor offices in each of the states where farm workers lived and worked. The systemic living and work conditions were deplorable, the families' lives an embarrassment to America; the workers' children's experiences were particularly pathetic. The case built like a drumbeat, and the judge was visibly shaken by the descriptions and scenes Micah's team presented. The press interest in the case grew, and soon national coverage of the case began on the evening news and the Sunday talk shows. The presentation lasted three months; Micah's life had been overwhelmed by this case for a year. He had lost weight, but an energy and integrity shone through his demeanor. The media portrayed him as a simple, honest hero fighting an unjust system.

Judge Marks ruled from the bench the day the case concluded. Obviously, he had become convinced about his course of action earlier and prepared his opinion. It was far reaching and eloquent. "Farm workers have been historically denied fundamental rights by a country they fed and which prospered because of their labor, but ignored their basic needs. The government has failed them. This court will not." There was electricity in the courtroom. Anne embraced Micah. Chavez hugged Micah. Micah hugged Valdez. The national media crowded around Micah in the courtroom, outside the courtroom, followed him to his office, and hounded him for days.

But Micah's work was not done. The judge had ordered fundamental changes and a time frame to accomplish them. But courts do not execute orders nor design laws to carry them out. Micah's orchestrated strategy had planned for legislative hearings to begin on the heels of the court decision. Micah's team soon moved to Sacramento, and then to Washington, D.C. In both places, hospitable and well-prepared legislative committees were ready to continue Micah's slide show, hear his articulate witnesses, and propose a Worker's Bill of Rights to provide relief in situations where new laws and appropriations would help. California's law would become the nationwide model. Other states followed. The federal government would complement the state laws where common interstate features of the problems were presented.

House and Senate committees of Congress completed the cycle with televised hearings. Micah had prepared the presentation to engage a television audience; his staff had prepared the legislative staff for the substantive work at the televised hearings. He showed pictures of dilapidated migrant camps and subhuman housing projected onto a large screen in the darkened hearing room. He played tapes of conversations surreptitiously made of supervisors and farm owners exploiting farm workers. He brought in workers and children disfigured by illegal pesticides that were spread over the worker-populated fields. Witness after witness described the ordeals of the workers who brought the food to America's tables, while Micah's pictures flashed before the legislators and the press in attendance. The whole presentation was stunning. The hearings captured the nation's attention as nothing had before on this relatively new medium.

It was a victory for the blacks and the whites. When all the work was done, there was a day-long festival of thanksgiving at Chavez's mountain retreat and farm workers headquarters for Micah's team. Media covered it, too. Their story was told nationwide; it became the cover stories of *Time* and *Newsweek* magazines. Politicians followed the media, and the bandwagon grew. Union donations poured in in unprecedented amounts. Change began.

Finally, when the celebrations ended, an exhausted Micah disappeared with Anne to be alone, and to decide what to do next. They drove south into the desert, to Joshua Tree National Monument Park. There, they backpacked into the wilderness where the Mojave and Colorado Deserts came together. For days they saw no one; they walked the trails all day with Charleston, camped out, and fell asleep each night in each other's arms in their sleeping bags, looking at the stars, as they had done on their ocean voyage years before.

On their last night in the desert, their second son was conceived. They would name him Joshua, appropriately. A third son, Daniel, was born two years later. "That's three out of three," Anne said after Daniel's birth. "I guess we'll never have a daughter." Micah thought they should try one more time, and several years later, their daughter, their last child, Cassie, was born, and named, as was her brother, after their dear Cambridge friends.

❧ ❦ ☙

When he returned from the desert, Micah was a famous lawyer, but he and Paul could barely pay their rent. Paul's local work on behalf of his clients was the firm's chief income. A few faculty members retained Micah to work on briefs they were paid to do, and he took some court assignments. Micah felt guilty and offered to leave his partner, but Paul insisted they stay together. Somehow, their practice would flourish. They were smart, worked hard, and the firm had received extraordinary publicity for two rookie lawyers.

Micah had talked jokingly about switching his recent interest in the "war" over laws to writing about the laws of war. But how would his scholarly expertise in international law, initiated in his studies in Cambridge, ever translate into business for a small California law firm? He had written about the subject at Cambridge, and wrote law review articles on the subject at UCLA as well. But how would a fledgling lawyer in Los Angeles ever find a client in need of such exotic expertise?

The client found him. It happened that a World War II refugee, living then in Los Angeles, had read Micah's articles and was impressed by them. When he attempted to find the scholar, he was surprised to discover that the author was a young man, just out of law school, however much he had been celebrated in the news. The refugee, a young survivor of the World War II death camps, had devoted his life to bringing war criminals to justice in memory of his murdered family. He had little money, but a profound cause and an indomitable drive. Micah agreed to help him with recurring legal issues, delighted for the chance to put his theories to practice. The refugee, Eleazor Berenbaum—called Elie by everyone who knew him, the press, and all who knew about his work— was happy to take advantage of this free but unusually wise counselor.

The marriage of convenience paid off for Micah when several very wealthy Holocaust survivors set up a foundation for Elie to expand his work, and eventually arranged for its perpetual funding. Elie remembered Micah's generosity and respected his professional advice, so Micah went on the payroll as counsel, and stayed on it for decades. The foundation grew. Elie's work expanded. Fascinating legal issues arose in the countries to which Elie's pursuit took him. Lost assets of war victims, survivor claims for insurance, retrieval of confiscated property, return of stolen artwork—all gave rise to interesting legal claims. It was a legal frontier and Micah was an early pioneer. Gradually, unpredictably, Micah became an active international lawyer.

During the early days of Micah's law practice, other serendipitous events occurred that set the stage for the extraordinary success that followed for him and Paul. Some of his writings, in the academic journals and in opinion sections of newspapers and magazines, made Micah a recognized name in the growing legal community, and also led to cases that led to more cases, so his practice grew exponentially. In a town of narcissism, his modesty combined with his brilliance made him stand out from others in the burgeoning legal community. His reputation grew as he carved out an eclectic practice, a unique one, and eventually a profitable one as well.

Micah's idiosyncratic views and standards led the firm into a mix of work that resulted in the firm doing well by doing good. It also led Micah and Paul into their first personal disagreement. Micah had decided when he began his practice that he would not do the dirty divorce work that was common in L.A. It had a petty and mean reputation, it concerned small intellectual issues, and he had no heart for fighting over the division of joint bank accounts and the distribution of merged record collections. He especially criticized the typical intense feuds over innocent children who were often the victims of their warring parents' battles.

At one of their informal lunches at their office desks, Micah mentioned to Paul that he had turned down a few requests to represent people at the UCLA center involved in divorces, whom Anne had steered to the office. Paul was outraged, and for the first time the partners had a stressful spat.

"How could you nonchalantly turn away business, Micah, when we are barely eking out a living?"

"Because this isn't how I care to make my living. You know that!"

"Might you have discussed the potential cases with me, see if I wanted to handle them? I'm not as pure as you, and we need my fortune, such as it is, through income generation, as much as we need your fame."

"And what if more clients follow, and we have a real fortune, earned on the back of law practice I don't want and frankly didn't think you did either, Paul?"

Paul had no answer, but uncharacteristically threw down his napkin and walked away, back to his office. It was their first personal quarrel.

Fate intervened. When by chance a resolution presented itself, Micah opened the door, and Paul walked through.

When a local newspaper editor he knew came to Micah to represent him in his divorce, Micah refused. He was not interested in the costly, combative, acrimonious, hurtful nature of divorce practice; he thought it hurt the only innocents involved, the children, and he believed there had to be a better way to mediate the end of a personal partnership.

The editor challenged Micah to suggest such an alternative, saying that he would follow that course. At his client's request, Micah called the wife's lawyer, and told him that his partner would take the husband's case if the parties agreed to mediate a resolution in good faith in a private, rational, reasonably priced setting. It was, after all, Micah reasoned, an end of a private and personal partnership. It made sense—personal and economic—to negotiate, not litigate, questions of alimony, property division, and child custody. To his amazement, the wife's attorney agreed. Not only did the firm have a happy client, but the editor told others and even wrote a column about his experiences. The firm's doors began to revolve with citizens from Los Angeles and eventually beyond who preferred a mediated alternative to the destructive litigious paths that typically led to divorce. Taking over this part of the firm's new work, Paul's ship rose on the wave of Micah's ultimatum.

Paradoxically, the more emphatic Lehman & Lee's idiosyncratic system for accepting cases became as they raised their eligibility levels for new clients, the more the new clients came. Eventually the firm had a staff of paralegals, child psychologists, and social workers assisting a small group of lawyers who did extensive family mediation work for the firm. Paul became the guru of rational divorce. He spoke on panels, was interviewed by the media, and eventually wrote a book that the American Bar Association published in a series it promoted for practitioners in the field, *The Right and Wrong Ways to Divorce*, which became a standard reference book in an endless field of law practice.

The firm's clientele included many of the famous Hollywood stars who preferred their route to the bloodbaths that awaited them if they followed the traditional approach. It turned out that the firm's integrity—their approach of taking no sides except to attempt to be fair to all parties, especially children—and Paul's efficiency at mediation skills impressed clients, many of whom came back for other work, including theatrical representation, which interested Micah. The partnership worked.

Los Angeles being the film capital of the world, interesting and very visible legal work naturally would be associated with it. Micah's good press and Paul's estimable domestic relations reputation with some of his divorced producers, directors, writers, and actors soon led the firm—mostly Micah—into another field of work. Micah's fascination in law school with the law of intellectual property—the protection and exploitation of ideas—led one of his professors at UCLA to refer cases to Micah.

This professor had written the leading treatise on the subject, and was often brought into cases to write briefs or appear as an expert witness. When he had conflicts of interest, or too many demands on his time, he referred some important cases to Micah. Micah's successes led to more work in this burgeoning field, and with time he was the counsel of choice to a star-studded cast of film personalities. They, too, admired Micah not only for his skills, but also for his modest personality and strong moral character, which was distinguished from his coarser competitors in the entertainment law bar.

There was a paradox. Paul remained the money-maker, combining his growing reputation in the now-large Los Angeles community due to all his extracurricular efforts and his growing reputation in the new but expanding field of mediation. But Micah was the more prominent face of their firm. The more that unusual matters were referred to Micah, the more choosy he became about what positions he would and would not espouse—an attitude not shared by most of the local lawyers, who sold what time they had to the highest bidder. The more selective Micah became, the more the bigger clients wanted him. Paul was busy and popular and enjoyed the notoriety his partner brought to the firm. Their office became a place where many of Hollywood's celebrated citizens could be spotted most days. Young lawyers wanted to work for them. The press remembered Micah from his farm worker case and gave him more attention, responding to his modesty and seeming lack of self-advancement, and that coverage raised his public visibility all the more. When Anne and Micah hosted a party at their family compound—they occasionally had to because they were invited everywhere, and though reluctant to join the party scene, they felt a constant obligation to reciprocate—it was an event that people connived to attend. And everyone adored Anne. In a town of pushy starlets, her beauty and sense of class shone all the brighter.

In addition to all the firm's new commerce, what really interested Micah was the emerging public interest law phenomenon that began during the era of his law practice, and to which he became devoted. It was here that Micah's reputation as a special breed of lawyer soared; it was his small seminar that Micah taught at his alma mater that made him happiest and most proud. Micah kept putting off the decision to leave law practice for teaching, yet he kept up his involvement with the law school throughout his busy career. As an adjunct professor, he created a course on the practice of law, composed partly of legal ethics, partly jurisprudence, and partly his own moral and ethical views of the profession. The course was perennially oversubscribed, and often faculty colleagues, visiting jurists, scholars, and celebrated practitioners attended and engaged in engrossing debates with Micah and the students. Micah's work in this field filled a void and became the model for a movement in law practice that developed during the years he practiced, as one of its pioneers.

The seminar focused on the obligations of the bar and of individual lawyers. Large law firms had always provided pro bono services to needy clients, but Micah viewed that as noblesse oblige, a charity that substituted for needed systemic changes that would come only when the nature of law practice changed. The direction and nature of that change was what Micah asked students to consider.

The legal establishment resented his critical views. Legal aid and public defenders are enough, his critics argued. Underfunded and overwhelmed, Micah responded. Systemic reform was called for.

"There are options other than legal aid and public defenders," Micah advised. Students had other possibilities beyond what he provocatively called "the greasy pole of big money corporate law practice." Idealistic young lawyers, even those who entered the profession with debts, mortgages, and an enviable view of the rich life they heard about from rookies sweating away in the large law firms, had options. There were interesting jobs for lawyers in government and charitable organizations, he told them, and he brought to his class—along with the big-firm lawyers to make their case and argue against his—practitioners in these nonprofit fields to explain how contributing to society could be an admirable road to follow, and that pursuing social justice could be a rewarding life that didn't require taking an oath of poverty.

Micah's seminar was charged, characterized by contentious, if respectful, dialogues. Micah argued, for example, that attorneys take on the coloration of their clients; they shouldn't hide behind the artificial claim that they have a professional responsibility to represent clients and should be deemed personally arm's length from them. The traditional legal "artifice"—as Micah called it—was that since doctors who treated sick Communists were not considered Communists, why should lawyers who treated criminals be deemed criminals or facilitators? They were simply carrying out a fundamental professional obligation. If doctors are instructed to do no harm, Micah posited, why shouldn't lawyers be ordered to do no injustice?

"If one spends all his professional life representing professional criminals, is it unfair to call them mob lawyers, as we label labor lawyers or corporate lawyers based on what they do?" Micah continued. Hands shot up, and critical observers leaped up, challenging that provocative claim. But Micah calmly continued.

"Doesn't a lawyer take on the coloration of his clients, add his honorable imprimatur to the client's reputation?" Micah asked. "If lawyers are permitted to turn away clients for the reason they cannot pay for their services, why can't they turn them away because they don't approve of the proposed client's views (the Ku Klux Klan, say) or practices (selling cigarettes that are a leading cause of death)?"

"Because," one of his dissenting guests responded, "most bar codes state that a lawyer's representation of a client does not constitute an endorsement of the client's political, social, or moral views or activities."

"Yes," Micah answered. "And lawyers who make their fortunes doing so must live with their reputations and self-estimation when they do choose to represent professional criminals or corporate polluters."

"You are sanctimonious, my friend," one corporate lawyer guest responded. "We provide neutral advice. If clients choose to apply that advice in ways some people—not all people—disagree with, what is wrong with that?" When there was some partisan snickering by students,

Micah shushed that, instructing that students could speak out for or against any and all positions discussed, but only respectfully.

Micah continued pressing his points to students and guests. "If lawyers claim that they are fulfilling honorable professional obligations by representing certain classes of defendants, how come *so* many people—invariably poor ones, many with good claims—can't find a lawyer to represent them?" Micah paused. "Might it be because lawyers adopt these arm's-length ethical stances when paying clients call on them, but not when poor ones do? What does that say about us our noble work for humanity?"

"Virtue," one large law firm manager Micah had invited to his seminar argued, "is in the eyes of the individual. The largest firm in Chicago represents major financial institutions in trouble, and its partners are all millionaires whose values Professor Lehman deprecates. Yet that firm also supports the city's ballet and opera in major ways, and funds a scholarship program for inner-city youth that the government and social welfare agencies fail to serve."

"And," Micah retorted, "most people in power can make the same claim, and offer their good works as justification for the more questionable parts of their professional lives. My question is, which of their work characterizes them professionally? What they do day to day? Or their extracurricular efforts?"

"Come on, Micah," his irritated antagonist protested. "You assign greater virtue to a small-town teacher who helps students year after year than to the manufacturer in that town who funds a charter school that provides systemic reforms. Who says a mediocre teacher or a public defender is better than a public-spirited banker or corporate lawyer? You're sounding like a socialist and pseudo-moralist."

Micah invited two partners in a boutique firm that specialized in start-up businesses to his class. "To prove I'm not a socialist," Micah told his class, smiling, "here are two young lawyers who will tell you about the joys of enriching themselves while they enrich the marketplace." His guests were recent graduates of UCLA, high minded and very bright, who told Micah's students how exciting it was to help create and launch a business that provided useful products and created jobs and revenue. "By taking an idea to reality," they told the students, "we feel we've worked within the marketplace and done well by doing good."

"See that?" Micah added. "There is no one true way."

While respectful of his guests' point of view, Micah didn't back off from his, though he responded in a cordial manner that defused the tensions implicit in the exchanges with his guests. But the classroom debates could become passionate. Once Micah suggested that students consider the question, when do corporate strategies created and implemented by their lawyers create a confederation in crime? A guest from a prestigious large law firm roared back: "That's outrageous, Micah—the Codes of Professional Responsibility require that we provide counsel, and the Constitution gives all people a right to that counsel. You know that!" Micah reminded him that the Sixth Amendment assures the right to counsel only in criminal cases, and the bar codes do not shield lawyers from participating in prospective misconduct with their clients. "Where is the line between advice and participation?" he asked.

Micah noted the class distinctions that divided lawyers and their practices. "Take the divide between plaintiff lawyers suing, on behalf of a client, alone or in a class action," Micah said to his class when a well-known, highly regarded managing partner in a multistate, widely populated law firm came as his guest and debate opponent. "We don't take one-third of our clients' judgments, nor run after clients," his dapper guest had told students.

"The big firms representing corporations charged with discrimination, or selling faulty products are paid *very* well, by the hour, to defend their clients," Micah responded. "But the plaintiff lawyers are considered second-class lawyers—worse, shysters and ambulance chasers—when they fight for their fees, which cannot be paid by their poorer clients but may be paid when a statute provides that legal fees can be demanded when the complaining party succeeds." Micah continued, "Corporate lawyers are paid and paid well, up front, for defending clients accused of mischief, or more; but lawyers who swing their cudgels on behalf of citizens seeking justice for wrongs done to them may never get paid, or are paid after risking their time and revenue on the chance the imperfect system of justice will eventually reward them. Yet, these lawyers are cynically called 'hired guns' for doing the work that, arguably, shouldn't have been necessary."

Micah editorialized to his students: "I cannot ascribe an ultimate virtue score to the financier versus the charity worker. My role, here in this seminar and in my personal life choices, is to point out and demonstrate the options fledgling lawyers are about to encounter and sensitize them to the choices they will eventually make regarding meaningful lives and money making . . . their responsibilities to their profession, their community, and themselves."

Micah pushed ideological buttons, and the word went out that this course was fun, and listening to the notable guests argue with Professor Lehman was good sport.

At one seminar, near the end of the course, Micah would end with a provocative summation: "Among our most esteemed members of the bar and the community are wealthy lawyers who made their fortunes in effect defending rich clients who are keeping bad drugs on the market, cigarettes in stores, dangerous cars on the roads, poison chemicals in our air, soil, and water. All this is done along with their pro bono work as community elders, enriched by their clients and honored by their communities for their beneficence. I conclude this seminar asking you this question: Are they honorable men, or are they facilitators of actions against the public interest? You must consider this fundamental question and decide for yourselves as you join our profession.

"Every lawyer makes choices. One lawyer may care deeply about the notion of capital punishment and spend a career fighting it through handling Eighth Amendment cases. Others might question devoting one's professional life to or even participating in helping vicious criminals who committed the most vile and horrible offenses, violating the social contract that citizens must follow in any decent society. They would prefer to prosecute those same people, and never would represent them. Those are personal choices lawyers make; no right and wrong should be associated with the choice. Others may simply enjoy solving tax puzzles and decide to do that in their careers for reasons of personal predilection. Again, there is no moral element. Some lawyers may want to make the most money and will practice near the largest honeypot, probably corporate law. That work probably leads them to representing rich clients seeking to enhance their riches. Rich people get the biggest cars and homes and best services, as a rule, so no surprise they get good legal services as well.

"My central point is this: All clients are entitled to legal representation for whatever their problems are. *But*, they are not entitled to *me* or *you* or any one lawyer in particular," Micah preached, pointing to all the assembled students as he concluded. "That is the point I ask you to consider; *you* decide what you do with your professional lives. You do have choices to make, and your answers will define you. As you set out in your careers, ask yourselves this important question, and answer it as you deem right."

Micah didn't tell his students what they should do or conclude, but he left them with no question where he stood, without saying it directly, while also exposing them to the best thinking by lawyers and scholars he invited to attend his seminar to make their cases against his.

One of Micah's intellectual adversaries reminded the class that the Shakespearean line from *Henry VI*, a line that has been regularly misquoted—"First, let's kill all the lawyers"—"doesn't stand for the proposition that we lawyers all are on the wrong side of public policies. Shakespeare meant to point out that bad public policies would only prevail if we killed all the lawyers, because we need them—us—to keep due process of law and order, fairness and justice."

"Bravo, amen, and a good note to end on in this lecture," Micah concluded.

The seminar ended with students lingering, lining up to discuss these subjects with their professor and the guests, as others scurried to their next classes in meeting rooms down the hall. Eventually Micah and his guest would adjourn to lunch at the faculty dining room, where their debates continued. Micah's seminar became notorious and was oversubscribed. Originally once a year, it was expanded to twice a year to satisfy the limited number of students each class could accommodate. Interesting guests—many of whom disagreed with Micah's views—added luster. Micah hated to miss these seminars when he had to travel.

Micah's interest in the laws of war—first aroused as a student, later written about in serious periodicals and eventually in a book, and honed working for Elie's foundation—also would lead to occasional special governmental assignments in war crimes trials abroad, in special pleadings before the United Nations and the Hague, and to lobbying efforts on behalf of controversial treaties concerning a ban on land mines, the jurisdiction over captured Nazis and wartime treasures, and other humanitarian causes. His book, *The Law of Wars*, adapted from an article he wrote as a student at Cambridge and enhanced by references to some of his cases, was published by Cambridge Press, and, as Micah laughingly told people, "earned me in the high three figures." But all his successes at work took a toll on Micah's time and energy—and on his attentions to Anne, the love of his life, but often his neglected spouse.

Whenever possible in later years, Anne traveled with Micah; when she could not, he was an unhappy man and raced home to her from around the world whenever he could. Anne would say facetiously, "Micah is an airport traveler..." Anne did accompany Micah on one of his business trips to Australia, as she did occasionally when the children were independent, and the place interested her. They were hosted elegantly by Micah's governmental client, residing for a week at a luxurious hotel in its deluxe suite. Her days were filled with sightseeing arranged by their hosts while Micah met with the officials who had retained him to provide advice about ancient treaties with aboriginal tribes and their impact on current government plans to develop untouched lands for tourism expansion. The tribes argued that no compensation would be acceptable because the lands were holy to their culture. Micah was sympathetic to their claim and a credible mediator, as his public interest views were known. Aborigine representatives agreed to meet with the government agency if Micah was the mediator.

One night, as Micah and Anne lay in their luxurious bed, drowsily talking about the day's events, Anne shocked Micah.

"Darlin', don't I attract you anymore? Physically, I mean?"

"What are you talking about? Of course you do. You know I think you are the most beautiful woman in the world. Here we can add another continent," he added, attempting levity in a conversation he found strange.

"We don't make love much anymore. What could it be, then?"

"Yes we do. Maybe not so much or the same way. We're 55 years old. We have as much history as biology. You know I adore you. What's prompted this? You must be reading romance magazines."

There was silence, as Micah wondered what was on Anne's mind, and Anne wondered if they would ever be at the place again where they fell in love, physically as well as spiritually. She never doubted Micah's commitment, only his ardor.

"Darlin', I think something has gone from us. After we married, first I was sick and recuperating for years, then I was pregnant for years, then you worked yourself to exhaustion, and when we were together the house was filled with kids and life's distractions. Then all of a sudden we looked up and have all the opportunity to come back to ourselves, and . . . ." Anne's rumination trailed off, but her conclusion was implied.

"Aren't you happy?" A weak and baffled Micah responded.

"Darlin'," Anne spoke into space, a note of frustration in her voice. "I think you got so used to treating me—so carefully and gingerly—when I was sick, and later when I was pregnant, that the passion disappeared. We never recovered it. Now, we are devoted"—she emphasized the word—"but not loving, if you know what I mean."

Micah interrupted, impatiently. "Great! We live in a time and place where men are not devoted to their wives, and you accuse me of what most women complain they don't get!"

"And," Anne interrupted, "we live in a time and place where men are too sex-driven with too many women, and I live with one who doesn't seem to be interested in sex at all!"

"Well, not at this accusatory moment," Micah snapped, turning his back to Anne and pushing his head into the soft covered pillow. They fell asleep in that estranged and distant atmosphere, surrounded by the silence and opulence of a setting that might have been designed as a perfect trysting scene.

"He doesn't understand," Anne thought. "Well, I can't be angry, only resigned. He is a good man, and I know he loves me," she concluded as she fell asleep, wishing his affection were less dutiful, less mechanical, more demonstrable, if not more passionate.

"What's gotten into her head?" Micah wondered as he fell asleep. "Tomorrow we'll have a romantic time. A dinner alone, some wine, she'll see." But tomorrow moved past them quickly and impassionately amidst planned events and separate schedules, packing and arrangements, and they never returned to the subject of that conversation.

Lehman & Lee had become, in a relatively short time, a well-known, well-respected, large, and profitable law firm. Micah and Anne were successful life partners, too. With three growing children, a growing bank account, and a life they designed for themselves and in which they seemed to thrive, they appeared to everyone who knew them as the perfect couple. It all seemed, especially after their painful start, too good to be true.

NINE

Life Moves On

❧ ❦ ❧

When Micah earned his first major fee by settling a studio's claim that a competitor studio had interfered with several of its stars under contract, he bought the large piece of property in the Pacific Palisades that Anne and he had discovered on their drives when they first came West, days when they had planned their future dream house. It was a knoll of land on the side of a mountain in the Santa Monica Canyon that had a spectacular 300-degree view of surrounding woods and of the ocean off in the distance. First, they built a large family house; several years later, they bought an adjoining, flatter area, where they built a tennis court and large pool (perfect for Anne's continued rehabilitative swimming, but also for family fun and games), and a small one-room guest cottage. The little house was always filled with visitors—family, their Cambridge friends when they could visit, and friends of their children. As Micah's fortunes increased, he bought more of the surrounding undeveloped land to protect their views and privacy. They never considered living any place other than their growing compound.

Although he was a very public person because of his work, Micah led a very private life. Anne remained his closest friend, on an everyday basis really his only friend. Micah worked long days and had no time for anyone else but Anne, and as much as possible their children. He wasn't a joiner of organizations and had no hobbies or side interests. Partly because it was his nature to be a private person, partly to preserve an island of calm and reflection and attention to his family amidst their busy and distracting professional lives, Micah and Anne lived by a rigorous schedule. Each of them worked hard all week, and Micah often traveled to handle cases in distant places. But every night he was in Los Angeles, no matter what else was going on in his life; there was a period between the time he got home, usually around 7:00 p.m., until 10:00 p.m., when the family was together and only private family affairs were discussed. Micah might have to return to work he brought home, and he and Anne usually spent time reading in their library after the children went to bed. But the five of them always followed a schedule that included tennis and a swim behind the house, dinner together with voluble conversation, and discussions about everyone's day, starting with the youngest and proceeding to Anne and Micah. Then Micah put the children to bed while Anne closed the kitchen. That done, Micah made a fire, poured each of them a scotch (a lingering Cambridge habit), and he and Anne would talk until Micah finished his work and they walked hand in hand to bed.

Weekends they observed a unique, self-designed Sabbath of sorts that began on Friday night and lasted until Saturday night. No phone calls were made or answered. Guests were welcome if they subscribed to the schedule. Candles were lit at the Friday night dinner, a nod to Micah's family practice, one Anne thought was lovely and adopted. Conversation often was about religious issues. They did not attend a church or synagogue or celebrate conventional holidays or rituals. Instead, Micah and Anne tried to imbue the ethical and humanistic underpinnings and moral lessons of all religions in their children through conversation, debate, and ecumenical and Sunday school education. Anne knew her Bible and was the family instructor. Micah had a more jurisprudential and literary view of religion. He subscribed to an idea from a Walter Lippmann book that modern man has ceased to believe but has not ceased to be credulous, so is alone and at rest nowhere. Find your place. Develop your personal moral compass. Pray as if everything rested upon God, but act as if the right choices depend on you, a biblical injunction he repeated to his children. Religion is private. Theirs was the religion of family and rational thought. When questions arose, in the family or from others, about church attendance, Micah often quoted the Ethical Culture maxim: "Where men meet to seek the highest is holy ground." Their family compound fit that description.

After conversation about religious ideas at dinner, music and reading aloud followed; then everyone retired before midnight. When Micah's sister, Ada, and her husband visited, or when Cassie and her husband and children or Daniel (who never married) visited, they joined the family's practice. It was never solemn or formal, and all five Lehmans came to consider it a special preserve in their family's life. Micah and Anne always considered their special family Sabbath as the highlight of their week and the special time of their lives. On Sundays, Micah slept late; Anne took the children to Sunday school, then after a bounteous brunch they competed in family tennis matches, swimming, long hikes on the nearby beaches, and climbing the local cliffs. They returned home at the end of the day physically spent, reconnected to each other, and ready to pursue their individual daily schedules.

Micah and Anne kept in touch with Cassie, the Flemings, and Daniel. Once a year, Cassie and Daniel, most times separately, sometimes together, visited and stayed with Micah and Anne, or traveled with them to places of interest in California and the West. Once a year, usually during school breaks, Micah and Anne and the children visited England, toured London, and took walking trips in the country. Once when the children were old enough to enjoy it, they took a grand tour of the continent with Cassie and her family. Cassie had married a museum curator and they had two children the same ages as Micah and Anne's. Daniel, a perennial bachelor, came alone, and Micah and Anne prodded him, without success, to marry and raise a family. The Cambridge gang of five liked each other and maintained their annual excursions.

Daniel's career at the bar had been filled with successes, professional and commercial. His brilliance and energy as a student led him to a prestigious judicial clerkship. His judge—a revered and esteemed national eminence—became an invaluable mentor who promoted him into London's most influential law firm, and eventually into an unusual partnership at the time when Jews were rare in such clubby societies. Daniel's work consumed his life, as one unique opportunity followed another, each demanding all his skills, energy, and time. He became known as a lawyer's lawyer, a barrister who specialized in complicated, high-stakes appellate court cases. His clients' admiration for his work led to friendships, positions, and assignments of immense consequences, prestige and reward.

But his professional life permitted him little personal life, and Daniel evolved into a distinguished and sought-after London bachelor, invariably paired at parties and social events with an elderly woman client or a partner's daughter who needed an escort. His professional interests and commitments kept him from the typical social life of young couples who were his contemporaries. He was taken too seriously by contemporaries, so he missed the frivolity and insouciance of his age. His elders doted on him, and he was a favorite at elegant events where he was perennially the very junior person in attendance.

It seemed that when Daniel looked up he was well into his middle age and had overlooked the family stage of life that consumed most men and women his age. He became everyone's favorite guest at dinners and weekends, the adopted uncle of every friend's and colleague's youngsters, the one all his acquaintances (Lehman's included) tried to fix up with the perfect mate. He was also the associate who could always be counted upon to drop everything else and contort his personal affairs in order to dash off to a bar conference in Geneva, replace a colleague at an important but protracted arbitration in Berlin, or sacrifice a summer holiday or a weekend retreat or even a planned birthday party to go to Israel or Russia or the United States on an important mission. Everything he did was first class, and Daniel evolved into a worldly traveler and influential counselor.

But all that he ever had to come home to was more of it.

Daniel's friendship with Cassie and her evolving family continued to be a close one, and his friendship with Micah and Anne, though long distance, survived and became more and more important to all three of them. Daniel and Micah worked on international projects occasionally, talked regularly and visited infrequently—Daniel on business trips to the United States and Micah and Anne and later their children on summer jaunts to England and to the continent.

One of Daniel's most interesting special projects was with an immensely powerful but scrupulously private unofficial group, known to each other but by very few others as "Our Committee." It was composed of 20 of the richest men in the world, all of whom were Jewish and had a passionate commitment to the survival and economic success of Israel. Organized during the mid-century Zionist days that led to the creation of the state of Israel in the aftermath of the Holocaust, the informal group of influential men met privately, often in London, where several members lived, though sometimes elsewhere to initiate action out of the spotlight, often in emergencies, always with the sub rosa approval—or instigation—of the government of Israel. Daniel was well known to one of the committee's leaders and was recruited to be their unofficial secretary, expediter, and representative. He did not have the vast resources or money or the individual power of the committee members, but he had their trust and the weight of their presence behind them. The members respected his intelligence, discretion, and availability. These were men who made decisions and issued orders to make things happen; Daniel was the perfect executor of these orders. As such, he traveled widely and was treated on these missions as royalty. He occasionally used his old friend Micah in this context, including in one notorious international case, which, though not intended, would do much to damage Micah's health and reputation.

Micah and Anne led such insular and personal lives, so different from the lives of their neighbors and friends and colleagues, that they had reputations as being loners. People who knew them wondered whether their relationship with each other was obsessive, unnatural. But people liked them and seemed to respect their eccentricities, benign and old-fashioned by local standards. Their children's friends liked the active but wholesome environment at the Lehman compound, and their families encouraged their children to spend time there. Josh and Dan and Cassie never felt isolated; in fact, their invitations to stay over at the guest house were coveted by their classmates. Saturday nights and Sundays at the compound were active, well populated, and bustling with athletic activities and group events.

Anne's work and involvements at the UCLA center increased. She had created a new alternative treatment approach, involving music and writing and other nonmedical activities, which interested professionals in the field. That special section was funded by prestigious research organizations, and eventually Anne became its director. She thrived on her work and was well regarded by her professional colleagues. Micah was proud of Anne's accomplishments and assisted in the fund-raising and special events that increased the center's prestige.

Anne rarely took vacations so that as their children got older she could accompany Micah on some of his cases in interesting places. Micah encouraged that, and always rushed home when Anne could not accompany him. Their lives together were absorbing and consuming, and they were happy and unquestioning about their path to their good fortune.

When Josh developed into an extraordinary tennis prodigy, the family often traveled to places where he played competitively. Special dispensations from the sanctity of the family's traditional Friday-Saturday conclaves had to be made on occasions when Josh's opportunities could not be avoided or manipulated. Everyone took pride in his accomplishments, however, and Josh brought teammates home to practice on their family court whenever possible. Cassie and her friends swam with Anne. During those years, the bustling compound seemed like a sports training center.

Micah tried to persuade his mother to leave Chicago and come and live with them. His sister and her family had attentively watched over their mother for years, but they had moved farther away from their mother's neighborhood into surrounding suburbs as they prospered and had children. His mother's neighborhood had deteriorated, and although many of her old companions had drifted away or passed away, his mother refused to move. Micah and Anne wanted to add an apartment to their guest house so his mother could stay with them, be looked after, enjoy the easier climate, and be a fuller part of their family. She refused, but she did come for month-long visits each February when the Chicago cold was most harsh and the Los Angeles winter rains ended.

Anne's parents had stayed in contact, but as a result of their estranged relationship remained distant. They wrote. They visited once a year, for progressively shorter times. They spoke often of their growing involvement with their son, Philip, once the family outsider. Philip had married young, badly, then remarried an extremely wealthy woman from a notable South Carolina family. They became involved in all the right social events in the state, and Anne's mother took delight in their ascension in the local society. She and Philip's wife, Marcia Ayers, now Strong, became constant companions at social affairs in Charleston and Columbia; they traveled to New York City for shopping, theater, and parties. Philip and Anne had reversed roles in their original family, as Anne turned all her attention to her new nuclear family in California. She genuinely wanted Micah's mother to be part of their new life, and was attentive to maintaining a warm, if long-distance, friendship with her sister-in-law and her children. But essentially, Anne, Micah, and their children had become a tight, self-sufficient family, self-absorbed but widely admired.

Micah's solicitousness of Anne's fragile condition while she lived through her long convalescence had an oddly perverse effect on their personal relationship. One evening, years after her recovery from the birth of their children, Anne probed Micah for a second time. They were sitting on the porch doing their habitual late-night chores, when Anne said, "Micah, I have a question. About us."

"What's that, my dear?" Micah responded without looking up from the work papers he was reading.

"Do I still attract you?" Anne asked, looking straight at Micah as he looked up, startled by her question.

"Are you serious?" He waited for an answer, but Anne stared at him without saying anything.

"Of course you do," he added. "I've never loved anyone else as much, and don't ever plan to. How could you even ask? What's gotten into you?"

"We rarely make love anymore. I believe the passion has gone out of our life—not that you don't still love me. You just don't *love* me," Anne continued.

"What's going on?" Micah asked, completely mystified by his wife's question. With long days of work, travel for work, busyness at home with children, guests on weekends filling the house with life—and distraction—there was little time for passion. Sex was infrequent and formal—never impromptu or aggressive or, for that matter, very satisfying. "Isn't our situation like every other middle-aged, long-married couple?" Micah asked.

"Yes," Anne replied, curtly for her, as she stood and walked out of the room, turning off the lamp light on her way out. "Yes, precisely," she added, talking straight ahead as she walked out of the room they shared. "That's the problem."

Micah didn't understand. He shrugged off the moment as woman's mystical romanticism, as a rhetorical question not really aimed at their own marriage relationship. He did not speak of it again, nor did Anne, who was in bed with the light off when he got to their bedroom ready to demonstrate his ardor to the love of his life. He did not try to awaken Anne, more solicitous of their need for a good night's rest than the need to revive their romance.

Anne lay there, eyes closed, and felt Micah's body carefully, quietly slide in next to hers, wondering at first, then disappointedly daydreaming about them in Cambridge, until she eventually fell asleep, long after Micah had.

Despite their isolationist social practices, Anne and Micah had grown into well-known public figures in Los Angeles. Anne's role as director of the Department of Alternative Treatment at Morrison-Pomeroy, and was written up in feature stories about her work there. Josh was well known because of his precocious tennis career. Micah's legal work received regular coverage in the popular press, and his writings had a respectable following in the professional journals.

Anne and Micah had a reputation as old-fashioned sweethearts, characters from another era. Because Anne was so beautiful, inevitably men had made passes. She had a way of dismissing those men so peremptorily there could be no mixed message. Soon, most men didn't even try; those who did invariably got the point, and that was that. In the fast-track social whirl of Los Angeles, word got out and around fast. The word on Anne among the players was she looks hot, but acts cool.

Once, at work, there was—a conversation. Just that, and months later a resignation. Anne had recruited Neil Fisher, a young physician who had conducted research at the National Institute of Health in Washington, D.C., on alternative treatment techniques. Anne was curious to know more about its application to physical therapy. She sought out the young doctor, who eventually came to work with her at Morrison-Pomeroy Rehab Center. He mistook her intense interest in him and his work for more than Anne had intended. One day, as Anne was doing her daily workout in the physical therapy room, Dr. Fisher came into the room and, seeing that Anne was alone, approached her.

"You look beautiful, Anne," he said in a tone that clearly was not all business. "Do you know how beautiful you are, to me?"

Anne stopped her workout. She was wearing the black leotard she wore during her exercises and she was perspiring; her hair was wet and clung to her forehead. Her long, lithe figure revealed the taut body of a young woman while her face showed enough of the wear of life to reflect a woman of experience and worldliness. She exuded an animal attraction that led the younger Dr. Fisher to suggest out loud what he had been thinking since he first saw Anne. Her first reaction was to not take her colleague's remark seriously.

"I'm sure I'm beautiful. Huffing and puffing to keep some semblance of conditioning at my age ain't easy, Neil. What's up?" She stopped her exercise and wrapped her towel around her shoulders.

"Anne, don't tease me. I've been struck by you from the first time we met. I look forward to our work together each day. I think about you every night. Surely you must know this." The young doctor took a step toward Anne, but she turned to face him and looked him straight in the eye.

"Neil, I'm going to forget this conversation, and you are *never* going to repeat it. I respect and admire you for your brilliant work. If I ever suggested more by anything I've said or done, I apologize to you. We have important things to do here together and it *cannot* go on unless this conversation is forgotten and not revived." As Anne turned and left the room, she said, over her shoulder, as if the last few minutes had never occurred, "I'll see you at the Friday staff conference."

Dr. Fisher never approached Anne again after that incident. Several months later, he accepted a position at a hospital in Portland. There was a going-away party, but Anne was unable to attend.

Micah gradually became an institution. His firm prospered, even though its eclectic practice included many nonremunerative battles over contentious social issues. He lost many of his fights, but always emerged personally elevated in his public reputation. He regularly lost cases challenging capital punishment. He saw it in black-and-white terms: people shouldn't kill people, and the state should not become the precedent for doing so. To kill prisoners is to tolerate an inhuman power and thus to lower the standards of public behavior. Time after time, Micah argued his cause on behalf of prisoners he did not even know. Regularly, he lost the cases, but grew in his public stature as a dynamic man of principle.

Micah sued the city of Los Angeles several times, seeking to keep crèches and similar Christological symbols off public property, and also challenging its compounding the public sin by erecting giant Hanukkah menorahs. The central idea of American freedom of religion, he argued, is not to equalize the exceptions to a good rule, but rather to observe the rule with absolute rigor. Memorialize religious messages privately in religious institutions, Micah lectured, and not publicly in state institutions. Religion should be private, he pleaded in these cases; it is cheapened and vulgarized and made divisive if it becomes part of any state action. Again, Micah never succeeded in his cases, though his efforts enlightened the public about these important issues.

While Lehman & Lee prospered and grew in the 1960s and '70s, its fortune had not yet equaled its fame, though it did well. Micah became a leader by example in what came to be known as the public interest law movement. His openness and commitment to justice led Micah into other landmark legal battles, and his example became an inspiration to others in the profession. After the Valdez case, the work that captured the most national attention was his advocacy on behalf of the homeless. In the wake of intended reforms based on the deinstitutionalization of prisons, jails, and mental institutions during these mid-century years, many people who had previously been locked up in squalid and inhuman public institutions were released. However, no private or public programs were devised and funded to provide alternatives for these people. As a result, many of them suddenly appeared on the public screen—living in parks and doorways, libraries and terminals, and on the streets. They were unattractive, often offensive, so they engendered no public sympathy. They were a problem most people preferred to hide from sight.

Their presence bothered Micah. He saw them daily in the beach-side parks in Santa Monica, and it seemed every public place he passed. Micah was repulsed by their presence but more so by their neglect. He questioned city officials about what might be done to deal appropriately with their problem. Budgets did not provide alternatives for their assistance. The public had little sympathy for them because they were so offensive. They had no constituency to push for their betterment; by their very nature, they were not equipped to organize, militate, or act in their own interest.

Micah came up with a scheme. He'd read an article in a law journal by an East Coast law professor, advocating that the constitutional right to life includes minimum standards of subsistence—income, shelter, medical care. How could a rich country founded on popular "little *d*" democratic ideals not assure these minimum rights to the weakest among it? Micah lobbied the city council, the state legislature, the federal Congress to create such programs. He wrote about this subject whenever a newspaper or magazine would give him the space. Many considered him a scold and were impatient with his lectures. But slowly, Micah gained respectable allies. First, some church leaders harkened to Micah's prodding, and spoke from their pulpits in support of his ideas. Then, some legislators took up his pleadings. Several foundations funded studies of the costs and nature of proposed social programs promoting solutions. Eventually, presidential candidates were dealing with the subject. A people's rights platform was proposed in Congress, an incipient legislative program that was the result of decades of Micah's work. It seemed reform might happen, but it never did.

Several times, Micah was offered positions in government, but he always refused. He was completely happy where he was his own boss and couldn't imagine changing his private universe. He was tempted to teach at the law school and write full time, but something always came up that he couldn't ignore—a test case, a unique challenge, a special assignment. So he taught as an adjunct professor and maintained his ties and friendships at his alma mater, but did his academic work in addition to and not instead of his other work. Micah always promised himself, and Anne, that he would change lives and become an academic full time, but after the big case of the moment that he could not desert, that dream invariably disappeared. When his longtime partner was offered a judgeship in compensation for many years of dutiful organizational work on bar committees, community organizations, and political campaigns, the firm became Micah's. He felt an institutional commitment to the young lawyers who came to idolize him and to their firm's reputation as the place to come if the cause was worthwhile and the need for representation was clear.

"How lucky we are," Anne once remarked to Micah, out of the blue and for no reason.

"What do you mean, dear?" Micah asked.

"Well, after Cambridge, I thought we'd been cursed, that the gods were conspiring against us. My mother. My family. Your father's sudden death. My accident. Losing our baby . . . ." She paused, but clearly wasn't finished with the thought. "I never doubted your love for me, our love for each other, but in that hospital room in London, I thought our balloon had burst. I believe I was unconscious when we came here. I was following you and not really sure where it all would lead. I'm so, so amazed we've made this life."

Micah didn't know what prompted Anne's ruminations. She wasn't usually so sentimental, and never seemed to doubt anything about their life together. She seemed so vulnerable to him. He was sure his protectiveness of their lives and of Anne's health was correct. He didn't answer Anne, except to put his arm around her and kiss her, smiling, very secure and content about their lives.

TEN

A Family Affair

Is there such a thing, really, as a perfect lifelong love affair? Or is such an idea merely a romantic naïveté? Is the purest love one unfulfilled yet profoundly felt, like Dante's adoration of Beatrice? If one has a moment, or a period, of perfect love, can it be sustained for a lifetime? These were the questions people asked when they talked about Anne and Micah. Some who knew them or knew of them were envious of what they thought the two had. Others were cynical, couldn't believe that beneath those pure appearances there were no ghost stories. One incident had fueled these speculations.

The city had been divided then. Did the famous lawyer have a cheap and sordid affair with his client, or was he the victim of innocent circumstances and evil forces? Cynics said this intrigue was another case of a hero who turned out to have feet of clay, as they all do; romantics insisted that a good man's reputation had been recklessly sullied by a skeptical public, feeding off an irresponsible press.

Whatever people concluded—and it seemed at the time that everyone knew about it and had an opinion—all wondered. How could it be that a lifelong love affair that seemed ideal and a unique professional career that was maintained at a high moral standard for decades could come to be questioned by one cheap and ambiguous incident? Wasn't there some alienation as a result between the father and one of his sons? Must this be the way it always happens, or are people too quick to condemn? Is the way we lead our lives a game played by elusive public rules or a private journey to be judged by enduring principles? Was Micah and Anne's love too good to be true?

In an imperfect world, being good isn't always enough. The cynical public has an insatiable requirement for heroes, and a predictable propensity for turning on them. Micah and Anne's love of each other was well known, even envied, in a town and at a time when fidelity was part of a Marine Corps slogan but a matrimonial rarity. Both Micah and Anne had created idealized images of themselves and their marriage. Though they had taken pains to live very private and honorable lives, in retrospect it seemed they protesteth too much. So a sordid story about Micah naturally was the buzz of the town. Only he, Betty, and God knew the truth. Micah knew the facts; Betty disappeared; and God was a silent witness. Anne had faith in Micah. But people wondered.

It began on one of those insouciant Sundays when the family and a group of their friends returned from sailing and a picnic. They arrived at the rambling hillside house on the Pacific Palisades late in the afternoon. As Micah listened to his weekend phone messages, one sounded urgent. "Micah. Please call me immediately. I don't care what time. Betty Pincus. (310) 555-1933." Micah recognized the name. Betty was the wife of studio head Irv Pincus. Irv, a rough and tough businessman who had come to Los Angeles from New York City years ago, lived under a cloud of financial scandal. He was coarse, profane; he had made a fortune, first in X-rated movies and later in the legitimate end of the film business. He was rumored to have ties to the mob, no scruples, and an insatiable libido that thrived on would-be starlets. Betty, his long-enduring wife, was increasingly out of place and out of patience since coming to Los Angeles. She was a tough-mouthed, hard-edged dame. Micah knew Irv; though he'd not had dealings with him personally, he had negotiated deals with some of Irv's studio chiefs, directors, and contract actors.

"Please, you've got to see me, Micah, tonight, please," Betty had pleaded when Micah returned her call. Micah had a few things to do in his office anyway, so he agreed. The weekend was winding down. Friends departed. Anne and the children were busy at their routine chores. Micah washed, picked at some leftovers from the fridge, and standing at the kitchen table had a quick snack. He said good-byes and gathered his papers and briefcase. It was 7:00 when he reached his offices in Santa Monica. He parked in his reserved place behind the building. He noticed a flashy looking white convertible there; it was the only vehicle in the otherwise empty private lot. He guessed it was Betty's. He'd called ahead to arrange for the security officer to let her into the building. She was waiting on the bench outside his office when he arrived on the second floor still wearing his Sunday garb, faded tan sports slacks, green sport shirt, and a worn and baggy white tennis sweater.

"Hello, Betty; come on in and tell me what's up." Micah unlocked the door to his suite and led in his would-be client. Micah glanced at some papers on his desk. He offered Betty a cold drink, and finally sat down behind his desk, looked across at his guest, and asked, "Tell me."

Betty looked awful. Her outfit was garish. She was dressed in tight yellow slacks, a pink knitted sweater, and spike heels. She wore too much makeup. She had a head of blond hair that had been dyed and sprayed more than once too often. Her story was worse. Irv had embarrassed her repeatedly with his affairs. He was never home anymore. She'd given him an ultimatum and he'd physically thrown her out of their lavish suburban house. After a few nights staying with a divorced friend, she'd moved into an expensive hotel and forwarded her bills to Irv's office. She would shop and wait; her girlfriends had advised her to bide her time waiting for his standard apology and a romantic rapprochement. The tactic failed. In a few days, Irv called and gruffly told her to get a lawyer; their marriage was through. But Betty couldn't find a lawyer because no one wanted to take on Irv. The one she finally retained had suddenly dropped her as a client—Irv probably got to him—and there was a hearing scheduled for next week. Micah had the reputation of being incorruptible and unafraid. This was like a civil rights case, she urged him. He had to help; she didn't know where else to go.

Micah explained that he did not handle divorce work, except when the parties agreed to mediation. Irv would never do that. And furthermore, he did too much business with Irv's minions and companies; he would have potential conflicts of interest, even if he wanted to take her case. But Micah might be able to help her, he said, and he called several lawyers he knew who he thought might take her case. He was surprised at the chilly reactions he received. Divorce lawyers usually did not turn away high-profile cases, especially when they involved wealthy litigants. But Irv was ubiquitous in the business and his fierce reputation was frightening. After several surprising turn-downs, Micah remembered a former law student he'd taught who had recently opened his own office after a successful stint as a public defender. He was smart, tough, good in court, and hungry. Micah called Jeffrey Bentman, who agreed to meet Betty the next morning. He was eager to take her case. A high-visibility divorce with a lot of money at stake was just what Jeff needed to launch his practice.

His mission accomplished, Micah told Betty he'd walk her to her car so she wouldn't be alone at night in the dark and deserted lot and alley. Before they departed, he looked over some papers, left his assistants and secretary some Monday morning messages, and called Anne to say he was on his way home. When they got to their cars, Betty gave Micah a hug, thanked him for his help, and they both drove off. The security guard later recalled that it was about 9:00 p.m. when the two left the building.

That was the truth, the whole truth, and nothing else had happened, Micah later swore. A different story became public soon after that Sunday night meeting. It included all the same facts, but one other suggesting that more had happened between him and Betty Pincus in Micah's quiet office that night.

It wasn't until weeks later that Micah realized that his brief encounter with Betty had been turned into a piece of Irv Pincus's scorched-earth strategy to beat down Betty. Irv had called a meeting of his "team"— his lawyers, his public relations assistants, and his security and intelligence thugs—the night he threw out Betty. His defensive strategy was to conduct a ferocious offensive against Betty and everyone who might be enlisted to help her. "She doesn't take what we offer her, Herbie boy, we rip her insides out," Irv shouted at his longtime, all-purpose lawyer, who winced at the prospect before him. "See that no fuckin' lawyer who wants to work in this town takes her case. Tell her she gets a lump sum that takes care of her, leaves town, and we settle this thing *fast*. We got no kids. There's nothin' to decide in court, right!" he shouted. "And you guys find out if she's *shtupping* anyone. If she isn't, she must be a lesbian, because we sure ain't doin' it much. She better know that one word about my sex life and hers gets raked over worse."

That was it. The word to stay away was passed on to the first three lawyers Betty tried to engage, and each found a reason why he couldn't proceed. The night she met Micah, one of Irv's investigators had followed Betty and surreptitiously snapped a picture of their good-bye hug. Innocent in fact, it was an evil enough suggestive scene for the tabloids. Betty in her gauche outfit, Micah in his sports clothes, a nighttime scene behind a deserted office building, a hug that the cynical gossip columnists would gobble up. Irv's public relations people painted Betty as the unfaithful member of the family; her accusations about Irv, they argued, clearly were retaliatory. Irv didn't know or care if Betty was really fooling around; he'd gotten what he needed. His cynicism about morality overcame any embarrassment he might have felt about his wife's apparent affairs.

"And she's complainin' about us bein' in love, honey; how dare she," Irv's squeeze of the moment complained, staring at the picture of Micah and Betty, as she held the hairy hand of her victimized sugar daddy.

Micah received a copy of the picture in the mail. He shrugged and stuck it in his desk drawer. The tabloid reporter who called for a comment wrote that Micah hung up and refused to discuss the photograph with him. The day after the article and photo appeared on the cover of *L.A. Confidential*, Micah received a call from his son Josh's tennis coach. He didn't comprehend it at the time, but later it would make sense. Josh had come home the night before with his right arm in a sling. He'd had a fall, he told the family; it was nothing. His tennis coach called Micah the next day to say that Josh had been in a fight at school the day before. The coach didn't know what had happened to provoke it, but Josh had slugged one of the boys on the team, breaking his nose and spraining Josh's hand—his serving hand, to make matters worse. The coach had learned from the school grapevine—off the record—that the injured boy had said something about Micah to Josh, and that was what provoked the brief fight. The victim was not talking about it or pressing any complaint, so he took no action against Josh beyond a friendly warning. But the coach thought Micah should know about it.

When asked, Josh wouldn't discuss the incident with Micah, who decided to leave the matter alone until Josh decided he was ready to talk. When the picture arrived, Micah realized what had happened. That night over dinner, after all the family events of the day were discussed and before everyone headed off to their evening tasks, Micah made a low-key announcement.

"I learned today that Sir Joshua slayed a dragon on my behalf yesterday." Josh looked down, and the others looked puzzled. "I appreciate your faith, son, and thank you for it. I just don't want anyone else here thinking you need to do battle against the forces of false gossip on my behalf."

"Would you like to tell us what you're talking about, darlin'?" Anne asked.

"Yes, just once because it isn't worth more. About a month ago a woman I knew slightly, Betty Pincus, asked me to represent her in a messy divorce. I didn't, but I got someone for her. When we left my office, she gave me a platonic hug to thank me for helping her find a lawyer. Her husband apparently had a photographer hiding there and a picture of that silly scene has made it into the scuz magazines. I'll live with it. I'm sorry you all may be embarrassed by some ripples. Just ignore it. Anyone who knows your mom knows I've got all the love of my life right here."

"Why don't you sue them? They shouldn't get away with dirtying your reputation," his younger son, Daniel, argued.

"No, counselor," Micah responded. "First of all, I did hug that lady. So what? It was polite, antiseptic, and dirty minds can see what they want in it. But suing would give the story credibility and life. The photo isn't false; it's only the innuendo that's false, and you don't sue over innuendos."

His youngest child, his daughter Cassie, and Josh, the eldest, were silent. Dan, an incipient lawyer, didn't understand Micah's view of the situation.

"But if you don't deny this ugly story, people will think you're guilty," Daniel was passionate, almost teary, his voice rising.

Micah's precise, calm answers were in stark contrast. He was patient and respectful, but resolute. "Dan, we don't always do things because we fear what people may think. In fact, if I argue with those sleazy reporters, I come off looking guilty—and for what? I know what I did and didn't do. My friends who know me will not give this story credence. Why care about strangers or fair-weather friends?"

"What about us?" Dan shouted. "What are we supposed to say to people who read the story? And what about what people think about us all?" He threw his napkin on the table, pushed his chair back, and fled the table and the conversation.

Micah stood and quietly followed him to his room. He knocked at the door. "Dan, may I come in?" No answer. "Dan, I'd like to finish the conversation with you, son." No answer. Micah started to say something more, but decided not to and walked off. "Okay; I'll respect your privacy, son." Micah left Daniel to his sanctuary.

Micah returned to the dining table and the quiet company that remained. "Okay, so that's my story. Josh has fought for my good name, and one lionheart in the family is enough. But this trashy incident doesn't belong on the tennis court or the law court, and I don't want my boys defending what needs no defense. If I need a passionate lawyer, I know now that I have Danny. Now let's move on." Micah never returned to the conversation with his children, but he and Anne did talk about the incident.

That night as they were undressing for bed, Anne said to Micah: "That was so sweet of Josh. But I'm worried about Cassie and Dan. She's too quiet and he's too upset."

"There's nothing to it, dear, nothing. They're kids. Of course they are hurt. But they know us. Let's not give the thing any life," was all Micah said.

"But the children idolize you, darlin'," Anne replied. "They don't understand how anyone could criticize you and you not fight back."

Matters got uglier a few weeks later, when Betty's deposition was taken by Irv's lawyers. Their divorce was heading toward trial. When Irv's lawyer showed Betty the picture of her hugging Micah and asked if that scene had taken place, she replied that it had.

"Were you having an affair with the man in that photograph?" Irv's attorney pressed on.

"I refuse to answer on the grounds that it might incriminate me," Betty replied. At that, Irv had what he needed, and his surprised lawyer was smart enough not to ask more questions. She might qualify her answer and they would lose their fortuitous advantage.

Her testimony was leaked the next day and the press—even the legitimate press—had a field day. "Show Biz Wife Takes Fifth over Affair with Celebrity Lawyer," one rag proclaimed. The trades and the local newspapers covered the smarmy story, too, with only slightly less reek. "The wife of movie mogul Irv Pincus, in a sworn deposition filed in the Los Angeles Superior Court, Matrimonial Division, said it would incriminate her to answer whether she had an affair with an attorney who advised her. The lawyer involved is Micah Lehman, who is not Mrs. Pincus's lawyer, but she consulted with him early in her bitter divorce battle with her husband. When questioned about this matter, Mr. Lehman refused to talk with this reporter. Mr. Pincus has said through his representative: 'I'm sad for my estranged wife. She'll answer for her conduct in a court of law. But I'm shocked that a lawyer would take advantage of a potential client in distress, and I'm forwarding my wife's deposition to the Bar Ethics Committee.'"

The incident had taken on a life of its own, and had soon gained more notoriety than the Pincus divorce. With the deposition, Irv Pincus had what he needed. He called Betty's young lawyer to his office a few weeks later, well before the scheduled trial. Irv asked his lawyer to step out of the office for a minute. Jeff started to protest, but Irv shouted at him, "Shut up, sit down, and listen." He spoke bluntly. "You're a good lawyer, kid. You got smarts and you got guts. When this case is over, I can see a tough cookie like you doing well in this town, maybe even on my team. Right now, though, I got an offer for you that's on the table for 24 hours, and if you're really smart you'll talk your client into taking it. What Betty's asking for—10 million dollars in cash and half my property—is a bad joke. What I'm going to give her is $250,000 a year for ten years. Period. And I'm going to give you $50,000 to cover your lawyer's fees. She's taken care of until she's 65; then she's on Social Security, Medicare, and on her own. She gets a quarter of a million bucks for each year we were married. She'll be a lot better off than when I met her in Queens where she was makin' $4,800 a year as a salesgirl. That's the deal. You take it or leave it, tomorrow. My lawyer writes up the papers and we file it then, and this case is finito. Got it? She says no, and we go to court for 15 years, you starve, and everyone in town sees you as a palooka. You settle, and my public relations team lets it out you brought down Irv Pincus. I'll live with that."

Betty's lawyer swallowed hard. He was dead and broke if he didn't persuade Betty to go along, and he'd never feel good about himself if he capitulated. Sick to his stomach, he thought about Irv's proposition all the way to Betty's house. It took him an hour to persuade her it was in her interests to take the money and run. He didn't sleep that night thinking about his heroic image of himself fading after his first big ethical test. But by morning he was able to rationalize that he couldn't beat Irv Pincus; he couldn't prove Irv's affairs, and perhaps Betty had had one—with Micah Lehman, of all people. He'd save her a fortune in legal fees she couldn't pay, in a lost cause at that. He'd have a nest egg and a rosy future practice. What was to be gained by tilting at windmills?

Jeff Bentman called Irv's lawyer early the next morning. The settlement papers were filed in court the following day. The newspapers had another field day. This time, Micah's picture was plastered next to Betty's—over a story about Irv's generosity in paying off his money-grubbing, straying wife. Betty had left town to stay with her sister in Arizona, and could not be quoted. Again, Micah had no comment.

He had no comment a month later, either, when the press learned that Micah had been summoned to a Bar Ethics Committee hearing called to determine whether he had violated Canon 2c of the California Rules of Attorney Conduct, prohibiting lawyers from having sexual relations with their clients. Stiff-necked, Micah hadn't discussed the divorce and the stories about him with his family after the night he told them about Josh's injury. He told Anne he thought it wasn't necessary, that if it was, it was useless, as he would have failed in the way he'd lived his life. That, and that alone, should provide the solid ground to support their family's faith in each other. Anne understood Micah's rigorous sense of honor. She shared his private hurt by respecting his preference, even though she feared what her children might be hearing. She put aside whatever self-conscious thoughts she might have had about the inevitable whispers and averted glances.

On the day of the ethics committee hearing, Micah refused to present a full or extensive defense to the committee. Micah was the only witness. His sworn denial was all he offered the committee. As a result, then, he knew, there was insufficient evidence for the committee to recommend any disciplinary action. Betty Pincus couldn't be found, so she was unavailable to the committee. Her sworn deposition at her divorce hearing was the only evidence before the committee. Micah told the panel that nothing improper or sexual had happened the night in question, and asked if they had any questions. After answering one perfunctory question, he was excused. A member of the panel asked Micah why Betty Pincus would have taken the Fifth Amendment when she was asked if she'd had an affair with him. "She was ill-advised and wrongly motivated," was all Micah replied. "What I told you happened is all that happened. I don't blame this committee for making this inquiry. But there is absolutely no truth to any untoward suggestions: the only physical contact I ever had with Mrs. Pincus was an amiable farewell hug to a woman in distress."

Micah knew why Betty Pincus had taken the Fifth Amendment, because he'd called Jeff Bentman when he first read about Betty's deposition. Too ethical to call Betty, who then was a party in litigation and had an attorney, Micah called Jeff at his office and asked: "Jeff, why in the world did Betty say that explaining our innocent meeting would incriminate her? You know what happened that night. I called you to take her case."

It was early in his representation of Betty, and Jeff had not yet sold out, so he was solicitous of Micah. "Micah, when she blurted that out I excused us and took a recess. I asked her what the hell she was doing. She said she wanted Irv to eat his heart out. She didn't want to lie and accuse you of something you didn't do, so she took the Fifth. She thinks she didn't say you did anything, and she thought it would drive Irv up the wall to think that you did. That's confidential, Micah, but I don't want you to think I put her up to this, or that I didn't try to talk her out of it."

So Micah knew. And Anne knew because Micah had told her at the time. But he couldn't tell anyone else because he couldn't force Jeffrey to reveal a confidential communication from his client. Betty had been dumb, and Irv had seized on her zany tactic and used it to crush her, as well as to corrupt Jeff, and to tarnish Micah in the process.

"Can't you tell the ethics committee?" Anne had asked Micah before he appeared.

"No. Betty's conversation with Jeff was confidential, lawyer-client. It's hearsay to me. And I can't disclose that Jeff told me what his client told him—he really wasn't supposed to tell anyone. Besides, I don't need to," Micah replied stoically. "They will have my sworn denial. There is no sworn accusation that I did anything beyond what I swore happened. What other evidence is there? The exercise of a constitutional right cannot be taken to mean any particular crime—adultery or anything else—ever happened. Only that an answer might tend to incriminate the witness."

"You know that, darlin', and so do I, because you've told me so and because I know you and love you. But, just as Danny asked you that night you told us about this, doesn't not talking leave open questions you could answer? Won't an ethics committee think what most people do, that a witness doesn't take the Fifth if she hasn't done something wrong? And, if she's guilty, how can you be innocent? In people's minds, I mean?"

Micah didn't say anything. Anne continued, "What if I came to testify that I know you and everything about you, and know you are a victim of a perverse and bizarre circumstance? Wouldn't that help?"

"No! I won't demean you or our marriage and put you through that, Anne. I know you want to help, but it shouldn't be necessary, dear. Thank you, though, but no."

Micah's position was that he wouldn't be pushed to act like a guilty man. He couldn't conceive that some people thought his pretense of virtue was comparable to a witness taking the Fifth Amendment. If a person who takes the Fifth suffers the insinuations that invariably follow, the accused person surely would be stained all the more by publicly denying he did something he did not do, Micah reasoned. What he did not comprehend was that he was in an impossible situation, because it was also logical to conclude that his silence suggested he had no good answer, or that he did not want to perjure himself. To Micah, the mere idea that he would have a sordid affair was unthinkable, and he wouldn't involve anyone else in his defense, however well-meaning their offers.

He refused as well when Paul Lee, his former law partner, called to say he'd be there to testify on Micah's behalf.

"Not necessary, Paul, thank you, but not necessary. What do you know about it, anyway?" Micah argued.

"I'm a federal judge. There's an Asian American counsel to the committee, Billy Chung. It can't hurt if I appear as a character witness for you. I may not be able to testify about the fact in issue, Micah, but you know very well I can testify about your reputation for honesty, even if I don't know anything about the truth or falsity of the issue in question. Your credibility is the issue, and I've known you for 40 years. Why won't you let me help, you hard-headed SOB!"

Micah laughed weakly. "You don't want my shit on your shoes. Someday you'll be up for confirmation to the Supreme Court or something, and you don't need this mess on your record. And at this stage of my career, my good character shouldn't need witnesses."

"They're going to screw you, Micah. Don't let them. I've heard—don't ask me how—that they have some over-the-transom bullshit about you and Ella Reed. You can't just be a fireplug and let folks piss on you," Paul pleaded.

"No, Paul. No. Thank you, my friend, for believing in me and for caring, but no." Micah hung up.

So now the Ella Reed gossip had currency. Micah had been asked by bar counsel whether he wished to respond to anonymous accusations he had received in the mail regarding this case. A copy of the unsigned memorandum was sent to Micah. It urged bar counsel to investigate Micah's relationship with his junior partner, Ella Reed, because it would be consistent with his matrimonial unfaithfulness and would corroborate what kind of an unethical lawyer he was. Was there no end to this garbage? Micah wondered.

Ella Reed was a bright, handsome young woman—charming if a bit earnest—who worked in Micah's firm. She idolized Micah, but so did most of the young lawyers there. When Paul Lee went to the bench, Micah made Ella and two young men in her class at the firm junior partners. Her promotion was notable because Ella was the first woman partner in a major law firm in Los Angeles. Ella made it because she was smart, helpful, and hardworking. Because they lived in a sexist world, and because Ella was good-looking and single, some cynical observers snickered—never to Ella or Micah—that Micah had a sexy little protégé, and who could blame him for working late with her alone at the office, or bringing her out of town on cases. Some mentor! Until now, no one would have given serious credence to the gossip or said it out loud. But someone—probably a still-vengeful Irv Pincus—had gone to the trouble of vacuuming up all the rumors and fantasies for the ethics committee to consider while it judged Micah.

Micah was outraged. He told bar counsel that there was nothing to the malicious suggestions and that he would not dignify them by publicly denying them. There was nothing to deny. To do so would be to put a fine young woman's reputation needlessly into question. It was like denying you ever were a Communist or that you beat your wife. Everyone would wonder for the first time and forever after if you were, or if you did.

But to those who knew about Micah's predicament, now there were two innuendos. Those same skeptics who had joked privately about Micah and Ella for years were among the people who believed the worst about Micah's alleged affair with Betty Pincus. It all added up, didn't it? Where there's smoke, there's fire, right?

The bar counsel, unsure what to do with the unsigned memorandum, called his friend, Paul Lee, and told him about Micah's obstinacy. "What am I supposed to do?" he asked. "I don't want to muddy two people's reputations, but I don't want to be charged with not looking into charges. Can't you get your friend to be a bit more forthcoming?"

"I'll handle it," Paul replied.

The next day, bar counsel was called by Ella Reed. "Mr. Chung. I've learned that disgusting and false accusations have been made about me and Micah Lehman. For the record, I'll present you with an affidavit attesting to the fact that these suggestive accusations are completely untrue. It is my professional judgment that with my affidavit you have the right—indeed the obligation—to disregard the baseless and unsworn charges. If you publicize my affidavit, you are unnecessarily sullying two attorneys' reputations. I hope you will agree."

Later that day, Ella Reed's affidavit arrived. Bar counsel wrote a note to the committee's file that the anonymous charges in the memorandum were unconfirmed and had been denied under oath. He considered the unsworn accusations untrustworthy and inadmissible. That part of the case against Micah Lehman was formally dismissed, and the file was sealed as confidential.

The ethics committee's finding on the Betty Pincus question was publicized several weeks later. It was less than cleansing of Micah's reputation, couched as it was in legalese: "There was no evidence to corroborate the rebuttable presumption implicit in Mrs. Pincus's sworn testimony that she had an affair with Micah Lehman in violation of the California Penal Code sanction against adultery. The attorney had never been retained by Mrs. Pincus, so he'd not entered into a professional relationship with Mrs. Pincus. He denied under oath that they had an affair."

"A pyrrhic victory," the press notice of the committee's action had reported, "for one of the area's leading lawyers."

"I suppose now no one will ever know what really happened one night with that pathetic woman in her friend's law office," a hedging columnist wrote.

"Everyone can judge my ex and Mr. Lehman for themselves," Irv Pincus's press statement pontificated. "I'm moving on with my life."

And so all the parties did. But the event marred Micah's relationship with his impressionable son, Dan. Nothing more was ever said about the incident in the Lehman household. Five Lehmans lived on with their own private conclusions. The public would be left to wonder who was the bigger fool, the father or the son? Micah or Daniel? Who really was at fault? In the ordinary but profound battles between fathers and sons, must the father always bear the blame? Is youth an invariable defense? Shouldn't a father be wise enough to know that people cannot return to those defining moments, nor redo them? When is the time for the son to grow up? When must a father relent, even when he may be right? Was there something more, something below the surface only the two of them knew and were hiding?

ELEVEN

Pressures at Home and Abroad

❧ ❧ ❧

Virtue is supposed to be its own reward, but sometimes—in the short run, at least—it can create serious pain and problems. Virtue is for the hearty.

It seemed that after the Betty Pincus mess, suddenly Micah's good fortune was turning bad. President Reagan had appointed Paul Lee a federal judge. Reagan needed to prove he was attentive to the needs of the Asian American community, and Paul was a Californian who had performed all his local political duties through the years. There weren't many Republicans who filled this bill, so Paul was the natural choice. He had come of age in the Eisenhower years and stayed Republican, as few of his community did in those times.

Micah was happy for Paul, and the firm gained prestige as a result. But Micah was forced to become more involved in the firm's administrative chores. They had been Paul's responsibility because he enjoyed organization and Micah cared little about it. Their partnership was perfect. Now, Micah realized just how much time Paul was required to spend doing these invisible, irritating jobs—meeting after meeting about insurance, leases, pension programs, policies for this and procedures for that. It took Micah over a year after Paul left to work out systems and find responsible junior partners to run them so he could step away from this administrative part of the law firm in which he had no interest.

But the year and a half wore him down because he did not lessen his workload in the cases he handled; indeed, he had to supervise more work in areas Paul had managed. So Micah's work weeks, always full and consuming, became intolerable. He preserved his Friday-night-to-Saturday Sabbath routine, but Sundays were given up to meetings and catch-up work that wasn't taken care of during the busy weekdays. Vacations were out of the question. Micah's long devotion to Anne's health was ironic considering his negligence about his own. The wear began to show. His boyish looks suddenly were replaced by notable signs of aging. His decisiveness that had been a sign of strength was changing to a more assertive, sometimes imperious style that showed up primarily in his dealings with those people closest to him, his family and his partners and employees at the firm.

These changes might not have come about after Paul's leaving, if the other incidents hadn't arisen at the same time. The Betty Pincus scandal took its toll. Once the hero of his law firm as the idealistic battler for the downtrodden, the one who brought in the glamorous cases the young lawyers competed to work on, and the partner who stayed out of the edgy dealings about sensitive secretaries and inappropriate conduct that Paul handled, Micah was now the arbiter of all these troublesome administrative problems. And, he had become one himself. Most of the people at the firm who knew Micah doubted the suggestive stories that had appeared during the Pincus fiasco, as it was referred to sub rosa at the firm. But those people who had experienced the short end of Micah's administrative rulings, or who themselves had crossed comparable lines in their private lives, weren't so sure. Even Micah's relationship with Ella Reed had become more formal. He had always favored Ella and looked for opportunities to use her on his interesting cases. She was devoted and hardworking and had charmed Micah. Now, he was self-conscious about their relationship, and distanced himself from her to avoid the stressful gossip. In doing so, he not only reinforced the beliefs of skeptical observers but also lost his closest admirer and most ardent assistant. For the first time, life at what had become the Lehman firm was not ideal.

The worst fallout from the Pincus affair was the unpredictable damage it caused Micah's relationship with two of his children. Because he was older, and because his nature was less intense, more extroverted, Josh handled the Pincus event without it affecting his feelings about his father. But Daniel and Cassie were traumatized in ways Micah didn't realize until it was too late. And he wasn't good at the personal repair work that might have made a difference. Josh had gotten out of his system what he needed to with one punch at his sarcastic classmate. He was a hero in a juvenile, macho way, and he never looked at the incident as more than an unwarranted insult that he had responded to appropriately. His hand healed fast, and so did his wounded family pride.

Less simple was the impact of the incident on two of his children, Cassie and Daniel. At 12, Cassie was the youngest. She witnessed one brother's physical reaction in unblinking support of her father, and her other brother's more personal, more questioning, more condemning emotional reaction. That her father never dealt with Dan's young teenage fury and hurt about the charges left Cassie with unanswered questions. Her youth, her adolescent sensibilities, her not wanting to take sides between brothers she adored and who reacted so differently left her baffled, uncertain. That there was no family conversation about the incident beyond the one peremptory announcement by her father meant she could not digest the facts and issues as she might have if there had been long discussions of everyone's ideas. Cassie saw Dan's alienation as a position she had to support or be guilty of sibling desertion. She looked up to Josh as her protector, and to Daniel as her soul mate and intellectual model.

Anne sensed that Cassie was baffled and troubled by the meaning of her one brother's sound and fury. Her silence shielded what was on her mind, and Anne tried to talk to her about it privately. Typical of youngsters of her age and nature, Cassie denied there was a problem and remained uncommunicative. Anne hoped the problem would dissipate in time, but she doubted it. Micah relied on Anne's usually dispositive interventions. A formality developed in Micah's relationship with Cassie. He always had been stiff about just how to treat a young daughter; it didn't come naturally, as with his boys. Cassie never took on her father over the question, or turned away from him as Dan clearly had done; nor did she forget it. There simply was a chill, and a distance that neither diminished nor extended.

Daniel was the real problem. After the night of his fight with his father over Micah's refusal to publicly deny the charge against him, and his storming away from the family conversation and retreating to his room, a deep alienation set in between Dan and his father—indeed, between Dan and the whole family.

Micah tried once more to make Daniel understand his position. Anne had insisted he do so. It only made the problem worse, and the distance between them became chasmic. The Saturday after their first explosive conversation, Micah approached Daniel when the family was engaged in their afternoon athletics.

"Danny, can we talk a bit, son? I'm bothered by our debate the other night, and I don't want to leave things between us as we did."

"Debate? That was not a debate, Father. It was a pronouncement by you. I guess you don't believe the First Amendment works at home."

"I do, son. And that is why I want to talk to you now."

"What's to talk about?" Dan looked down and tried to walk away from Micah. He called out, over his shoulder, "You spend your life defending other people . . . why can't you defend yourself? Why can't you defend your own family?" With that, Dan stormed off.

Micah followed him, and they strolled away from the pool where the rest of the family was frolicking. "Dan, please try to understand what I meant to say the other night. There is nothing to contemptuous stories, and to publicly plead my case against them creates a lot of smoke that cynics will say means there probably is fire. It demeans me to get into the pigpen with these scandalmongers. You step into that kind of mess and inevitably you come away with some stink on you. I don't want that. It would only hurt your mother more to drag out this story. She knows me. Why should I care about what some others think?"

There was no response. They walked a while in silence. "The conversation you wanted to have," Micah finally said, "I felt shouldn't have been necessary—not between us. Do you understand why I feel as I do, son?"

Dan turned toward Micah, tears in his eyes, in a rage. "Yes, Father, I understand. You are so self-righteous, so fucking stubborn, so above it all, that you don't care about what your rigorous, patronizing position does to anyone else. You can't understand that people have questions. That charges that go unanswered leave most people believing they are true."

"We in this family are not most people," Micah blurted out, in an angry interruption.

"Oh, no, we're above all that. Well, maybe you are. But not everyone is!" Dan answered, and he hurried away, leaving Micah alone, angry, stumped.

Micah didn't try again. His son grew estranged from the others except for the unavoidable formalities of family life. He was closest to Cassie, but she was too young to be a real confidante. Josh had left the issue long ago, and was gone most of the time as his tennis career blossomed. Anne and Micah were consumed by their routines at work.

The next year, when his college plans were discussed, it didn't seem related that Dan applied to college abroad. His godfather and namesake, Micah and Anne's friend in Cambridge, encouraged Dan to come there. "Nothing would make me happier than to have you in the middle of my life, Dan," he'd implored. But young Dan applied to Oxford, citing reasons of curricula. It really was his way to get away from his family, immediate and extended, particularly Micah, without it seeming to be a statement. Anne and Micah saw Dan on their annual visits to Cassie and Daniel; Daniel the elder was extraordinarily hospitable to young Dan throughout his tenure at Oxford, acting as big brother and London tour leader whenever his young namesake had the time and inclination.

Four years at Oxford were followed by a period of continental travel, and then Dan decided to go to law school. When he was accepted and decided to go to Yale, that seemed natural and sensible, too. As a result, it would be almost a decade before Daniel came back to Los Angeles.

Dan left as an alienated boy; he returned almost ten years later as a resolute man. He discussed his career plans with Micah in a formal correspondence that revealed the degree of their estrangement. Dan wrote a very proper letter to Micah saying that he would pursue corporate law and was considering offers from the two largest firms in Los Angeles. Did Micah have a view? Micah couldn't resist asking why "so brilliant and well-educated a mind with various interesting options would spend itself on preserving and expanding the riches of the rich."

Not everyone cares so much for the purity of the law and the protection of the downtrodden, Dan replied sardonically, "but you and I have differed historically about the application of the law." He would not forget their decade-old disagreement. Micah silently acquiesced, and Dan returned to a home and practice of his own. He called his mother regularly, but his communications with Micah were infrequent and formal.

"I should have tried harder," Micah reflected. "You can't get those times back." Micah and Anne had more contact with Cassie after she left home, though not much more. She moved to Berkeley, where she went to college and graduate school, and then became an undergraduate teacher and a poet. Since college, she had lived with her boyfriend, Simon Van Rhym, an avant-garde architect who joined an innovative firm of architects and planners in San Francisco after graduating from Berkeley. Cassie would never leave Berkeley; it had been her home for a decade since leaving her parents' house after high school. She visited Micah and Anne, with Simon, twice a year, and while those visits were relaxed and pleasant, Cassie was remote from the family, no longer part of its parochial patterns and practices. When her first book of poems was published, Anne and Micah hosted a big party for her, inviting all her old friends, as well as their connections in the Los Angeles literary world. Both brothers came, but even then, with everyone focused on an event and person about whose well-being they all shared good feelings, there was a formality and distance between them and their children that bothered Micah and Anne. They had invested so much in their nuclear family that when each of the children left for lives of their own, Anne and Micah were lonesome and confused by where life had taken them all.

"Children," one of their friends said. "What would we do for aggravation without them?"

Geography, circumstance, and the fallout of the Pincus affair left Anne and Micah isolated as a couple for the first time in over 20 years. They became closer and even more dependent on each other, if that was possible. Anne worked at the rehab center every day. It had grown more active and was more prestigious than ever, and Anne's reputation and association with the center was highly regarded and well publicized. In every spare hour, she tried to be with Micah, whose work was consuming and who often had to travel away from California. Their private time together became more precious than ever.

"I miss Cambridge," Anne mused one night, apropos of nothing, it seemed, while they sat in their favorite big chairs on their screened porch after dinner, listening to music by candlelight.

"What made you think of Cambridge?" Micah asked. "You want to return to the scene of your young romance?"

"Yes," Anne said, sighing. "We had all that good special time together, all the freedom to do what we wanted, to discover new things. Now we are free—supposedly—the children are gone, we have lots of money, and we have so little of what we had then. We have each other, of course, but—" Anne stopped in mid-thought.

Micah waited to hear the rest, and eventually asked, "But?" Micah waited again. "You're not unhappy with your life—our life, are you?"

"Unhappy, no. But sad in a way that our time in Cambridge was cut short. I loved it so. I feel cheated that our love affair was too brief. I suppose I have a sappy, romantic notion about how we should have married, and how it should be now. I want to feel the way I did then again. Know what I mean?"

"I think so. Should we go off for a while? Go back to England and visit our old haunts? Go some place we've never been? Get back some of those old feelings?"

"And how are we going to do that, darlin'? How am I going to get away from the center? And how in the world are you going to get away for any real time from tilting at all your windmills? You'd hate it if you did."

"I want to," Micah responded. "We will."

But they never did.

❧ ❦ ☙

The conversation, and others like it Micah recalled through their years together, stayed with him. He did not understand what Anne meant, but he was sensitive enough to her words to keep pondering them. They led him to a course he never dreamed he'd take: to the office of a well-known and highly regarded psychoanalyst, Marvin Lukacy.

"Marv, thanks for seeing me." Micah was looking over his shoulder as he slunk into his friend's office. It was one large room off a small anteroom where Marv listened to the distraught and anxious population of Los Angeles and environs, mostly successful professionals upset by their lifestyles and coping with the demands of their success, along with some seriously sick patients, people with schizophrenia and addiction or attempts at suicide. Often nine or ten each day. Two large cushy chairs faced each other with a small table in between, holding the standard equipment in psychiatrists' offices—a small wall clock reminding how many of the 50 minutes remained, and a box of tissues available to dry the tears of distress. Marv pointed to one chair and Micah self-consciously dropped into it. He looked around the room at the oriental carpet over a parquet floor, the nondescript leather couch with a heavy quilt folded at one end, the maze-like paintings on the walls. The scene was strange to Micah, who shifted in his seat and eventually began a torrent of monologue.

"Marv, as I said on the phone yesterday, this is off the record. I'm here because you're a friend and I need to discuss something *very* confidential.

I don't like this. No offense, but I never believed in complaining to shrinks, sorry, to anyone about my personal problems. But I just need you to hear me out, give me some advice, and forget I ever was here. Is that okay? I don't know how these things work."

Each time Micah paused, his friend looked at him passively, not responding, and Micah picked up on his train of thoughts. "Can we say I consulted you on behalf of a client? How do you keep records of these things? Will you have notes about what we say?" Still no response. "Marv, talk to me!"

"Micah, you're a lawyer. Whatever your clients tell you, as well as your records, are totally confidential. You know that privilege applies to me, too. And you wouldn't have called me if you didn't think I was as professional about my patients as you are about your clients. So put that concern to rest. Please."

"I know. I know. Yes. I'm sorry. I just . . . ." Micah shifted in his seat, looked off into the distance over his friend's shoulder. Highly regarded in his profession, Marvin Lukacy was a casual social acquaintance of Micah, not a close or intimate friend, even by Micah's standards, which included no one at a level that would allow a baring of one's soul even at times of great anxiety. But they'd met at the homes of mutual friends several times through the years and Micah had found him to be very proper and smart and poised in their conversations. He could think of no one else he could rely on and whom he respected. Lukacy guessed when Micah had called that he wanted to discuss his recent folie à deux that had been a topic of gossip in the community.

"Why don't you begin by telling me what has upset you so much that you feel compelled to come for help, which obviously is very difficult for you to do?" Marvin Lukacy had the right blend of authority, directness, and palpable kindness that permitted Micah to proceed, however awkwardly.

"It's about Anne, Anne and me," Micah began. "I thought, think, we have the perfect marriage. I adore her. Never looked at another woman. Totally believe she has never had any love but me. But, I don't understand this, she keeps telling me our love is, is, is perfunctory, really inadequate. I don't know what this means. And if she hadn't alluded to it several times, I'd have overlooked her remarks. But I'm concerned I'm missing something. I *love* Anne. Adore her more than anyone in my life. I can't imagine she could not *know* this. If anything happened between us . . . ." Micah's words faded and stopped as he looked off into space.

"Have you asked Anne what she means when she says these things?"

"No, no, I'm baffled about what she means; what can I say?"

"What exactly is it Anne has said in these instances that has you perplexed?"

Not responding to these questions, Micah mused: "I thought it was men who always wanted sex, and women who wanted respect, and faithfulness from men. Anne knows I love her, respect her, wouldn't . . . even that time when the tabloids ran that bullshit about me, I knew Anne never believed one word of that."

There was silence. Lukacy was giving Micah time to say what was on his mind. Micah was waiting for—for he didn't know what. Lukacy was smart about these things. What advice would he have? Eventually, Lukacy asked, "What do you think is on Anne's mind, since you both are faithful and don't seem to have problems you know of?"

"I don't know. I really don't. Maybe I'm just away too often, too tired when I'm with Anne. I thought when we're together it's just what we want and need from each other. Peace, quiet, friendship." Again, a long pause. "Let me ask you an embarrassing question." Micah continued. "How much sex does a woman want, need . . . I mean, we're not kids any more. We've got three children, and we . . . ." Again Micah's words trailed off.

Lukacy picked up the conversation. "Different people have different sexual needs. Men and women. People with long, monogamous relationships like yours and Anne's usually are aware of each other's needs, preferences. But if you have questions, as you and Anne obviously do, the obvious first step to answering them is to discuss them. Have you ever asked Anne about her remarks, what is on her mind?"

"No. Yes, I mean, when she says these things, I answer her."

"What is it she is saying to you?"

"I think she, she means she wants to make love more, for us to be more romantic. Maybe I should go off with her someplace, just us. Bali. I hear it's very beautiful, romantic. But how the hell do I get away with all my commitments?"

Then, Micah suddenly snapped from his thinking-aloud meanderings to a more matter-of-fact summary, like the take-charge lawyer he was. "This is good, Marvin; I think I needed to talk this out. Thank you. Thank you. I'm going to buy tickets to Bali, maybe, maybe Japan; I've got to go there for business next month. We can stay after that and just travel around. Yes, that's it." Micah stood, and Lukacy stood up too. The traditional time was not up, but Micah was finished, a reluctant patient not wanting to go further with their conversation. Micah had been about as ruminative as he'd ever been, and a half hour of it was more than enough for him.

"Wait," Dr. Lukacy interjected. "You came here for help, and you are running off without getting what you came for. You seem to have cut off conversations with Anne about the tricky subject of sex. Now you are cutting off our conversation. We have time left today to continue, even if you decide not to return—though I do believe there is good reason for you to explore this question, here and now. To open up, difficult as that is to you."

Micah wasn't listening. He dropped two 100-dollar bills on Dr. Lukacy's desk.

"This enough?"

"Yes, of course." And that was the end of Micah's exploration of the mystery of his and Anne's love life.

Almost the end. Micah, a decisive man who made his decisions instinctively, wasn't sure what to make of this confusing dilemma. What he did do was perfect. Impulsively, a week later, for no particular occasion, he invited Anne to meet him for dinner at their favorite restaurant on the beach at Malibu. When Anne arrived, she found Micah seated at a corner table, displaying a wide smile. He stood and helped Anne to her seat across from him. On the table was a small package, elegantly wrapped. A bottle of their favorite white Bordeaux was cooling in its ice bucket.

"What's this?" Anne asked as she sat opposite Micah.

"Open it and see."

Anne opened the small box, and then a smaller box that was enclosed. In it was a platinum ring. "The ring I couldn't afford in Cambridge when we married," Micah explained. "My vows are no different today, Anne, but at least I can improve the ring."

Anne slid on the glistening ring over the simple antique one her mother-in-law had sent to their hospital wedding. A typed note inside the box included lines from Micah's favorite poet, Mary Graynor, Anne's mentor at Sweet Briar:

You were and always will be my love.
All in my life, all in my heart is you.
You have to know that.

Anne was stunned; she dabbed at her eyes. Then she stood and came around the table to embrace Micah. "You old sentimentalist. I am so touched. So . . . ." At a loss, she could say no more. She sat down again, and silently they held hands across the table.

Their dinner was a quiet one. Their mood was special, as Micah had hoped. And that night they loved each other as they hadn't since their crossing to Cambridge.

❧ ❧

Soon after Micah dealt with his family predicament, out of the blue his professional career received an unexpected jolt of reality.

The year young Daniel returned—1991—was also the year Micah took on a case that lost him friends and clients and exposed him to professional criticism in the press and vilification in private conversations. It also consumed his attention and energies and eclipsed his resolve to be more attentive to Anne. Micah's reputation as a respected advocate of important issues of international law, usually on the side of the angels, was severely tested in the Hornizek case. It began when his friend, Daniel Barth, called from London; he was calling as the intermediary between the Israeli government and his old friend Micah. Daniel represented Israeli companies doing business on the continent and spent time in Tel Aviv frequently. On one of those trips, over a long dinner at a seaside restaurant famous for its fresh fish and moonlit views of the water, Daniel's host introduced him to the Israeli attorney general. The casual conversation soon focused on a notorious trial that would be occurring in Jerusalem.

The Israelis had been tipped off by friendly lawyers in the U.S. Department of Justice that Herman Hornizek had been located by American intelligence sources. He was living in Detroit in his daughter's small, nondescript home; he was 80 years old and suffered from diabetes. Israeli clandestine agents arrested him one afternoon when he was returning from a medical appointment with his daughter and granddaughter. They summarily spirited him to Israel in a private jet; he was jailed and charged with committing heinous war crimes almost five decades ago, when he was a Gestapo officer. The Israelis intended to prosecute Hornizek to publicize his crimes against humanity, but they were facing world criticism for kidnapping an old man who claimed he was a victim of circumstance and not an evil Nazi as the Israelis charged. If he were defended by someone who was respected in the international legal community, preferably by a respected Jewish American lawyer, the case could go forward with less international furor and censure.

At Daniel's urging, Micah agreed to take the case. It meant long periods of travel away from home, which bothered Micah more than the unpopularity of his client or the financial cost of ignoring his prosperous practice. Intrigued to visit Israel, Anne accompanied him for the trial, but she could not travel with him when he had to be gone repeatedly to several places in Europe to prepare his case. Micah was always unhappy when Anne was not with him, so the strain grew and compounded the other pressures on him.

Civil libertarians questioned the hunting down of old men for offenses committed many years ago, as well as the methods used by the Israelis to snatch Hornizek off an American street and transport him to a jail on another continent thousands of miles away. Some of the American press and many foreign magazines portrayed Hornizek as a victim of wrongful identification, a defense his children were able to propagate with the help of a sophisticated public relations campaign. By becoming their antagonist's unwitting poster boy, Micah incurred the wrath of Jewish groups, who portrayed him as a self-hating Jew, a traitor to his murdered ancestors, and in the extreme, a Holocaust denier.

Micah took the case because his lifelong writings about international law were founded on ideals of justice that were flouted by the nature of Hornizek's arrest. He was trapped by the ethics of his often-stated professional commitment that required the best lawyers to defend the most hated defendants. Critics twitted him for his past criticisms of corporate lawyers for representing their rich clients. Micah saw a fundamental difference between representing an unpopular client who needed representation (even if he was an alleged war criminal) and defending a rich and corrupt client who had all the help he needed. Years before, he had chaired a professional committee that applauded the defense of a Russian spy, Rudolf Abel, by a highly regarded Wall Street lawyer, William Donovan, who was appointed to represent Abel by the court. Micah thought his representation of Hornizek was a comparable undertaking, but few of his friends and clients agreed. The most poignant example of the latter was his very public and personally disappointing dumping by Elie Berenbaum, whose organization Micah had created and represented for decades.

Having to cross-examine and undermine the testimony of elderly Holocaust survivors who were witnesses against Hornizek was the most painful assignment Micah ever undertook. He was spat on in a popular

Tel Aviv restaurant by an elderly woman, a survivor of the concentration camp that Hornizek had policed. She shrieked, "You call yourself a Jew!" as her family pulled her away from her shocked, scorned target.

Matters became worse when he discovered that a prominent member of the Israeli government had been connected to a long-ago dragnet of ghettoed Jews that led to their deportation to concentration camps. Micah had followed the evidence, but it led him to a situation where everyone was antagonized. He was a pariah to the Israeli public during his long stays there, despite the fact that it was the Israeli government that had secretly recruited him for their own sub rosa reasons. No one knew that; no one who did could say so.

Micah was able to demonstrate, through rigorous examination of old documents, government records, and sworn statements provided in other trials, that the evidence against Hornizek was contradicted in repeated and serious respects. It was onerous research work and painful courtroom examination of witnesses that allowed Micah to paint a defense that would have persuaded most juries in most cases in most jurisdictions. But no evidence in the world was going to persuade this group of Israeli trial judges to acquit Hornizek. When he was convicted, Micah didn't even have a courtroom victory to show for all his hard work and the obloquy he endured for over a year. That the Israeli Supreme Court years later (after Hornizek had died in an Israeli prison) reversed the conviction based on the proof Micah had produced would give little solace to Micah. Nor did the special award the Israeli Department of Justice gave him for his services to the government, an award given in secret and never made public for security reasons. It was comforting but of little solace that his friend Daniel hosted a dinner for Micah in London on Micah's stopover return trip to the United States, which was attended by several committee members who honored him for his selfless work.

Micah returned to Los Angeles physically depleted from the ordeal of his long and arduous trial, and from a year of living in hotels and enduring hostile receptions wherever he went. He was working himself too hard, Daniel had counseled his friend as he left London. "Take some time, go off someplace wonderful, restful, with Anne, my friend," he'd commented at the airport.

That good advice was not to be. Micah's center had fallen away. Anne could not be with him much of the time. Josh was either away competing on the tennis circuit or at home developing his popular tennis camp in his free time. Cassie was in Berkeley living a very private and distant life. And Dan was estranged from Micah at a time when Micah would have turned to him particularly for help and understanding. He was a brilliant lawyer, highly regarded in his professional community, though his world was very different from his father's. Micah often thought how wonderful it would have been if he could have recruited his son to work with him on this challenging assignment, how close such a mutual adventure would have brought them. He pondered that thought to his friend, Daniel Barth, when they talked over a long dinner in Jerusalem in the early stages of Micah's work there. Daniel had called his godson that night, unbeknownst to Micah, to urge him to volunteer to help his father in his daunting assignment. Daniel was tempted intellectually, but too frozen in his contrarian position of personal animosity toward his father. It was a moment of lost opportunity for the two men.

Micah returned to his life in California diminished emotionally, physically, even professionally. At one of his regular lunches at the courthouse catching up with his one close friend, Paul, now Judge Lee—meetings that had grown fewer and more infrequent as life intruded—Paul asked: "Micah, are you taking care of yourself? You seem exhausted."

"I'm fine, really, too much travel and the case in Israel took a lot out of me. I'll be okay, my friend."

"I hope you will take some time and do that, Micah. That's a court order!"

"I will. I just need some time with Anne and the kids."

All Micah had—all that mattered—was Anne. He dealt with his loneliness and worn-out physical condition by doting on Anne. He seemed to thrive only on looking out for her well-being, as if he were her doctor, as if she needed his help now as she had years before.

But the years had taken a toll on Anne, too. She felt the loss of her children more immediately than Micah did. He seemed to miss them intellectually; she felt almost a physical and certainly an emotional void from their absence from their lives. She resisted Micah's patronizing attentions to her for the first time. She was well physically and engaged professionally, and she didn't need what now seemed to be his suffocating manipulations. For the first time in her life, she thought critical thoughts about Micah, and she felt guilty for having them.

Anne and Micah exchanged words of exasperation occasionally; at times they were frustrated by one or the other's behavior. But they never had spoken to each other with harsh or angry words. Micah's words or acts might irritate Anne, but she said what was on her mind and that was the end of the issue. When Anne's comments sometimes mystified Micah, he pampered her in a solicitous way that exacerbated her irritations. Neither ever had chastised or spoken cruel or hurtful words to the other, except for that one time earlier in the pub in Cambridge.

The unusual event happened after Micah's return from his arduous trial. His behavior no doubt was attributed to his feeling besieged by all the pressures he had endured, his travel and work weariness, his return to unwanted office administrative pressures that greeted him. Anne's out-of-character snappish remarks emerged from a reservoir of buried complaints that gushed at a spontaneous provocation.

After dinner the evening after Micah returned, Anne told him the news of Cassie's pregnancy. At last, they would be grandparents. She'd saved the sentimental news for a suitably private moment at their favorite candlelit dining table. After dinner was served, Anne raised her wine glass: "Well, Gramps, let's toast to very good news. Our daughter is having her daughter!" Anne smiled radiantly.

Micah was stunned by Anne's news; he silently listened as she reported. "Cassie was in the middle of her doctorate thesis, on Coleridge and Keats, when she learned she was pregnant. Always the academic, she is naming her C. K. Van Rhym! Quite a moniker for an infant, eh?"

Micah's response was not what she expected.

"Thanks for telling me. Don't you think some good news might have added some cheer to my ordeal these months? How long has this news been kept from me? Why?"

Anne was stunned, shaken, silent for a moment.

"Damn, Micah. Cassie had a difficult time with her pregnancy, and we didn't want to burden you. Everything isn't about your schedule. We are not your law firm, around whose orbit the sun and moon must circle. Is that your reaction to our wonderful news?" Anne began to weep.

Most times, at such a response from Anne, Micah would have risen and gone to Anne, supplicating. He did not this time. He recoiled.

"Thank you very much! I'm in a hostile land battling a bruising war. I'm called with problems and bad news, but my own child won't share her good news. Makes no sense!"

Where this uncharacteristic sarcasm came from, Anne would never understand.

"Yes, your history of communicating with your children—Daniel, for instance—is such a sensitive one, what must Cassie have been thinking?"

At first, Micah didn't even comprehend Anne's response to his historical problem with his younger son. When in a moment her reference dawned on him, he felt betrayed, outraged. He threw his napkin on the table and rose angrily, upsetting the table before them. Glowering, he stormed away, declaring, "Thank you for the warm welcome home. Before you dredge up more old grievances, I will leave."

Micah didn't know then where he'd leave to, but the motions begun, he stormed out of the room, leaving Anne, head in hands, weeping silently.

Anne heard the car start and drive off. She left the table and walked to her porch, wine glass and bottle in hand, where she sat in the dark, brooding. Micah would return in a while; they would fix things somehow, call and visit Cassie, and they would never return to this atypical unhappy incident.

But Micah did not return as expected. He'd driven aimlessly, bemused, hurt, offended, unsure what to do. With nowhere to go, no one to turn to in his insular world, Micah found himself at his darkened, closed office. He distracted himself mindlessly, occupying himself with matters that might have waited. Late that evening, exhausted, bewildered, he drove home. It was near midnight when he arrived at his darkened house. He let himself in, quietly went to the guest room, undressed in the dark, and fell into a fitful sleep.

Matters were left unresolved, unspoken of—neither Anne nor Micah felt forgiveness or saw a way past their argument. In the morning, they went about their daily routines, passed each other silently, exchanging only perfunctory remarks. Each drove off later and busied themselves in routine chores.

When they returned that evening, they ate a silent dinner together, never returning to their past angers and disappointments, saying very little. After days like this, with no rapprochement, no conversation, no forgiveness or further rancor, each returned to their quiet, dutiful lives of family and work. The daily flow of life becomes scripted, except that it really never can be. If we knew the future, we would alter the present.

TWELVE

Bad Press

❧

Micah and Anne's names appeared in the *New York Times* a third and final time—45 years after the first time, almost to the day—on the obituary page.

> Micah Lehman, the noted trial lawyer and legal rights expert, died yesterday in his home in Pacific Palisades, California, of a sudden, massive heart attack. He was 65.
>
> Mr. Lehman was born in Chicago and educated at the public schools there and at the University of Chicago. A Thayer Scholar at Cambridge, where he and his wife Anne met, he later graduated from UCLA Law School, valedictorian. He started his own firm, Lehman and Lee, with a former classmate, now federal district court judge, Paul Lee.
>
> Lehman was known as an advocate of the needy, and his roster of famous cases began with his representation of the California farm workers whose landmark case proved historic discrimination. He took that case as a public service, as he would do many times thereafter on behalf of social causes,

while his firm prospered. Lehman was recruited several times to handle celebrated trials, by the government of Israel and the International Court of Justice in war crime cases. His book on this subject, *The Law of War*, is considered the classic work in its field. A passionate critic of capital punishment, Lehman represented countless death row inmates in vain attempts to change the law on this subject. He also served as pro bono counsel in many cases dealing with the First Amendment freedom of religion's application to schools and other government institutions, and the constitutional implications of poverty.

Lehman taught as an adjunct professor at his law school alma mater for 40 years and was honored twice: once as the most popular faculty member by students, for whom he was a constant mentor and champion; and again by the alumni association as its most honored graduate.

Among the many comments about his career by Lehman's friends and admirers was the statement by Supreme Court Justice Everett Marks: "Micah Lehman represented what was the best in the legal profession—brilliance brought to bear on the critical issues of our times and a commitment to the fundamental notions of justice."

Mr. Lehman is survived by his wife of 43 years, Anne Marbrey Strong Lehman, and three children, two sons, Joshua Lehman, a tennis professional, and Daniel Lehman, a lawyer, and the youngest, a daughter, Cassandra Van Rhym, a poet who teaches at the University of California campus in Berkeley, and one granddaughter, "C. K.," an infant. Their first child, a son, Samuel, died in childbirth.

The burial will be private, but there will be a memorial service at the University of California, Los Angeles, time and place to be announced. The family suggests that those wishing to mark Mr. Lehman's passing consider a gift to the Lehman Fund at the UCLA Medical School Rehabilitation Center, which he, along with his family, friends, clients, and law firm, started ten years ago. The fund is administered by his widow.

It was an irony, really. Micah had always been the caretaker in his life with Anne. He was rarely sick, even with a cold. Good genes, he said, are what count, or good luck, when his doctor urged him to rest more or have preventive checkups. Then, one night, a quiet evening passed peacefully at home with Anne, after a favorite dinner, quail roasted on their outdoor grill and a bottle of chilled Vouvray, as they sat in their screened porch talking about the day's routine, Micah died. Suddenly, as his father had at the same age.

Anne had just finished talking to Micah about an event planned for the rehabilitation center. He sat silent, unresponsive, looking straight ahead. Anne sensed something was wrong. After a strange silence, Anne asked: "Micah, darling, are you asleep? Are you all right?" Micah did not answer at first, then said a few slurred words Anne did not understand. She stood and walked toward Micah, who was staring, silent, dazed. As Anne reached out to Micah, his hand felt cold, clammy. And suddenly Micah fell forward, collapsing at Anne's feet. Stunned, she called out, "Micah," dropping to her knees and lifting his cold head. He showed no sign of life. "Oh my God, Micah, what's wrong?" She ran to the phone and called the emergency medical number, pleading for them to hurry. Anne ran back to Micah's slumped body on the floor. She lifted his head. His face was cold, his lips blue. She dropped to the floor, straightened his limp body and covered him with a throw rug that lay along the side of the couch. Anne knew emergency measures from her work at the rehabilitation center. She began CPR, breathing three times into Micah's mouth and pressing his chest 15 times, a second apart. It was exhausting, but it seemed to have no effect.

By the time the ambulance and emergency crew arrived, Anne had called the family doctor, who was not home; a colleague from the rehabilitation center, also not there; and her son Dan, who was working late. "Mother, I'll be right there."

The attending emergency medical technician took Micah's pulse, touched his neck and wrist, asked Anne questions about Micah's medical history and what had happened that night. He listened for spontaneous breathing while his assistant called the hospital on a walkie-talkie for instruction. They placed Micah on a board and shocked his body with an electrical defibrillator. His body jerked, but his breathing did not return. For 30 minutes they tried again and again, adding injections of atropine at the emergency room doctor's telephoned instructions. Anne hovered, asking, "What is it?" "What did they say?" "What's happening?" "What can I do?"

Finally, the EMT stopped his frantic efforts and turned to Anne. "Mrs. Lehman, I'm sorry. He's gone. Your husband has passed away. Probably a heart attack; it could be arrhythmia, lethal irregular heart. It can happen suddenly, as it did with your husband, no warning. The only good thing is that he undoubtedly lost consciousness and felt no pain. He never knew what happened to him."

"The only time in his life you could say that about Micah," Anne mused. Unimaginable as it was, beyond her comprehension, just like that, in a second, life was over for Micah. For them.

Micah's funeral was a private family affair attended by only a small and select list of close old friends who had been invited by Anne. Micah had bought a family plot in a picturesque grove not far from the ocean at the edge of a nearby nonsectarian cemetery. The remains of Sam and Charleston already had been buried there. Years later, his mother's remains would join them. A simple white gravestone stood atop a mound of fresh earth. At his request, Micah's name and the dates of his life span were all that were inscribed on it.

Several days later, there was a memorial service that had to be moved from the UCLA chapel to the university's vast field house in order to seat the impressive number of friends, colleagues, lawyers, and press who scrambled to be there—as well as observers who merely wanted to be seen. A large group of doctors and administrators from the rehab center came, not only in respect to Anne, but also because Micah had been a major benefactor ever since Anne first arrived there as a patient. He'd supported all their funding drives, attended most of their public events, and made a testamentary donation to set up an endowed chair—the Anne M. S. Lehman Chair. Anne would be its first and lifelong occupant.

From Micah's professional world, there was an A-list of stars from the movie community, many of whom considered Lehman a father confessor and big brother (along with some who thought it was a status symbol to be present, or who "didn't want to miss a chance to *schmooze* with all the right people," as one wag commented). A contingent of farm workers from the fields of California and Arizona had driven all night and arrived in time to show respect for the man who, along with Chavez, had made such a difference to their lives. A row of grim-faced, tattered-looking citizens from the homeless shelter sat in a front row the moment the doors opened. A large contingent from the Asian American community, led by Judge Lee, arrived to pay their respects. One producer wisecracked to his associate, "What the hell is this, the U.N.?"

It was the "event of the year," according to the *Hollywood Reporter.* "An incredible display of respect toward one of the city's first citizens," reported the *Los Angeles Times*, on page one. "There wasn't a dry eye in the house," a gossip columnist noted.

Even amidst the starlets and well-maintained matrons in attendance, Anne shone as the most beautiful woman in the room. She wore no makeup or jewelry; she wore Micah's favorite of her dresses, a simple but elegant straight black dress that showed her still-enviable, refined stature. As ever, she exuded a class and charm and beauty that left every woman admiring and every man respectfully infatuated. The mood was serious as guests arrived at 10:00 a.m. and were seated while Micah's favorite Mozart and Vivaldi selections played.

An eloquent passage about the need for morality in the law and about society's obligation to assure standards of humanity to all citizens, adapted from Micah's argument to the court in the famous Valdez case, was printed in the program Cassie had prepared with suggestions from her brothers and Anne. Finally, a brief printed note from Anne was included, touching words of thanks to Micah for their life together, and polite thanks to all who honored his passing. She kept a printed copy and enclosed with it the private note to her from Micah at their dinner when he'd given Anne her second wedding ring.

Josh had agreed to speak for the family. Cassie was too shattered by the event and was not able to do more than contribute her poem, "For Father," which was the final page of the memorial note. Her infant daughter C. K., whom Micah had seen only once, slept in her mother's lap. Dan was asked to gather Micah's papers from his law office, while the others in the family made arrangements to cope with the sudden business of death that was imposed on them. Micah had handled all family affairs, so new divisions of labor had to be created quickly. When Daniel returned to the house that night, he seemed very subdued. Others presumed he was coping with his feelings about his estranged father, feelings he could never alter now. Anne was surprised when he asked if he could say some words at the service. "Of course," she agreed without asking more. They had presumed he would leave that responsibility to others and respected his distance. But his name was added to the program.

Strikingly handsome, tall and muscular, dark and curly haired, Josh was well known to most of the people in attendance. He had been a junior tennis star, captain of the Stanford team, and was now on the pro circuit. He'd played before many of the people in the audience, and with a few at family parties at the compound as well. He was usually very informal, so his tie and jacket seemed tight and out of style for him. But his big figure, movie-star good looks, and magnetic smile charmed everyone, even at such a formal and sad moment.

"I'm the jock in the family, and not much of a public speaker. But as the older sibling in the group," he smiled as he nodded to his brother and sister seated next to Anne in the front row, each holding one of her hands, "I've decided to tell some revealing family stories about Dad.

"You know, in my work, there are some ugly stories about parents of athletes. So I really appreciate how my father dealt with his stubborn, erratic, know-it-all kid. Until I reached my ripe old age, I didn't really appreciate some of his—and Mom's, because they always acted together, much to us kids' outrage—his acute child management. First, he never *gave* me a point, *ever*." There were chuckles in the audience. "Second, when I was deciding—and they always let me make the decisions—whether to go into competitive tennis, he so covered his feelings on the subject, that to this day I don't know what he thought about it. It's up to you, son, is *all* he ever said. Third, he was my best fan, came to most of my matches, and watched tapes of the ones he couldn't make because he was far away saving someone's life." More laughs. "But he was never a hanger-on, backstage father sublimating his game through mine. And last, and most important, he never made me feel that somehow or other what he or Mother or Dan or Cassie were doing was somehow more important than what I was doing—even though, of course, it was." Now some smiles turned to tears.

"Our father, the private man, taught us the primary values of life by the way he lived his and affected ours. Whatever the swirl of pressures that surrounded his public battles, our family life was a reserve of spiritual calm and close friendship that we all will cherish, all the more so now that its source and inspiration is gone. What he gave us we will never lose, and could never repay.

"When I stop playing for money, I'll look back on the best matches of my life. They were with Dad, and him and Mom when I could get a date to play with me." More laughs. "They provided the class I'll always try to emulate, and if you can hear me, Dad, you are the man to whom I'll always be grateful." He sat down, loosened the top button of his shirt, and smiled as Anne leaned over to kiss him.

Dan rose to speak. The brothers hugged as they passed coming and going to the rostrum. Dan looked like his mother, lean and patrician and elegant, even if his professional life seemed to reflect that of his father. "You got the best of both of us," Micah had teased. "Her looks and my legal mind."

To the people present, Dan had always seemed distant, cool, unemotional. Today, his words displayed another part of him.

Dan looked over the assembled crowd. He paused before beginning his remarks. There was an awkward moment while the audience—especially those few in attendance who knew of the strained relations between Daniel and his father—wondered what would follow. Finally, Daniel began.

"Why do we wait?" He paused again. "Why do we wait until it is too late?" A pause again. Every face looked toward him, focused by his silences as much as by his words. "Eulogies are indulgences for the living; they are wasted on the dead." Now there was some suspicion, an awkward concern amongst those listening that this youngster might be going off the deep end. Dan continued, and the flow of his remarks picked up, and his message grew clearer.

"My father died too soon. As all of you make clear, for my mother especially, and his family, as well as those for whom he labored for many years—all his life, really—he gave of himself completely. What he offered me, I realize now, is a sense of honor and of the importance of personal integrity. My father's commitments to people and to fundamental values of family and the law were beacons from which he never—never—deviated. Often, his steadfastness and persistence were costly to him. Costly because he chose to live with the risks of life that flow from all human activity, and which most people seek to avoid by . . . compromise, dishonesty, lower standards, to name just the common excuses we all use. I regret that I neither understood this about my father when he lived, nor had the faith in him that he had in me, in all of us to whom he dedicated his life, the faith he earned and received too little of in the currency of human relations."

Anne covered her eyes with her handkerchief. Those close to her could see her shoulders heave. Cassie took one of her hands. Josh put an arm around her shoulders. Anne's friends noticed her abandon to emotion—outward emotion—for the first time any of them could remember.

"Many of the kind commentaries about Dad's life that appeared in the press and in the notes to Mother and our family commented on his many legal triumphs. I, therefore, will mention only one of my father's legal battles—the one that most observers considered his big defeat. We in our family know that Dad never thought of it as a defeat. I speak, of course, about his case against this city about religious displays. Dad always said so many people were mad at him over that case that he knew he must have been right. Four Supreme Court justices agreed with his position; alas, five disagreed. We talked about religion a great deal around our traditional family meals—gustatory colloquia might be a better word for it."

There were knowing titters in the audience from those friends and associates who had been to a Lehman family dining-discussion session. Daniel continued, pausing to smile back, as the mood of his remarks relaxed.

"When we kids questioned Dad about religion, we invariably got patient, full explanations that took years to sink in, but eventually did. We grew up with Dad playing Santa in respect to Mother's Christmas, and Mother lighting the candles every Friday night as our family shared a Sabbath. We went to Sunday school at the Ethical Culture Society because they both wanted us to know about the tyranny and divisiveness of avid religionists, and the beauty and wisdom of inspired religious writings. 'What do you believe in, Dad?' one of us eventually would ask. 'I believe in the perfection of my love for your mother. I am in awe of hers for me. I have faith in the virtue of my four children'—he never said he had three; he always remembered Sam, their love child. 'And I believe in the value and worth of honest work in the public interest.'

"'The rest is hokum,' he would say. 'Except for those who believe in anything else, and I believe in their right to do so. But when they try to tell me about the one true way, I head for the door, or when they try to entrench their ideas in public policy, I resist.' Dad truly believed in the First Amendment, that freedom of religion meant private acts unencumbered by public policy. 'Period!' as he would often say.

"So we were never surprised by his efforts in the *Five Unnamed Plaintiffs v. Los Angeles* case. And I expect some day the Court's five and four will be tipped the other way. I recall this case to note to you all that even in defeat my father was a winner, and that in the best of all ways he was a deeply religious man.

"So it was when he fought against what he saw as the mindless cruelty of capital punishment. Most people disagreed with him. Indeed, I did, both as a matter of legal principle and of social policy. But Father was a humanist, first and always, never a follower of trends or fashions, and the best friend of all citizens in need of honest representation. He thought deeply about issues, reached conclusions founded upon constant principles of justice, and acted without consciousness of the costs to him.

"But it is as a man that I realize now how unique he was. And how fortunate I was to have been raised in his and my mother's family. And I deeply, deeply regret I waited too long to let him know these feelings. I realize now that my father is my hero. Oh, that I had realized it sooner. That I had told him so. The Greeks had it, didn't they? Herodotus said that heroes are never perfectly heroic, any more than villains are completely villainous. But I know now that my father was—in the realest sense of the term—a hero to us all.

"God bless you, Father, and thank you for what you gave us all."

When Dan returned to his seat next to his brother and sister, Anne reached out to touch him and he leaned over to kiss her. Josh rose and hugged him, while Cassie, seemingly bemused by her brother's remarks, looked up at him silently.

Daniel Barth had flown to California with the Cambridge Cassie to be with Anne and the children and he spoke next. Daniel was not a remarkable physical presence, but his very British elocution and his skillful forensic abilities, honed by years as one of London's leading barristers, caused the ordinarily blasé audience to take notice. In elegantly tailored clothes and with a distinguished mien, he was—as the movie folks in attendance might have said—straight from central casting as the ultimate British barrister.

"Forty-five years ago, after a debate in which I deftly defeated my worthy adversary, a young man who had been lurking around the lectern during postdebate discussions stepped forward to compliment me and to challenge the position my adversary had ably presented to those gathered. Micah and I disagreed about that debate, and we have been arguing ever since, and our conversations—always with Anne's wonderful presence to brighten every scene and lighten any charged moments—have been the single most joyous times of my life. Oh, Micah was very bright, no doubt about it. But so are many others whose accomplishments pale and whose character diminishes in comparison. About Micah it could be said that here was a man of stature, of fundamental good character, and commitment to the eternal verities of our profession—fairness and justice.

"Micah's devotion to principles of justice led him down eclectic paths, and into controversy, as happens to nondoctrinaire activists. Always there was constant soul searching by this man of action and principle. To observe this, as I have done in several instances, is to witness great work happening. And this is rare in the workings of law—indeed, in all important endeavors.

"I think particularly of the case Micah handled in Israel involving Colonel Herman Hornizek. Because Micah was a leader in international jurisprudence, he was brought in to defend Colonel Hornizek. Despite Micah's strong repulsion over his client's alleged wartime activities, he agreed to defend the case. It caused a great rift with many of his longtime friends in the Jewish community and ended an association with an organization he had helped bring into being and had represented honorably and well for decades."

Everyone present knew about Micah's public dismissal and condemnation by his old friend and colleague, Elie. But they did not know what Daniel was about to tell them.

"Micah would never allow me, or any of the few people who knew this, to disclose what I will now tell you. But the record needs to be clear about this incident before the book is closed on my dear friend's noble career.

"The Israeli government knew that it would suffer international condemnation, and that it risked losing important American financial support, because it had arrested and whisked away the notorious and evil Colonel Herman Hornizek under questionable circumstances. They knew, too, that Colonel Hornizek claimed he was mistakenly accused of the crimes he was charged with by the Israeli court. Only if the notorious war criminal was represented by someone of international stature and respect could Israel argue that any conviction it might produce was merited and that it should be left free to administer its justice according to its own procedures.

"An Israeli official asked me to intervene on behalf of their government. They knew of my friendship with Micah, and that I could not refuse their entreaty because I was retained by them on other lucrative legal matters that I would not wish to give up. I did ask Micah to consider the case. Just consider it; the decision was his. He did, and when he concluded that important issues of international law were at stake, he accepted Colonel Hornizek as a client. In doing so, he endured a year-long arduous trial, at great personal sacrifice. When the Israeli court dismissed most of the charges against Colonel Hornizek, imprisoning him for lesser crimes that were proved, but not taking his life, Micah endured widespread and greatly undeserved condemnation from communities that should have known better and that were in his debt. He never responded to the unfair charges of betrayal leveled against him. So far as I know, the only time he explained his reasons for taking that case was at a dinner with Anne and their children before announcing that he would be taking on a very unpopular client. He told them he'd be 'taking heat,' to use one of your apt phrases, and wanted them to know why. Of course, their devotion never wavered. The Israeli government in a private ceremony presented Micah with its rare award for service—similar to your CIA's secret list of honorees—for his work on that case, and I probably breach confidentiality telling you this today. I don't think anyone besides Anne knows that."

There was silence for a moment, and some heads turned toward a conspicuous Elie—who sat in the audience with tears coming down his face—before Daniel continued his remarks.

"I take the greatest pride in recalling that as a result of our student-day conversations over meals and mugs of ale in Cambridge about a half century ago, Micah Lehman decided to discard his plans to teach literature and instead to study law. My modest role as a bystander to this decision is the crowning accomplishment of my career at the bar.

"Through the years, our friendship continued, in visits here with Micah and his family—his son Dan is my namesake and my godchild, and his other son and daughter and his wonderful wife are my lifelong friends. During their visits back to England each year, we walked the countryside by day and relaxed at the village pubs at night. Those very happy times I will cherish and deeply miss.

"Goodbye, old chum. Now I must admit: You were right. You always were right."

Law school dean John Sawyer concluded the remarks. Dean Sawyer was young for a law school dean, trim and proper, with a gray crew cut and a suit with a vest, not a traditional garb in this Western city, but a habit carried forward from earlier Ivy League and Wall Street days. He put on wire-rimmed glasses but took out no notes when he stepped to the rostrum to speak. He looked out at the vast audience, waited a long moment, and then spoke.

"Our law school will have no greater representative than Micah Lehman. Everyone there feels pride and good fortune to have been touched—however briefly; much too briefly—by Micah, and by Anne, because one cannot consider anything about Micah without noting the extraordinarily close relationship between these two soul mates. The pride with which each glowed in the other's presence was truly unique and enriching.

"But in a time when my profession is attacked—too often justifiably—for its greed, its neglect of the needy, and for its failure to act as a profession instead of a business, Micah Lehman's career stands as a beacon and an example. That he prospered, financially and personally, demonstrates that one can do well by doing good, and that the standard of our profession need not be the double standard—justice for the rich, neglect for the poor.

"How Micah found the time amidst his staggering commitments to his work, his constant attention to his family, and his never-ending public services, to write his important books and articles amazes me.

Micah put the lie to the propaganda that there are only 24 hours to any day, and to the academic pretense that important writings must appear only in scholarly journals. Micah's writings are classics, they are comprehensible by ordinary citizens, and they make a difference. They changed how things get done, and changed them for the better.

"I'm proud to tell Micah's family that we at the law school will dedicate our next permanent funded chair to a professor of public interest law who will be the Micah Lehman Professor of Jurisprudence.

"Micah, my colleague, rest in peace. We *will* carry on in your name."

The dean was the last speaker. After the formal remarks were concluded, at noon there was a reception at the law school. Most of the crowd left the memorial service with a smile on their face, though most of the women and some of the men were dabbing their eyes with tissues as well. The suddenness of a world without Micah would touch many people in varied ways, but it would change Anne's world most profoundly.

THIRTEEN

Final Thoughts

When the memorial service ended, Anne went home with her friend Cassie and her family, her daughter Cassie and hers, and Josh. The two Daniels represented the family at the law school honorary proceedings. Anne couldn't face another public event.

The house overflowed with flowers sent by well-wishers. She would send most of them to patients at the rehab center. Despite notices that the family wished to observe this sad time privately, an endless stream of neighbors, professional associates, and friends came by with offerings of food and good wishes. After putting baby C. K. to sleep, Cassie persuaded Anne to have her ritual daily swim; she had missed it for three days and needed the release and refreshment it provided. Those present busied themselves, provided minor distractions, and answered a constantly ringing phone.

It wasn't until evening that quiet and privacy returned to the Lehman household. Of the immediate family, Ada and Les and their two children had returned to Chicago after the memorial service. Micah's mother had died several years earlier, and Anne's Carolina family sent flowers but didn't make the trip. Their friends from England changed into comfortable clothes; together they rehashed the day's events and waited for the deadly reality to set in. Micah had been away from home often, so his absence was not unusual. The permanence of his being gone would not set in for a while. They told warm and funny stories about Micah that only they would have known; it made it seem as if he was still there. None of them were ready to face the solitude of sleep. Their collegiality made the day's events easier for each of them.

Late that night after her children left and her Cambridge guests were occupied at different personal chores, phone calls home, kitchen cleanup, and private chats about being helpful, Anne walked off and lay down across the rattan couch in the screened porch. Alone on her back, in the dark and quiet, she stared into space. Cassie drifted by, noticed Anne, walked to her, knelt alongside her, and hugged her; Anne wept silently, her chest heaving in Cassie's arms. No words were exchanged. When Daniel walked into the room, he stopped, observed them silently, and walked away, leaving the friends to a private moment of womanly connection. It was the last time Anne publicly showed emotion that week after the ceremony and funeral.

Later, Cassie persuaded Anne that she needed rest, and after embraces she went to her bedroom. Then Cassie and Daniel sat around for a while longer, having a nightcap, chatting with each other, wondering what they could do to stay busy and be helpful. Eventually they drifted off to their beds, to what would be for all of them a long night and restless sleep.

Several days like this passed quietly. Anne flowed along with the motion of chores, obligations, and the private busyness that inevitably follows events like this. Conversations were formal, perfunctory, rote, as old friends and family, dazed by the sudden event that had thrust them together, mechanically followed daily routines. Only once did Anne speak about Micah's death. She was gathering flowers in her garden early one morning after the funeral. She'd wakened before the others, steeped a large pot of tea for her English friends, who would want it when they arose, and was picking flowers to arrange in her house—forgetting it was overflowing with floral arrangements sent by friends and business associates. Anne was startled when Daniel Barth stepped behind her: "Coals to Newcastle, I'd say."

"Oh, Daniel, I never heard you come outside."

"I hope I didn't startle you. Strange time zones, hard sleeping, you know. I saw you here, thought you'd not mind company."

"Oh, yes." Anne stood and gathered her basket of cut flowers. "I must give away all those gladioluses and basket arrangements. My babies here make me feel more at home."

"How *are* you, Anne?" Daniel had not had a personal conversation with Anne since he'd arrived and assumed dutiful roles and chores. "This must be terribly hard for you. You will tell us when you want to be alone," he said, trying to be light about a heavy conversation.

"Daniel, I don't know what I'd have done without you and Cassie and the children these days."

"Anne, this has been our loss, too. Not like yours, of course. But we couldn't *not* be here. Or not be with you."

Anne sat on the bench in the garden. Daniel sat next to her.

"Are you okay, Anne?"

"Yes. And no. It's the incompleteness of this that disturbs me most. One day we are planning what to do Saturday evening, what to have for dinner, complaining about some petty thing that Micah or I did, and then he's gone! I was always the sick one, and Micah the one in charge. Now I'm here, and he's gone."

Daniel took Anne's hand. Said nothing.

"Micah was all I knew for all my adult life. After we met, everything we did, I did, revolved around *us*, not me alone. Ever since I first left for England, for the Thayer adventure, some adventure, I had no life without him that Micah did not arrange and manage for me. We had no time to consider the end." Anne's words drifted off to thoughtful silence.

Daniel waited a moment, then offered words of consolation. "Anne, generations ago people were dead at our age. Now, we have decades left. And with time you will regain your own life. Not the same, of course. Nor should it be. It may seem impossible to imagine now, but you are young, healthy, you have the ability to live a whole other life, and you will. First, you have to digest all this. It will take time, but you will do it. You will. Anne, you do know that our friendship does not end here. We who are your past are here for you now, you do know that. However far away we are, you are in our heart."

"Dear Daniel, I do know that." Then there was silence.

In a week, Daniel Barth and Cassie returned to England. Anne promised she would come soon, see them all, and stay with Cassie for a while. For now, she needed to be alone. Eventually Anne persuaded her children they should return to their lives, too. She would finish going through the reams of condolence mail and send the necessary thank yous. In another week, she planned to return to the rehab center and the welcome distractions of work. Young Cassie had returned to Berkeley, promising to come home on weekends so Anne could enjoy grandmother time with her first grandchild. Josh and Dan made dates with Anne for dinners that week. When they all finally left, Anne felt relief in regaining some quiet and her privacy. She was allowed to be alone.

One of those quiet, private nights, Anne was going through the remaining letters, snacking on a light supper at a table outside the kitchen overlooking the pool and garden. She heard a car drive up to the front of the house, a door slam, and footsteps sounding alongside the house. Somehow, Anne sensed there was no danger; the path was one the family always took, and the footsteps seemed familiar. A moment later, Daniel appeared.

"Dan, darlin', you startled me. I'm happy to see you. Come sit with me. Want something to drink?" Anne was chattering.

Dan sat next to his mother. They held hands. For minutes, only quiet. "I need to tell you something, Mother. You never asked me what prompted my saying what I did at Father's memorial service. You—like him—never questioned anything any of us ever did. Dad expected that of us, too." Even in tense and emotional times, Daniel spoke with a stiffness, a formality, an awkward earnestness.

"You don't have to go into any of that, Dan. We were touched by what you said. Your father would have been, too."

"No. I need to show you something you need to know." Dan took an envelope from his jacket pocket and handed it to Anne. "Remember my assignment as the new in-house family lawyer was to go through Father's papers in his office and get his will? I found this in Dad's desk." Handing Anne a letter, Dan rose and walked inside and poured a generous splash of scotch into a large cut glass on a silver tray. He took a deep sip while his mother read the letter.

The letter, dated years earlier, was from a Mrs. J. Murphy in Sedona, Arizona. The handwritten page was simple and innocent-looking enough, but as Anne read it, she found the message was not.

Dear Micah—

When I read about your recent case in Israel in the newspapers here in Sedona, I had to write and tell you something that has weighed on me for years. I meant to write this letter sooner, but was always afraid of what you might say. It's unfair to you that I did not say this until now. You were very kind to me when I went through my divorce with Mr. Pincus. I wanted to hurt Irv because he had hurt and humiliated me. When I said what I did about taking the Fifth Amendment, I thought it would hurt Irv, not you. I never meant to lie or to suggest that you did anything wrong—of course you didn't—I only wanted to make Irv think that. Then, when it all got out of hand and Irv didn't care and you were the one who was hurt—I didn't know how to deal with it. I was worried Irv might say I perjured myself. So I ran away from it, from Irv, from California.

Then, I met Jack Murphy golfing here and we made a life together, and I let it all fade away like a bad dream. But as a woman I knew I must have hurt your wife. I didn't know how to write her—your home phone is unlisted so I don't know her address. I want her to know that her husband was an honorable man. I am deeply sorry for any hurt I caused you or her. I hope it's not too late to make the record clear.

I'm sorry,

Betty Pincus Murphy

Anne dropped the note on the table. Dan stood near Anne on the porch, looking off into the darkness. He spoke softly, slowly. "How arrogant I was. And how ironic that it was arrogance I charged him with. All those years. He lived with it. With my condemnation. Probably the one condemnation he endured that caused him real pain. Pain that he didn't need to endure. He could handle the public stings that I couldn't. He had the private confidence, that certainty at the center. He and you. You had that. Why didn't I get it?"

"You do, darlin' Dan," Anne replied, softly. "You do now, don't you?"

"Yes, but too late. Dad had it right. Even tried to understand me much later on. You know, he gave me a hard time about going to work in the big firm world originally. But later on, not so long ago, when we talked about something or other I was doing, he said, Dan, the big cases, many of the good issues, are being fought by you big firm lawyers. We little guys—even our firm is a relatively small one by current standards—we can't fight the big battles against tobacco companies and asbestos manufacturers and insurance companies; it takes resources you guys have. I know he didn't really like that reality, but he was even at the end reaching out to me. I never took him up on his outstretched hand . . . ." Dan's voice trailed off.

"Sometimes, one learns life's lessons after they can't redo things, darlin'. That's just the way it is. That chapter is done. Don't make yourself miserable wishing you could redo it. Just write your next chapter differently." Anne held on to her tall son.

Anne knew Daniel was crying. She heard it in his voice, if she didn't see it in the darkness of the night. It wasn't her consolation Daniel needed now, but the opportunity to unburden all the years of false pride and harsh judgment. She sat quietly and listened until Dan was done talking.

"Danny. Don't hold on to this guilt. Now that you know what we always knew, be relieved. Go on, knowing your father was an honorable man, and that our love was special. Special to us. Which we knew from the beginning. If you know that now, you're a young man and that can be your guide when your time to love comes. Then your father can be your model. And he will have given you the best of life's lessons."

For a long time they hugged each other, standing in silence at the edge of the garden. Anne felt wetness on Daniel's face, and felt his chest heave silently. After a long time, Daniel drew a deep breath.

"I love you, Mother. Please come to Dad's grave with me tomorrow. I'm going early before the traffic. I can pick you up and drop you before work. There's something I need to say to him. Maybe if you hear me, he will." Then he walked away. Soon Anne heard his car start, and the silence of the evening took over.

Anne sat on her porch for a long time remembering Micah. His sense of honor, his belief that denial would indicate there was something to the charge, his perfect love of her that wouldn't permit even the necessity to defend it. All of a sudden, Anne's feeling of loss was profound. The vivid memory of Micah and of the unique love they had overwhelmed Anne, and she sobbed inconsolably until she was exhausted.

When she felt an evening chill, Anne went up to her room. There, she sat on her bed and looked through a pile of scrapbooks they'd collected through the years. There were formal pictures of the Thayer group of 30, and snapshots of Cambridge and their friends. One picture showed Micah and Anne grinning and hugging, standing in front of their favorite pub. Then came the years of pictures of the children and the family activities. In those photos of walking trips in England and family adventures, the children grew before her eyes. There were scrapbooks of news clips about highlights of Micah's career that Paul Lee had brought to Anne from the firm library. Anne flipped through a kaleidoscope of their life together, almost half a century of full and happy days.

Anne felt the profound presence of Micah. She remembered how he had always—since her accident in Cambridge all those years ago—watched over and worried about her health. How ironic. Her parents were alive in a South Carolina retirement home, and Micah was gone. He never thought about himself, always about her. And now she probably had decades to live, without Micah. "I never had the chance to say good-bye—how unfair, to him, to me," Anne thought.

Anne was happy that she knew her love when he appeared, and that she savored it while she had it. "We go on," people had been telling her these last weeks. She would go on. But how long, she wondered, would it be before she could let go of what she—they—had had.

As she browsed through the old photographs of their life together, Anne felt she was in a vivid and continuous dream. For just a few moments, some of the feelings she had those nights on the deck of the ship that took them off to England returned. She remembered their crossing, almost felt the sway of the ship's motion as it rose and dipped on the waves, how lightheaded she—they—were in each other's arms. She remembered her feelings of falling deeply in love. Losing her sense of aloneness for the first time. The reality of being alone again, now, had not truly set in. She knew the facts. She would learn the reality.

A Second Crossing

FOURTEEN

Filling the Void

There are periods in our lives when time seems to stop or vanish. The usual routines that define our days and nights no longer do. We exist in a void, live without feelings, walk through days unconsciously. Sometimes we need and want such a time. We may have to repair, or forget, or simply just think. Anne needed such a time after Micah died.

The year after Micah's sudden heart attack slipped by quickly and quietly, but whenever Anne thought about it, the event seemed a lifetime ago. For the first few months after his sudden death, there had been the mindless distractions of the newly necessary family business, will probate, changing names and titles of their marital property, learning to do the mundane things Micah always had done. Learning how to go through the routines of her days alone, after living with Micah for 40 years, was the hardest part. She could barely remember when "she" wasn't "they."

Thankful to be able to lose herself in her work, Anne returned to her duties as director of the UCLA medical rehab center two weeks after the funeral, when all her friends and family faded away. Her work filled her days with purpose and distraction. Her children visited on weekends, most of the time. Josh was busy running his tennis instruction camp and traveling on his professional tours. Dan was working at his law firm longer hours than even Micah had. Cassie, now a mother as well as a professor, remained in Berkeley. Few friends in Los Angeles called after the funeral ceremonies. Dear old friends Daniel and Cassie called from London regularly, staying in touch and urging her to visit. But while touched, Anne couldn't imagine traveling to England, now, alone.

Long ago, when Anne had named her daughter Cassandra after her old friend from student days in Cambridge, they had decided the baby would be referred to as "Little" when they were together. "I was Cassie first, so I remain Cassie," her friend had joked. That became their practice when both Cassies were together. Now that her daughter was a young woman, the nickname was particularly inappropriate—except when she was in her godmother's company. It was all the more a joke because young Cassie was quite tall and lean, like her mother, and Cassie the elder was petite, and in the euphemism of high fashion clothiers, she had become "full bodied."

Cassie in England had conspired with her godchild and namesake in Berkeley to get Anne to begin life anew after the anniversary of Micah's passing. A mother-daughter holiday among old friends seemed a sensible scenario for concluding a mourning period. Young Cassie handled all the arrangements, and Anne went along with the plan. In fact, as the time to depart drew closer, she looked forward to a change of scene and lighter times with her dear friends. They would go to the theater and shop in London; visit Washbrook Farm, the Fleming family's retreat in Ashton Hill; go walking in the Cotswolds; and take a side trip to Dublin while young Cassie attended her poetry conference, the cover story for her suggestion to her mother that they travel abroad together. It was Cassie's first time away from baby C. K., who would be looked after by Cassie's husband and his mother for that brief interlude.

Daniel Barth, a part of all the plans, had arranged a welcoming dinner party at his London club, the Athenaeum. He had made reservations for the plays Anne chose to see, and he was included in the Washbrook

Farm excursion in the second week of Anne's visit. Daniel wrote to Anne asking if a trip to Cambridge would be too painful. He had meetings there as a member of the college board of trustees and would love her to join him for events at the school. Anne was curious how it would feel to be there without Micah, and she pondered whether to accompany Daniel for a few days of nostalgia. Daniel was such good company. With Daniel, Anne could cope with the inevitable poignant memories—her early love, her life changing accident—that were sure to emerge when she returned to Cambridge, as she knew she must eventually. Then, she thought, her daughter could attend her conference in Dublin without the needless distraction of chaperoning her widowed mother.

Anne stayed out of all the arrangements, enjoying her daughter's assumption of the role of planner and manager. But the week before her actual departure she was overcome with guilt and dread over what should have been a time of earned relief and relaxation. She told young Cassie that she had second thoughts about going. "How can I leave my work? I don't want to be a fifth wheel, a burden to friends." Was it right for her to be entertained so soon, especially in this special place where she and Micah had fallen in love and begun their life together? Cassie should go without her this year; next year Anne would be ready. But both Cassies refused to change plans. Tickets had been ordered; commitments were made. Anne had to come now. "You'll love it once you get there," they both implored.

The day before they left, Anne was uncharacteristically anxious and discombobulated. She misplaced her ticket, broke and had to repair the handle to her luggage, forgot to cancel the newspapers and mail delivery. Cassie arrived late in the afternoon and took charge. "Okay, Mom. You get dinner ready. I'm taking over." By early evening, the departure details were arranged. They ate a late, light dinner at home together, and calm was restored. But Anne didn't sleep much that night, worried about what, she did not know. The next day at the airport she took a pill so she could sleep on the second half of the flight from New York to London, and as a result, didn't remember much of it. When they arrived at Heathrow early the next morning, disheveled and groggy, the swirl of entry and greeting elder Cassie, who was waiting for them full of smiles and cheer, swept her up and she gave way to it.

Anne and the Cassies went directly from the airport to Cassie's capacious home on a green park in Belgravia, not far from her parents' place where Anne and Micah had visited as students. Anne and Cassie were assigned sunny rooms of their own, and shared a bath on the third floor. Anne was directed to the first bath, and after a long, hot soak she lay on her bed for a moment and sank into a deep sleep. When she awoke it was late in the afternoon. The light was leaving her room. Anne was disoriented. Gaining her bearings, Anne dressed quickly in a silk slip and robe and walked downstairs, where she heard familiar voices.

Cassie and "Little" were on facing love seats, having tea. They rose to greet Anne as she descended the long, curved stair leading into the sitting room. "We thought we'd lost you for the week," Cassie joked, walking to Anne and hugging her.

The three of them sat around the tea table that overflowed with small sandwiches and sweet cakes. They poured the strong hot tea from silver servers, and chatted about their lives since they'd last met. Young Cassie reported about her new appointment to the English department faculty, her forthcoming book, and how CK was growing so fast, so wonderfully. Elder Cassie brought them up to date on her family's activities. Anne described the new programs at her rehab center.

Eventually, Cassie noticed it was after six. "My goodness. Daniel is sending a car for us at seven and we've yet to dress for dinner." The three women scurried to their rooms to prepare for their first night out.

As Anne dressed in her now-darkened room, she stared into the full mirror. The face that looked back at her seemed to be someone other than her mind's-eye image of herself. The long black dress was simple, conservative, the proper projection of a handsome widow. Her string of pearls complemented her dignified outfit tastefully. Her figure was still trim, though fuller than it had been when Anne first visited Cassie as a graduate student years ago. She was long legged, high breasted, and quietly imposing. Her dark hair was cut short, and showed only a touch of silver. The chief difference from her earlier days was in her face. Anne had always been a classic beauty, but now her aspect and its mood were serious, settled and saddened. Minutes later, Anne shook herself free from her momentary reverie, placed a long silk foulard scarf around her shoulders, and walked downstairs to meet her friend and daughter. Anne didn't realize then that she remained extraordinarily beautiful, statuesque, and refined—still a head turner—despite the plainness of her private mood.

Daniel's driver stood outside the gate in front of Cassie's house next to an elegant, highly polished black Bentley sedan, its back door open to the three ladies. Inside, the old red leather seats and paneled appointments made the riders feel they already were at their host's club. When they arrived at the Athenaeum minutes later, they were greeted royally at every door and landing as if they were the only guests expected at the club that evening. Eventually, as they were escorted into an elegant candlelit dining room, Daniel rose from a set table and hurried across the room to meet his guests with energetic hugs and genuine greetings.

Dinner was active and overwhelming. Daniel had ordered more courses and different wines than Anne had ever consumed in one meal. The conversation all evening was animated and jolly. Daniel was an eager and indulging host. The evening sped by. It was nearly midnight when the wine master came to the table asking Daniel whether there would be anything more he could provide. Theirs was the only table still occupied, and the surprised guests insisted it was time to retire. "We're still on California time," Anne reported, "or is it New York?"

In the lobby, the friends exchanged schedules, and plans were laid for the ensuing week's events. Before they separated, Daniel asked Anne: "What about it? Can you come to Cambridge with me? My meetings start mid-mornings and end late afternoons. You could sleep late, troll the shops, visit old haunts. We would attend the chancellor's dinner Monday evening, or not. Your desire. I'd love it if you'd come."

"Little Cassie is going to Dublin Sunday evening until Wednesday. So, yes. I'll get out of Cassie's hair for a few days. I want to see Cambridge while I'm here. It's so kind of you, Daniel, to include me."

"Well, it's done, then. I'll book you a room with a view of the Cam and we'll drive Little to the airport, and be on our way Sunday evening."

There were more embraces and cheerios, and the ladies were whisked home in Daniel's car.

The rest of their days and nights in London sped by. Good theater and endless social conversation. Long walks. Deep sleeps. Anne was refreshed and removed and completely enjoying herself, as she had not for a year. Sunday morning, before the two guests left on their separate trips, the three ladies went to hear the chorale music at St. Matthew's church, a treat Anne and Cassie had shared in their earlier lives. After sherry at noon following the woodwind concert, they returned to Cassie's house for a light lunch and packed. Daniel's car was waiting for them, this time with Daniel in it, at 3:00. After warm good-byes to Cassie and her family, the three travelers drove to Heathrow, where young Cassie would catch her 5:00 plane to Dublin. Then Daniel and Anne continued their trip to Cambridge. For Daniel, it was a regular monthly sojourn for his lifelong devotion to university affairs. For Anne, it was a nostalgic return to the place where her life and love—now gone—had flourished.

Daniel and Anne chatted amiably during the drive from the airport to Cambridge. As they approached the meadowlands surrounding the old town, Anne became quiet and stared out the car window, her mind drifting back to the first time she arrived at the university as part of a bus full of new Thayer Scholars embarking on their prized fellowships. She would hearken back to those days often during this visit, but she was snapped out of her private recollections by Daniel's announcement.

"There. Recognize it?" The university buildings had come into sight.

"Yes, of course. How could I not?" Anne replied. "It has hardly changed at all in all these years."

"No, not even in 600 years," Daniel replied.

They drove slowly down narrow, cobbled streets dividing the ancient colleges and pulled alongside the small bridge at the Cam River, a narrow creek at this point that meandered through the town. Next to it was an old stone building that had been expanded and converted to a small and elegant guest hotel, where Daniel and Anne would be staying. Daniel checked them into their rooms, Anne's with a pleasant view across a lawn that ran down the river.

"I'm off until half after six, Anne," Daniel advised as their bags were carried into their rooms. "You relax, and I'll ring you when I return. Tell the desk if you don't want to be disturbed. Dinner is at 8:30 at the trustee's dining quarters, but we're to have drinks before with the group at 7:30 at the chancellor's garden. Cheerio for now; do whatever you like and I'll see you then. Is that all right?"

"Yes, of course. I may walk around and see how the town has changed. I'll be here when you return," Anne replied.

They exchanged friendly pecks on the cheek, and Daniel departed. Anne unpacked and freshened up. She wasn't tired, so she walked off to look at the colleges where she and Micah had lived when they were students. She browsed in an old bookstore, searched in some of the shops for presents—bound books for the Cassies, heavy cable-knit sweaters for her boys at home, a Cambridge shirt for little C. K.—and eventually made her way back to the hotel.

As many shops had closed early or altogether on graduation week, Anne's meandering was a brief one. It was not yet 6:00 when she returned to the hotel, and she was not ready to dress for the evening. It was an unusually hot day and she didn't want to be in the closeness of her room, so she sat at a table on the lawn. As she sipped a cold lemonade and watched the students punting by on the Cam River, Anne's mind drifted back to her days there with Micah. As students, they had been insep- arable and had spent many insouciant hours on these very paths and lawns along the river. Like a movie of their life, memories long locked up were released and rushed forward from Anne's subconscious while she sat alone in the last rays of the day's sun.

At one point, Anne drifted into a half sleep and a strange dream. She was on a streetcar in a place she did not recognize, though it seemed like a distorted image of Charleston. An older woman—also unrecognizable—stopped in the aisle next to Anne, who was seated. "Just who are you, child?" the woman asked in a drawl. The *child* sounded like *chile*. "I'm Anne Strong," Anne responded to her inquiry. "Oh, the *real* Anne Strong?" the woman asked. Anne could not answer. What did that question mean? Was she being sarcastic? Didn't she know? Was Anne uncertain? Anne felt a gnawing and painful sense of embarrassment and challenge. Who exactly was she? Why did the scene feel so familiar but remain so unclear? Who was this woman? What was the meaning of this question, at once simple and straightforward, but so profoundly pressing in the reaction it generated in Anne?

Eventually, the early evening chill awakened Anne. Her neck was stiff and her arms were cold. The sun had slipped away. For a moment, Anne wasn't sure where she was—in Cambridge, England, or a dream. The desk clerk called to Anne as she walked briskly toward the lift. "Madam, I have a message for you, from Mr. Barth." Anne opened the fine-etched envelope as she walked along the carpeted corridor toward her room. "Anne," it read, "sorry not to have returned sooner. But the consolation is that this evening is all social, no business. And the dinner is always splendid. I'm so pleased you can be with me at this one. Ring you up at seven. D." Anne looked at her watch, made the change-of-time calculations, and realized she had less than half an hour to be ready. She bathed and dressed hurriedly, and was groping to put on her pearl earrings and clasp her matching necklace when Daniel knocked.

"So sorry, Daniel, come in. I'll be a minute." Anne was putting on a necklace, reaching behind her neck, as she crossed the room.

"Here, may I fix that?"

"Thank you. I'll be ready in a moment." Daniel enjoyed a moment of physical proximity as he helped connect the clasps, close enough to Anne to inhale her fresh perfume.

"Don't rush. We are on time, and I'll be quite proud to make an entrance with such a beautiful woman on my arm."

As they left the hotel, a car was waiting to whisk them to the annual dinner of the Cambridge Board of Overseers.

The elaborate dinner and event was elegant and formal. The rooms at the college president's quarters were ancient and impeccably furnished with period furniture. Several fireplaces in the long dining room were lit, as were the hanging chandeliers and multiple candles on all the tables. The orange firelight cast shadows across the oriental carpets and onto the walls. Flowers were arranged copiously on all the surfaces.

The college officers and the board and all their spouses knew each other well, so the formalities of greetings were brief. Drinks were served on silver trays by gloved waiters in tails. After an hour of animated conversation and libations, a bell tinkled subtly and the guests all went directly to one of the foursquare tables set before a long, raised head table. The college provost in his black robe crisscrossed with bright academic colors toasted to "we band of old brothers and this hallowed place, the love for which brings us together—and our special guests," an inadequate but proper nod of acknowledgment to the women in that evening's company. Anne was the only woman in attendance who had been a student at Cambridge, which all who met her noted and doted upon. She was able—for the first time, she would note later—to recall her days at Sidney Sussex College and her friends from the era without pangs of sadness and without dwelling on the memory of Micah. She was engaged by the conversations and interested in the pronouncements of the governing body's decisions that had been made in the executive sessions during the day when she and the governors' wives were resting and shopping.

From her days at the rehabilitation center in California, Anne had been a good and active organization member, unlike Micah, who was a loner. She had always respected the good works that captured so much of Daniel's time as long as she knew him, and she easily involved herself in the inside Cambridge stories at dinner, and later with Daniel in their hotel's bar.

There, at one point midway in their conversation, Daniel paused and looked silently at Anne. Moments elapsed while they each sat quietly looking into each other's eyes.

"You've stopped telling me your stories, Daniel. Why?" Anne asked.

"I believe I've talked, how does your expression go, a blue streak, all the while with you kindly listening to me go on," he answered slowly, more quietly than he had been speaking.

"Your stories, your life really, is so interesting, so much more so than mine or the lives I know about; I always love hearing them. Besides, I want to know everything about you I don't know, and there has been so much going on in your life between all the times we've shared." Anne reached across the table, taking one of Daniel's hands in hers.

"I don't think so at all, really. I think I'm talking so much and so fast because, somehow, I am in awe of you. Always have been, Anne. You are the one who's lived the full life. Continued the line of descent. Left your mark in such a personal way on everyone you've been involved with. I've always felt, from the time we met as students, that we all were on roads to prove ourselves, while you"—Daniel paused, then thought of what he meant to say, and continued—"you were so supremely self-possessed, so sure of yourself and your position, you always seemed, still do, the most self-secure person in your world. In mine, certainly."

Anne shook her head slightly, smiled a smile of curiosity. "How could you have thought that? I truly can't imagine how you could think that."

"You were the epitome of the successful person ever since I've known you," Daniel explained. "Oh, we were all successful, but alone among us you always seemed the one with nothing to prove. The one to whom success naturally flowed. We were all so competitive. You seemed blessed, really, self-assured, needing to prove nothing, measured by your own standards, comfortable with all the accomplishments that came so naturally to you."

"Daniel, darlin'," Anne interrupted, shaking her head slightly, looking bemused. "I'm the one who hasn't talked to her family for decades, whose first year off on her own here amongst the intellectual giants cracked her head and had to stop her academic life before it really started. I lost my first baby. I'm a widow years before I should have been, and the only life I gave myself to has ended. Yes, I have three lovely children, but they are now and likely always will be, sadly, a very small part of my every-day, every-night life." Anne stopped and looked off into space. "Some super-star success!"

Daniel now took both of Anne's hands, imploring. "How naïve of me, Anne; how truly insensitive. I suppose I've confused your extraordinary charisma with a judgment outsiders would make about your enviable life. I'm so sorry if I've seemed to not be empathetic with all you've—you've—endured. Please forgive me, my blindness."

Anne smiled, looked away from Daniel. How interesting, she thought, what people think we are; how different from what we think of ourselves.

They sat alone, quietly now, until the bar closed, the fire in the fireplace banked, and their drinks were long finished. "My lord," Daniel gasped, looking at his watch. "I've kept you up until 2:00 this morning; how wicked of me. You must be very tired, Anne."

"I am, but it was such a pleasant evening. You were good to include me in such a special occasion. I never dreamed I'd . . . I hope I didn't offend you with my complaints. I have no right to complain, given all I've had—have."

Daniel interrupted. "You added grace we've not had before. And further, you've made an old friend surer than ever before how fortunate he is to be a small part of your life."

Sleepily, quietly, Anne and Daniel walked together through the empty bar and across the lobby, up a flight of stairs to their rooms; they exchanged pecks on the cheek as they entered their separate places, bearing their separate thoughts.

Anne begged off meeting Daniel for breakfast. "I need some beauty rest, Daniel; the time change still has my head pounding."

"To say nothing of the claret," Daniel smiled as they agreed to meet in the lobby in the morning at ten, packed and ready to drive to the Cotswolds to visit with Cassie and her family.

The next morning, refreshed and packed, Anne arrived in the lobby promptly at ten. Daniel had already checked them out and loaded his travel bags into the waiting Hillman. His driver and car had returned to London. The university provided its visiting board members with local transportation, and Daniel had paid the driver for the two-hour personal sojourn to Cassie's family country house in the Cotswolds.

Their days at the Flemings' cottage with all of Cassie's family was like being back in their old home for a week. The cottage was filled with children and old friends; the senior Flemings were there for a few days to see Anne. Omnipresent were dogs, chatter, clatter, good food smells, and fireplace fires. Long walks on the nearby footpaths each day were followed by naps, drinks before the fire, and long dinners that lasted until someone was sleepy enough to stand and retire. Anne and Daniel were there just short of one week, which flew by like one long and wonderful day.

The final evening, Daniel announced that he and Anne were in charge of the dinner. They shopped in the village markets nearby for breads and cheeses, and two main courses of lamb and fowl, which Daniel cooked over an open fire, and an assortment of wines for before, during, and after dinner that cost Daniel a small fortune. They relished their daylong project. They drove to villages with names Anne loved—Chipping Camden, Morton-on-March, Lower Slaughter—to buy the specialties Daniel had in mind. "After West Hollywood and Culver City," Anne kidded, "these village names just touch my heart."

Everyone dressed for dinner. The old stone dining room was gloriously illuminated by scores of candles and the fireplace glow. Toasts were warm and funny, as only dear friends can offer between themselves. And then around midnight it was done.

The next morning there was a rush of packing, last-minute planning, tearful heartfelt goodbyes, and promises to be together again soon. Then, Daniel and Anne were off. The car Daniel ordered drove Anne to Heathrow. Young Cassie was already there, having arrived earlier from Dublin to join her mother for the flight home. Daniel assisted with Anne's plane arrangements and waited until she had to board. They looked long at each other, holding hands. "How can I ever thank you enough for, for all of this?" Anne said.

"Dear Anne, the thanks are mine. I shall miss you very much."
What else might have been on both their minds was not said.

FIFTEEN

Old Friends

✤❦✤

When Anne returned to California, for the first time her work and daily routines failed to engage her. She'd never had to work, but always did as a love's labor. Her work at the center was something she'd always felt a commitment to, something that was hers alone. In the time after Micah died, her work provided a hiding place to shield Anne from her thoughts, regrets, some of her sadness. Even her house, so long a sanctuary full of life and activity, was too quiet and empty, too filled with strong memories to enjoy. The associations were overpowering. Instead of providing the repose of the familiar, it became a reminder of all she had lost and the emptiness she felt. Anne had always said she'd never leave their dream house. "I'll leave in a pine box," she and Micah both replied when they were asked by brokers if they would sell their home, or when their friends inquired whether they wanted less space and less responsibility, when their children left home. Neither of them could imagine living anyplace else. Now, the quiet, the empty rooms, the chores of upkeep without the pleasures of engagement all cast a pall.

One night, months after her return, her son Dan took Anne to dinner at a quiet seafood restaurant they liked in Santa Monica. Over a glass of cold Sauvignon Blanc while waiting to be served, Anne confided her feelings to Dan, not complaining, but in bemusement about her sudden apathy over all the parts of her life, parts that had been its heart and soul. Dan had become, since Micah's death, Anne's soulful listener.

Dan had also become a sensible advisor to his mother. "Mother, you really should consider passing the baton at the center. You've given so much of your life to it. You could remain involved as an active member of the board of directors. You don't need the money, nor the driving every day, or—frankly—the responsibilities. To your credit, it is so well funded and well staffed, you can walk away knowing all will be well. And feel very good about your having made it so."

"I know, dear, I know. I just can't imagine not going to work every day, whether or not I need to. What would I do?"

"Well, you'll find out. When you give yourself the chance, the time."

Anne sidestepped any definitive pledge. "I suppose you're right. I am going to think about it." Then she changed the subject to Dan. What was new in his work? Why wasn't he settled with a wife? Motherly concerns.

That night as she lay in bed, Anne thought about her son's sensible remarks. She was frightened because she didn't know what she wanted to do with the rest of her life, only that she shouldn't go through the motions of her past life any longer. But what did that leave her? She fell asleep distracted by these thoughts, by her quandary. For all her life, Anne had coasted along courses created for her, first by her family, then her accident, later Micah and her children. It now occurred to her that she never had made a fundamental personal decision about her own life, except falling in love, long ago, with Micah.

These thoughts remained on Anne's mind for weeks, while she followed her routines mindlessly, unenthusiastically, aware how unlike her this new attitude was. She was surprised at how pleasantly excited she was to find a long letter from her friend Daniel when she returned home early one spring evening. She poured herself a scotch on ice and sat in the late afternoon dusk on her screened porch reading Daniel's letter, hearing his elegant British voice in her mind as she read. She reread the part about his coming to San Francisco next month on business, wondering if she would meet him there, visit with Cassie in Berkeley, and then perhaps—"if you could spare the time and would agree to be my guide, visit the California vineyards one hears are quite good, and drive your lovely drive through Steinbeck country, isn't it?"

Impulsively, Anne reached for the phone and called Daniel, hoping he would be there and not asleep.

"Yes, Daniel here," a sleepy-sounding voice responded.

"Daniel, this is Anne. Oh, I hope I haven't wakened you."

"Anne. Never too late to hear your voice. Anything wrong? Everything all right?"

"Yes, yes. I just received your letter. What a wonderful coincidence," Anne lied. "I was thinking about making plans to visit Cassie and the baby, and she would love to see you, and so would I. How much time will you have for our tour? I need some time off myself, and I'd love to be your guide."

"It's open-ended, really. I'm engaged at meetings on the 10th, 11th, and 12th; would love you to join all of us for a formal dinner with spouses evening of the 12th, and then I'm free. I'll buy an open-ended return and travel with you long as you'll have me. My first commitment that I can't change isn't until a fortnight. I'm yours for whatever you arrange. Oh, Anne, I'm so delighted you called."

Anne sensed Daniel was as pleased as she about the trip, and in the ensuing weeks she threw herself into planning. Micah had always handled arrangements, and Cassie and Daniel arranged their trips abroad, so Anne was new to this assignment. She discovered she enjoyed the anticipation and planning. She called friends and travel advisors for suggestions, read up on the best operating vineyards to visit and places to stay along the way, rigged a map to calculate the stops, even read—at young Cassie's suggestion—*The Red Pony* and *The Pastures of Heaven* by John Steinbeck to help focus on the literary landscape of their slow ride along a scenic oceanside road from San Francisco to Los Angeles. She made reservations at an old Spanish inn in Monterey, at Nepenthe in Big Sur, at a funky B&B in Ofay, at a health spa near Santa Cruz. She sent Daniel a detailed agenda with reading materials to prepare for their journey. She felt like a high school girl before a prom date, but never focused on the fact that her enthusiasm might mean anything other than a release from her burden and her delight to be in social company with whom she felt familiar and comfortable.

There were many trans-Atlantic calls to refine schedules and complete plans. Anne reveled in her newly emerging management skills. Daniel was very busy and happy to leave the arrangements to Anne, even charmed by her energy and imagination in these efforts. One Saturday, when Anne was home making phone calls to arrange one lap of their tour, the doorbell rang. A deliveryman stood there, directions in his hand, and asked: "Are you Ms. Anne Lehman?"

"Yes, what have you got for me?"

The man walked to his car and returned with a huge bouquet composed of three dozen yellow-and-white daffodils. A dazzled Anne thanked her deliverer, rushed to the kitchen, and found the note:

And then my heart with pleasure fills,
and dances with the daffodils."
With thanks from your appreciative student, Daniel.

Anne filled several pitchers of different sizes and shapes, placed them all in the rooms she used regularly, and called Daniel. He wasn't home to receive Anne's call, so she returned to her planning, freshly energized.

The next day, Anne's enthusiasm was doused. Out of the blue, a telegram from Daniel arrived, without notice. "Anne dearest: I'm filled with remorse to have to cancel at this late moment. Something I cannot control arose, and I must attend to it. I pray you will understand and forgive my reluctant behavior. When I see you next, forgiven I hope, I will explain. This nasty piece of business involves an old problem that will not go away unless I attend to it now. Please forgive your abject and despondent friend, Daniel."

Anne felt as though an emotional rug had been pulled from under her feet. She cancelled all the arrangements. She told no one except her daughter, who was in on the plans. Anne was annoyed that Daniel's lifelong masters of law and business would intrude on their—whatever it was. For days she didn't even respond. Reluctantly, she eventually sent Daniel a curt note: "Daniel: Of course I understand. Frivolity succumbs before the call of duty. Best wishes, Anne." Daniel never responded, confirming her worst doubts and making her feel bitchy for revealing her jealous reaction.

For a week, Anne felt emptiness. She went through the motions of everyday routines, living a blank slate. One morning as she lay languorously in bed, not quite awake nor still asleep, her phone rang. It was the elder Cassie.

"Anne, darling, I've not woken you, have I?"

"Of course not. I was just having breakfast," she lied.

"Are you all right, love?"

"Yes, yes. And so happy to hear your voice. It has been *too* long."

"It has. And Anne, I have news to share. News I anguished about telling you."

Anne felt panic. Please, no more bad news. Please, she thought.

"Anne, Daniel made me swear not to worry you by telling you. But I think I must."

"What? Don't alarm me!"

"No. Daniel has been in the hospital. He had to cancel your trip. He was more distraught about that than what he faced."

"What? Tell me."

"Daniel's had troubling chest pain symptoms, and his doctors insisted he have exploratory heart surgery. He threatened to put it off until after your trip together, but his doctors insisted that this procedure be done immediately."

Anne barely heard the rest.

"I should come, now."

"Don't, Anne, dear. I can't have him think his confidence to me was a ruse to get you here. Let me tell you when; I'll keep you knowing what is happening. I'll ask him if I can let you know after the procedure tomorrow. Then, let's see what happens and what he says."

"Okay, but please call me the minute you can."

All day, Anne absentmindedly walked through her daily chores, distracted, guilt ridden, and worried. How could she, an old woman, be acting jealously, jumping to wrong conclusions, when all along Daniel had been the consummate thoughtful person?

Later in the evening of the same day, Cassie called.

"Hello, what is the news?"

"Darling, I have good news, good amidst the scary, that is. Seems Daniel was having a routine medical examination before your trip. The electrocardiogram concerned his physician. He gave Daniel a stress test, and that result left questions whether Daniel required bypass surgery."

"Oh, God, no . . . ."

"But hold on, they insisted on further testing by Dr. Marvin Sackner, a very renowned cardiologist here, and immediately—which is why Daniel cancelled his trip. He didn't want to worry you, if the worst was going to happen."

"Get to the end, Cass."

"Okay. They got Daniel into the hospital that evening—no easy trick here, but Daniel knows everybody and favors were provided. He underwent coronary artery catheterization with an angiogram, to look inside the vessels to his heart. Here comes the good news—goodish, I should say. There was very minor blockage; no major bypass operation was needed. They put in a balloon to open the one vessel that was blocked, and that did the job. Daniel can leave hospital in two days, and shouldn't have further problems."

"Oh, God, I'm so relieved."

"Now, here is the deal. You must promise to be surprised when he calls. He will when he is home. Until then, I'm sworn to utter secrecy."

"I understand. Thank you *so* much, Cass. I thought the worst at first when he cancelled our trip. Then worse still when you called. What should I do? Come there when he calls?"

"You and Daniel must decide that. If you come here, you must let me know and stay with us."

Anne had a private cry when Cassie hung up after their call. She realized how much she cared for Daniel, and pondered what would happen next.

⁂

Daniel did call Anne late the next day and told her what had been going on. Anne acted shocked, as if it were news. They agreed to jump-start their planned trip. Daniel would come to the final days of his business meeting, and then the trip Anne arranged would be his recuperation.

When Cassie picked up her mother at the San Francisco airport, she teased her. "Mother, you look so different. Your hair? Your clothes? What is it? And do you think you can manage with only three suitcases for ten days? What's up? Where are you and Daniel going—round the world?"

Anne ignored Cassie's remarks, busying herself with baggage and questions about her daughter's doings. She stayed at Cassie's apartment that night. Simon was out of town on a new project. Anne played with C. K., a name that seemed presumptuous, unfitting for a tiny baby, though Anne was certain—impartially, she assured Cassie—that C. K. was as beautiful as she remembered Cassie was at that same age. When the babysitter arrived, the two of them chatted and gossiped, and then walked to a neighborhood restaurant in Berkeley famous for its view and ambience, as well as its cioppino chocked with local seafood. They exchanged news about everyone they knew, grew tipsy from more California Cabernet Sauvignon than either usually drank, and walked home to Cassie's apartment, holding hands, more happy together than they'd been in a long while.

After several phone conversations to perfect their arrangements, when Daniel's conference concluded the next morning, Anne rented a car and picked him up in San Francisco. Daniel had planned to take Anne to lunch at one of the city's famous restaurants, but Anne suggested that they meet Cassie at her faculty dining room; it would be her one chance to see Daniel, and then Anne could pick up her bags, they could give baby C. K. a hug, and drive off together. The Sonoma wineries—the first stop on Anne's planned trip—were an easy drive northeast, and they could be there by dinnertime.

"You must try some of our native wines, Daniel; see that we in the New World aren't without fine, if young, vinous offerings."

Daniel smiled. "I shall be your rapt student, madam."

Thereafter, their days together were a blur of motion and talk and timelessness. They drove south on Route 1 toward Los Angeles and stayed at small, elegant inns, walked the streets, shopped, saw the local sites, and dined late into each evening, from place to place. Anne had found wineries and small country chateaux to visit. In Monterey, they read aloud from Steinbeck stories set in Cannery Row and other literary locales. Their final night before they reached Los Angeles, 400 miles and one week later, was in Big Sur. There, they walked in the fragrant park and stayed at Nepanthe, the hotel and restaurant set dramatically high on the cliffs, overlooking the crashing sea below. At dinner that evening, Anne was radiant and Daniel was more relaxed than she'd ever known him to be.

As they sat at a table outdoors with a dramatic view of the water crashing below the cliffs, lanterns lighting the evening around them, the sky filled with stars, Daniel ordered a rare Armagnac for a final toast.

"Anne, how can I ever thank you enough for arranging this extraordinary trip? And for being my tour leader. I shall never forget these days."

"Oh, Daniel, it has been a tonic for me as well. No thanks are necessary. I believe this is the first time I've felt happy since . . . ." Her voice trailed off and she looked down.

"It's all right to say the word, Anne. Micah. We both loved him. We can't allow our love for him to, to—"

Anne interrupted: "Daniel, I have to deal with this, this guilt. Of being happy. I've absorbed that, of all things, from Micah's Jewish side of the family." She finally smiled at the irony of her remark.

Daniel waited, and then spoke. "Anne. It is time, more than time, for you to enjoy life again. Don't waste these years. You have grieved long enough, forgive my saying so. You are such an attractive woman—I mean that in every sense, you know—that . . . ." His voice trailed off.

Anne looked at him long and affectionately. "Dear, dear Daniel. Thank you for making it easy for me to return to the world. I hate that you'll be leaving in a few days. That you will be so far away."

"Please don't make me think that we will be so far apart, so long again, Anne. I want you to think about something. I'll always be your friend, if that's what you want. Always. But I confess—surely you must sense this—that I want to be more for you, if you could share that feeling, somehow." Daniel was halting in his speech, more like an adolescent with a first-time crush than the sophisticated man of the world.

Anne smiled. "I know that. I think I want that too. Give me time to absorb the change. Next time, after we separate, I'll know. Can you wait? Is that too, too—"

"Don't," Daniel interrupted. "Let's just continue this perfect holiday, as we have been. I'm inviting you to meet me in Venice, in a month, for an open-ended visit. What happens, happens. No promises, no demands tonight."

Anne smiled, nodded. They both looked off, staring at the sea and sky, lost in their thoughts.

They spent Daniel's last day at Anne's house. Daniel had lunch with Anne and young Dan, who was happy to see his godfather and to see his mother refreshed and lively. They poked around in the garden, swam in the pool, and did domestic chores like an old married couple. Anne and Daniel had a quiet, early dinner at home before he had to leave to take a red-eye flight to New York to catch the morning flight to London he preferred. They stared at each other sadly over the dinner table, holding hands, avoiding the questions each had about the future, poorly hiding their feelings about their impending separation. When the taxi arrived to take Daniel to the airport—he insisted, despite Anne's pleas, that she not drive him so late at night—they embraced long and silently. "Leaving quickly will be easier for me," Daniel told Anne. "I don't want to be seen so sad in public." With that, he abruptly moved away. Anne felt a weight in her chest as Daniel picked up his briefcase and, baggage gathered, turned and left.

SIXTEEN

More Than Good Friends

❧❧❧

For Anne and for Daniel, the month after Daniel left California and returned to London was empty, their activities rote. It was as if their lives were on hold. Each conducted their routines evenly, neither happy nor sad. All else in their lives seemed tentative. Daniel was certain what he wanted—to have Anne as his wife in London. He would curb his work to be able to be with her more than nights and weekends. Perhaps they could have a country home near Cassie where Anne could live among friends most of the time. He would have only a few days each week to preside over a transition in his professional life that would allow him to have the domestic life he'd sacrificed all these years. He would maintain only those prime clients who would respect his new priorities and allow him to continue to feel he was active in his profession. Daniel had no doubts.

Anne was less clear what should be next. A transcontinental friendship or affair? Then what in between? Live in London? What of her children, grandchildren, home, and work? Anne had no doubt that she could be happy living with Daniel, but she was less sure that there would be no guilt about living with her husband's oldest friend. There was no one else Anne saw socially whom she could imagine living with. She felt empty being alone. Though her feelings about Daniel were sure, it was, deep down, her fear of an incomplete ending to her life that closed the question. Anne wanted to have a lasting personal relationship in the concluding years of her life. It was privately an overriding need more than a passion that finally made her realize she was going to make her decision in Italy. "I'll take a bungee jump," she thought. "Better than growing old alone."

Anne and Daniel's relationship changed without a plan or a word said. They were staying in adjoining rooms at the Pitti Palace in Venice. The film festival was their public excuse to meet again. Anne told colleagues and her children she would finally be using all her accumulated, unused vacation time at work. She had never been to Venice, and she felt like a child in a fantasy world traipsing through the narrow, complicated warren of streets that led nowhere, crossing small bridges, lolling in gondolas that meandered the crisscrossing waterways. She and Daniel ate royally. "The Italians are the only people who only serve their own food," Daniel remarked once over a lunch that dazzled Anne. "You never hear of a Chinese or French or German restaurant in Italy. Their food is so good they'd never think of serving anything else."

Daniel had been to Venice many times and was an enthusiastic tour leader. He knew where to stay and where to eat, took her on a vaporetto boat ride around the lagoon that separates Venice from the Adriatic Sea, and led her on endless walks through neighborhood mazes she never would have found. He showed her the thousand-year-old Jewish Campo di Ghetto Nuovo.

"Even here," Anne commented. "Is there no place Jews can live in society without being segregated?"

"There's a long history here," Daniel instructed. "It includes Napoleon, the Nazis, and more antiquarian, *Merchant of Venice*–like characters."

"Do Jews feel an obligation to visit Jewish ghettos wherever they travel?"

"No. Some do out of curiosity, I suppose. Even out of respect or . . . ." Daniel's response trailed off. "But don't Christians visit old churches and religious shrines in their travels around the world?"

"Yes, I wasn't criticizin'. Only tryin' to understand. The lonesomeness and alienation makes me sad. Always has. I can't understand it." Anne's comments faded, as did the conversation as they walked out of the ghetto, seemingly out of a page of history one of them had wrestled with lifelong and the other could only imagine.

They held hands as they strolled silently back to the hotel late in the afternoon after a long, leisurely, and very winey lunch. Anne usually held Daniel's arm in a traditional, formal, but friendly escort's style. Without a thought, this afternoon she took his hand. They ambled slowly back to the hotel, speaking little, inhaling the enchantment of Venice's ancient buildings and canals. A raking light illuminated the old buildings with a warm golden glow that reflected the two visitors' feelings. The hotel lobby was quiet and cool; it was between the busy hours of lunch and dinner. They got off their elevator at their floor and walked toward Anne's suite. Instead of opening the door, turning to brush Daniel's cheek with a sisterly kiss, Anne simply walked in. And Daniel followed.

Anne walked to her bedroom and turned, looking directly at Daniel, saying nothing, standing still. She looked, quietly, fondly, at Daniel. Daniel walked to her, took Anne's shoulders in his arms, delicately; they looked long at each other. Daniel began to say, "Anne, I never, I always—" Anne interrupted, touching his lips with her finger and moving closer. She didn't have to ask Daniel to make love to her.

Theirs was not the passionate love of youth, where physical demands overwhelm couples and are followed by quiet tendernesses. Theirs was a love of quiet, at first tentative, contacts. Their lips touched, softly at first. Their arms circled each other. They inhaled each other's presence, smells, breathing paces. Fingers touched hair. Lips came down to neck, and rose again to waiting lips. They stepped apart momentarily, looking deeply into each other's eyes, then returned face to face, lips touching again, now-open mouths growing more hungry. One hand here. One there. Feelings growing. A moan. A whisper. "Oh, my darling." Words mixed, mouth to mouth. Anne's hand now led Daniel's to another place. They sat at the edge of a bed, each helping the other loosen their clothes. Finally, touching intimately, falling back, reaching for and into the other, feelings building, unconscious of anything except the other's self, the growing pleasure within each other, from Anne a sudden squeaky gasp, from Daniel a soft, intermittent moan, and finally both cried aloud in joint pleasure and fell into each other's shoulders, and kissing, kissing, and at last falling into a sleep of a very special personal knowledge and connection.

They awoke in Anne's bed early in the evening. The room was in shadows. Now they could talk of it, of what happened, of them.

"I'm hungry, but I don't want to go out. Could we order dinner here?" Anne asked.

"I'll do it, yes. I'll go to my room and dress. Will you call me when you want me?" Daniel felt licentious staring at Anne walking, unashamedly, from the bed to the bath, her long legs still firm, back straight, cheeks discernibly soft.

She looked back over her shoulder, a sly smile on her face. "I think I did—call you, want you." She disappeared into the bathroom and closed the door as Daniel stared into the room, numb to every feeling except his overwhelming adoration of Anne.

That evening they ate a late dinner in Anne's room. Daniel ordered an Italian specialty, boar roasted country style over wood, dry and smoky tasting. They washed it down with a bottle of ancient Brunello that Daniel told Anne was special. It was. Anne and Micah had enjoyed California wines at their dinners, but however pleasant, they had been perfunctory. Daniel had chosen one that drew Anne in; it was deep, dark, and sensual and made her feel so. "Oh, Daniel, I adore your love of good food and wine, your impeccable taste. For us, it was all-fungible—whatever was, was."

"Well, one of the benefits of all my travels was to become educated, and I must say I do enjoy the right sole with the perfect iced Sancerre," Daniel replied, enjoying the admiration of his beautiful student.

They didn't talk any more of "them" that night; they spoke of little of import. On their minds were their remaining days in Venice, their plans after. The windows to Anne's suite were open, and the combination of salty air from the canals and the flowers in the room, music wafting in from nearby bars, even the slapping sound of the canal waters, drew them to the window. They stood—naked under cushy bathrobes—looking out at the Venetian scene, wine glasses in hand, close to each other in a special way each sensed but did not remark about. At one point, church bells rang, advising the city that it was 2:00 in the morning. Anne took Daniel's hand, led him to their bed, and they collapsed into a long and profound love and shameless exploration of each other's bodies.

Later, they lay entangled and spent; Daniel felt a tear on Anne's face.

"Are you upset?"

"No, very, very happy. I wondered if I'd ever feel this way—so alive—again. I'm happy I do." With that, they fell asleep.

They were awakened by a pounding of the door, which opened to an embarrassed "Bongiorno, oh scusi, Signore," as the embarrassed maid backed away. The room was filled with sunshine that made the evening's rubble of tossed clothes, open wine bottles, dirty glasses, and dishes look like a den of sin.

"Oh, Daniel, we've shocked the help. How nice," Anne laughed aloud as she scampered toward the shower.

"I doubt it, Signora," Daniel remarked. "I'm sure she's seen this scene before—but never presided over by such a grateful and happy man. I shall shower and knock for you in say about an hour, okay?"

"Yes," a shout came from the shower as Daniel left. "I'll be ready."

Over a long, late breakfast at the hotel's outdoor grill overlooking the Adriatic Bay, outlined by tall churches and antique buildings, with bobbing boats on the water, they did talk of "them" and how their lives had profoundly changed in 24 hours.

After sipping the blood-red sweet orange juice and ordering their food, Daniel took Anne's hand in both of his, leaning across the table as they waited for their hot rolls and fresh coffee.

"Anne," Daniel began slowly, signaling a shift from romance to reality. "You know our lives now are so very"—*veddy*, was how Daniel pronounced the word—"different. For you perhaps less than for me."

"No," Anne interrupted. "You surely must understand it is different for me as well."

"Yes, but, but you've—forgive me for this allusion, darling, but it is a shadow we must acknowledge, and deal with—though I'm not certain how." Daniel paused to collect his thoughts. "You've been deeply in love and committed to a man for a lifetime. I'm a first-timer at this. Happily, delightedly so, I should add. And to complicate things, we've both loved the same man. I do feel—felt momentarily—I don't know, some guilt, though there is nothing dishonorable about what's happened to us."

"No, there isn't, and you mustn't allow yourself to think so. Don't spoil this, whatever it is we have—late love—with ghosts. I shan't. I loved Micah, loved him long and constantly, for over 40 years—my God, almost half a century. You and I never dishonored my love with Micah, or our friendship throughout that time. Some love is fueled by young passion; other love comes from long friendship—more than that, of course—shared experiences and values, common tastes. . . ." Anne squeezed Daniel's hand and paused.

They stared at each other, leaning across the table, oblivious to their surroundings, as the silver pitcher of hot coffee and the platter of fresh breads and jams and fruit was being placed before them. They sat back silently and turned their attention to the fragrant breakfast before them. They ate quietly, wolfishly, as they were hungry, having waited to the point where breakfast service had been concluded and tables around them were being prepared for lunch. The veteran waiters were solicitous of the lovers' privacy, and after completing their settings and preparations, left them to themselves. Sated by their tasty meal, Daniel returned to their conversation.

"How do we proceed? You in California; I in London. You with your work, I with mine. And your children?" Daniel looked to Anne for answers.

"I don't know the future, but I care about now. After the loss of Micah faded and life continued, I found myself wondering if that was all there was of it. I read books about widowhood, and mature love—forgive the corny phrase—and living life past 60. Now I'm past 60. And I know this. I'm selfish, darlin', don't want to wait around to get feeble and die. I want to live my life for as long as I can. I don't think I can if I stay in place. Friends have offered to introduce me to men they thought were perfect for me. Men have called, some friends of Micah's and mine, some still married and professing hidden love for me. Nothing appealed." Anne paused, then continued: "Then—yesterday happened. I embrace it. I will take what it leads to, though I have no idea what that might mean. If I did, it would mean I calculated this—and, dear one, I'm overwhelmed by this—all. I want things with us to be as good as it gets, for as long as it may be."

"I, too, though I confess that I always envied Micah the love you two had, from that first night after my debate, when he was so earnest, and you were so charming. Perhaps I subconsciously wondered what it would be like to feel the love that seemed so palpable between you two."

"You must have had loves, Daniel. Not to pry. Micah told me you were always in the company of beautiful women in all your travels. Was there no one you wanted to marry? I'm going to be nosy now, so you must open up to me." Anne smiled and reached out to hold Daniel's hand in hers.

"Yes, well, of course you must want to know," Daniel said, pouring a last cup of the strong Italian coffee as he sorted through his thoughts, selecting, censoring, and finally opening himself to Anne as he never had to a woman before. He realized this as he spoke, and he relaxed and talked, in a stream of consciousness, for almost an hour, as they sat, absorbed, focused on Daniel's story, oblivious to anything and everyone around them, in a place of their own.

"I suppose my story is a classic workaholic's tale. One opportunity after another, each consuming my life for a period . . . first school, then my clerkship, then my apprenticeship. I became a victim of my successes, unable or unwilling to miss an opportunity to excel. I enjoyed my work. I wasn't hiding some brooding psychological hurt; I really loved each project—wouldn't, couldn't give any of them up."

Anne knew about most of Daniel's professional chapters, but the details interested her, and the personal parts she always speculated about slowly became part of Daniel's story.

"Oh, my school chums wondered if I liked boys, as one after another of them were married, and it seemed only I remained a bachelor. But that was never my bent—pardon a bad pun. No, when I looked up I was a mature man, and frankly, I must admit, one who grew to enjoy the irresponsibility and utter indulgence of that life. At a certain time, a time I never recognized or acknowledged, I concluded that family life was not one I was destined to have. I sublimated, I suppose, as the avuncular friend to all my colleagues, and doting godfather to Daniel, indulgent godfather to others. I frankly presumed I'd never live with a woman."

"But weren't there—" Anne started to ask.

"There were two women I had real love affairs with. One English, the other Israeli, actually. Each was ready to become my wife, but I was not sure—never sure enough, and let their ultimatums go by. I've wondered at times if that was a mistake. I wanted children, actually sublimated those feelings with yours, Cassie's, other friends. You know I do love yours, truly. I wonder how they will take our new relationship."

"Happily, I should think," Anne answered. "Cassie and Danny have both urged me to go out and have a social life. Josh always viewed you as part of the family. And your namesake and I have become closer since my—since Micah left—than ever before."

"Yes, but he loves me as an uncle. How will he think of me as your lover? He may view this as incest," Daniel joked.

They laughed and sat in silence for a moment.

"Then," Daniel paused, resuming his story, looking long at Anne, "then this happened. Perhaps I loved you from the first time I met you, but never allowed the thought to emerge, out of respect for you and Micah. And frankly, because it never occurred to me that you would even consider me as anything more than a dear friend."

Anne held Daniel's hand, saying nothing except what she told him with her eyes. Plans, agreements, details would come later. "Let's walk. Come, my dear friend." Hand in hand they strolled across an old bridge and into a labyrinth of winding streets, into a time and place of their own.

Where that "place" would be, in fact, remained an open question.

SEVENTEEN

Old Love, New Love

❧❦❧

A week after her return to California, Anne was not asleep, but was still lazing in her bed at 7 a.m. thinking about the day ahead, when the phone rang.

"Anne, good morning! I just couldn't wait to tell you my news."

"What news? Where are you? What is happening?"

"I'm at my club, actually, but I've just come from a meeting of the committee. You remember my telling you of the group of superstar businessmen who watch the world for budding anti-Semitism and problem solve—"

"Yes, yes, I remember."

"Well, they've made me a proposal that could resolve our dilemma about living on two continents."

"Tell me," Anne interrupted.

"When I told them at the end of our regular meeting today about us, that I was planning to retire to be with you and remain a consultant only with favored clients under some ad hoc arrangement, they all looked at each other smilingly. Appears they'd been hatching a plan to move their center from London to New York City. They'd like me to manage it there.

At my own pace. They know I want to get off the treadmill, and they agree. They want me, and accept my terms."

"New York?"

"Yes, what do you think?"

After a pause, Anne responded. "I never thought about New York. But I will. I like the idea of starting someplace fresh, without memories, someplace we can make our own." Daniel smiled to himself, pleased by Anne's sentiment. "But I'll miss my children. And my grandbaby."

"They'd have a reason and a place to visit," Daniel answered. "Think of it, my dear, and here's another idea. How about meeting me there next week? I'm to look for offices—no commitment for me to run it until you agree, they know that, but by looking around together we'd get a sense of whether you'd like it. You do, and I know I will."

"This is such a nice surprise. When? Where?"

"I'll make arrangements and call you tomorrow. Could you arrange to come, say, next weekend and stay, open-ended?"

"I don't see why not."

"There, then, it's a date. I'm excited to see you. I'll call as soon as I work out details. A bit later in the morning next time, darling."

"Oh, I'm awake now! What an interesting way to start the day."

Anne and Daniel spoke every day that week as their plans evolved. Daniel had booked rooms at the Lotos Club, which had a reciprocal arrangement with members of his club in London. Ms. Lockhart, the suave, white-haired real estate agent retained by the committee to help Daniel find office space—Anne would come along and advise—also showed them residential options. Daniel wanted to see co-ops in the midtown area near Central Park so he could walk to work. Anne wanted to see brownstones in Greenwich Village, which would feel more like a home in a neighborhood.

The week became two and then three, filled with busy days with the agent, learning the city's neighborhoods, much walking and gaping at the passing parade, and wonderful dinners alone at charming restaurants of every ethnic specialty, all small and modest and romantic.

They fell into their bed late each evening after a long postdinner walk, exhausted, exhilarated, and utterly happy.

"I thought New Yorkers were supposed to be brusque and unfriendly," Anne remarked one night over dinner at a family-owned Italian restaurant on the far west side. "I like 'em."

"Yes, I find it easier to know people here than in London. And they're more colorful."

"I like finding a place that can be our own, too," Anne added. "I'm warming to this adventure."

At one of their last dinners, they ate at a French bistro on the Upper East Side, recommended by their agent. Daniel clasped Anne's hand across the candlelit table. "It is time to talk about marriage, my dear one."

"You going to make me an honest woman, proposal and all?"

"Yes, I do want to do this. You must decide when and where."

"I've thought about it. Let's tell the children on my birthday next month. Can you come?"

"Of course. I'm not at this advanced age missing one important time with you. For anything or anyone."

"Well, we can tell them then. And actually do it, where, there? Then?"

"We could. Or we might do it here, in our new home, when we find it. Maybe Cassie and her husband Jonathan would fly over for a visit, along with the kids. What do you think?"

"I like that idea. Doing it at home is too compromised. It must be at *our* home. Let's do it here."

"It's settled, then. I shall try to arrange my affairs so after your party next month, I can come back here with you and, hopefully, settle us in a new place."

By the end of what turned out to be three weeks, three weeks that seemed a lifetime because they were so on the move, they'd found the perfect office for the committee, but not their perfect new home. That would come. But the decision to live in New York City simply occurred without an agonizing should-we, shouldn't-we debate. They both felt they'd found their new place. They would stay in a suite at the club when they moved there permanently until the right home materialized. Both had much to do before the move. Daniel would keep his apartment in London, so they would have a place on visits there. Anne would offer her home to her children, and sell it if none wanted it. "You can have your own investment portfolio then," Daniel advised, "and no expenses. Then the children can be sure their estate won't be affected and you will be provided for nicely should I . . . ." Anne admired Daniel's scrupulous sensitivity to her children and his protective attitude about her. But she blanched at even the idea of a second widowhood. "No, darlin'; I'm going first. If you leave me a two-time widow, I'll kill you," she teased.

And so, the lovers completed their plans. In remaining days when they were thousands of miles apart, they were giddy about their involvements with each other and consumed with their thoughts about their new future together.

❧⚬☙

Anne's birthday party a month later was at home, with the three children along with Cassie's Simon and baby C. K. and Josh's latest gorgeous girl of the month, an aspiring actress he'd been with whenever the tennis circuit allowed him to be home. Dan—like his namesake—was too preoccupied with his work to have a lover he'd bring to such an intimate family affair, so he brought a lady colleague, a best friend from work.

After drinks in the garden, all retired to a dining table lighted with a collection of candles and laden with bouquets of flowers, and all the best of Anne's china, glasses, and silver. "Ah, Mother, how beautiful. Your touch!" Josh said as they sat. Before anyone could say a word, Anne raised her glass: "I toast all the people I love so dearly, and thank you for being at my birthday party."

"No longer 64 and a half," Josh teased.

"Mother, we love you. I want to look as radiantly beautiful when I'm 50," Cassie added.

"To our role model, the love of our lives, our dear and perfect mother," young Daniel added.

In a brief moment, after he was sure that others had said what they wished, Daniel stood, wine glass raised. "My toast, on this very special occasion, is to the best person of *my* life. To one I have asked to be my wife." Daniel stared at Anne and she, silently, looked back at him only.

The long pause while Daniel's message was absorbed by the others at the table ended when young Dan rose and responded, "L'chaim. To life. To love, of two people all here love." Then Cassie rushed to hug her mother and Josh shook Daniel's hand while young Dan hugged him. Everyone chattered and moved about, until Anne said, "No one waited to find out if I accepted. So, let me respond: I do, my darlin', I do!"

The dinner, much planned and prepared with great thought and attention, appeared and disappeared over the course of the next hours, as all around the table chattered about the lovers' plans. "New York, no; Mother, why don't you do it here?" Josh pleaded. "Yes," Cassie agreed, "it should be here where all our associations are, not in some hotel room." "Hey, how about letting the parties decide their own wedding plans?" Dan suggested. Daniel and Anne listened, delighted at the children's reactions, smiling at each other as the banter continued until after midnight.

"Well," Daniel announced at a propitious pause. "We shall take all your pleas under advisement, as the courts would say, and Anne shall make the decision. My thought, after hearing all yours, is to elope to some justice of the peace with my bride, and then have a party for all of you wherever you please." Ceremonial plans were left at that point.

Anne and Daniel held hands as the children left, congratulating them, advancing final editorial comments, hugs and kisses. The lovers walked together to Anne's bedroom, tired and pleased by the evening, uncertain what was decided. "What do you think, Anne? You should decide this. Anything you like is fine with me," Daniel called to Anne, who was undressing in the adjoining bathroom.

"I don't know *what* I think, darlin'," she called back. "Let's sleep on it. I'm exhausted."

And so they did.

At their family brunch next day at noon, after greetings and orders and chatter and the consumption of a cornucopia of breads and jams and fresh fruit, Anne announced, "My dear ones. I've decided our question of last night. Daniel and I are going to Europe soon so he can conclude plans for his new life in New York. We're going to France and Italy and Turkey and Switzerland to see Daniel's lush conspirators. We will make an impetuous decision at some romantic time and place." Now Daniel was smiling, surprised but pleased by Anne's announcement. "And we will ask the ship's captain, or some small courthouse magistrate, or a rabbi in an out-of-the-way village, *someone*, to marry us. Then we will let you make a party wherever you wish, invite whom you want, and we will come, as husband and wife, okay, darlin'?"

"Okay," Daniel dramatically answered. "O, very, very, K."

And that is what happened. Their travels—Daniel's last walk around the international legal-political arena, really—were triumphant. In each city, they were treated royally by the committee members, who treasured Daniel. When they were in Milan, Anne asked Daniel one evening as they walked to their hotel after dining, "Darlin', remember that old synagogue you showed me in Venice?"

"Yes, of course."

"I want to go there with you and be married. There's something symbolic about that old quiet place. And then we can elope to *our* hotel. Can we do that?"

"I adore the idea," Daniel responded. "Yes, that's what we shall do."

When Daniel's work in Milan was complete, they drove to Venice, checked into their tryst hotel—they would always think of it so. They walked the next day to the Jewish quarter. The deserted synagogue, little used, was aged, its doors locked.

A store on that street that sold religious artifacts was open, but without customers. The proprietor, an aged and friendly elderly woman, knew a neighborhood rabbi who could open the synagogue and offered to run off and find him. "Aspettate, torno subito . . . one moment, yes?"

"Yes, okay, thank you," Anne and Daniel responded, then waited at a nearby small café at a table on the empty street, sipping small coffees. Not long after, a small group of people approached: the shopkeeper, a rabbi, and the rabbi's wife, all smiling, waving effusively. "Buongiorno! Prego, venite." Negotiations were awkward because no one spoke the same language, but through acting-out of nuptials, the idea eventually was understood. "Ah, un matrimonio!"

The small, celebratory group walked to the old building. The rabbi, using one of a collection of large antique keys on a brass ring, unlocked the marred, oversized wood door. The group entered the cool, musty interior where rows of aged benches faced a small altar with a crudely engraved arc of wood and metal. The rabbi's beaming wife left briefly and soon returned with a small bouquet of local flowers she handed to Anne with a hug and smile. "Per la sposa." With interlinguistic explanations and an ad-libbed exchange of Hebrew, Italian, and broken English, the rabbi eventually married Anne and Daniel, simply, without benefit of family or planners.

"Congratulazioni!" the rabbi said to Daniel, shaking his hand energetically. "Mazel Tov," the rabbi's wife exclaimed to Anne, with hugs.

The shopkeeper brought from her store an old, engraved wooden music box that played Baroque music by Antonio Vivaldi for this impromptu event. After the ceremony, Daniel insisted on buying it for Anne as her wedding present, and the shopkeeper, initially reluctant, eventually was persuaded to accept Daniel's outsized offer. When all was done, the small wedding party parted with embraces, gesticulations, and waves. "Arrivederci!" "Goodbye!" Daniel made a generous gift to the rabbi for his service and for the synagogue fund.

Anne and Daniel walked back to their hotel, where they enjoyed a grand lunch at the outdoor grill, watching the gondolas, the passing parade of walkers, inhaling the lazy afternoon, holding hands, sipping wine, ecstatically happy with life, with each other.

Daniel learned later, from their ever-informative concierge, that indeed Vivaldi had composed sacred music in the early 1700s for a historic orphanage in Venice for abandoned girls, many of whom became accomplished musicians at Ospedale della Pieta—Vivaldi's Virgins, he called them. There is a museum at that site, the concierge told them, offering to direct them to it. "I don't want to go there," Anne whispered to Daniel, "I just want to believe Vivaldi—or the spirit of Vivaldi—wrote this piece of beautiful music for us—for our wedding."

How different from my ceremony in a hospital room, Anne thought to herself later in their room. Except that the best man was now the groom.

The "old" married couple left Venice the next day and flew to London. Daniel met with his organizational mentors for a long day of transition arrangements, while Anne celebrated with her friend Cassie and shopped for special gifts—wedding presents for her children. "At this age, the bride buys her offspring presents after the wedding, for encouraging her, or at least reserving their condemnations," Anne joked.

The next day the new couple flew to New York City so Daniel could begin the office transition, made easy because the organization's longtime administrative assistant in New York was a formidable organizer who liked Daniel and was delighted to be now in the center of the group's action rather than alone in a satellite office. Daniel and Anne were still to find their perfect home.

Next the travelers flew to Los Angeles to officially celebrate with the children. At that point, they were travel weary, and accepted the children's joint offer of a week's vacation in Hawaii as their wedding present. They'd rented a small house on a private beach on Oahu, which was just the tonic for Anne and Daniel.

"We're sexagenarians, you know, running around like pups," Daniel kidded.

"This is perfect," Anne added. "Just what we want and need."

EIGHTEEN

Love at a Later Time

On their final evening in Hawaii, after a languorous beach day, they dined at their private seaside retreat. They'd walked and swam all day and been bleached by the sun, refreshed by the soft, steady sea breezes. When they returned to their beach house, in her Greta Garbo voice, Anne purred to Daniel, "Darlin', tonight let's not dine out; I just *vant* to be alone." Daniel quickly arranged for dinner to be delivered to their lodge from their favorite small, local restaurant with a shack in back that roasted local fish and served it packed in rice and wrapped in leaves. When dinner was delivered, Daniel perched a bottle of white Bordeaux in a silver wine holder to chill. They had long, hot showers, dressed comfortably—Anne in a flowing linen muumuu, Daniel in a long white shirt and tan slacks, both of them barefooted—and sipped iced rum drinks, sitting side by side on their deck. As they sat, silently at first, dreamily staring at the florid sunset, listening to the soft sluicing sound of water at the edge of the beach, Anne eventually looked over at Daniel, and took his hand.

"Darlin', you know," she started, then paused, slowly continued. "I'm so happy, in a way I never felt before."

"How's that, my dear?"

"Well, you know, with Micah it was different." Anne for the first time talked openly about Micah, reflecting with candor. "Our fallin' in love on the boat coming to England, it was a surprise, young people finding first love. We were full of romance and the world seemed—new—ours alone. As if we'd invented love. And he was tender, and dear, and for those, it seems minutes now, those months before my accident when the world changed us into old people without our realizing, everything was natural, intimate, privately so, just what I'd dreamed falling in love would be."

Daniel listened. In a while he stood to bring them a fresh drink. He wanted Anne to continue her openness, and he feared any comment from him would interrupt, take her off that track.

"Did I embarrass you, darlin', talkin' that way about my love life?"

"No, no indeed, *please* do go on. This is something we needed to get to, but only when you wanted. You must continue."

"After the accident, it was as if we were old people. We lost our love child. I was working to recover for years. Micah worked so hard, in law school, and building his practice. Then our family came, it seemed 1, 2, 3, and every day was a routine, work, family, you know. Not that *any* of this was bad. It was fine, and real, and we were very fortunate. But, I don't know how to say this without feeling selfish, darlin'. I don't want you to think I'm a spoiled . . . ." Anne trailed off and was silent for a moment.

"I don't think that. And I'm curious, embarrassedly so, to know everything about you I don't know—your life and thoughts, happinesses and sorrows, everything."

Anne continued, "But, you know, something is lost, this is probably heresy to say, something is lost in a long love life. One never recaptures the romance. Of course, one can't. And, yes, there are all the compensations—devotion, shared good times, dutiful respect, certitude, I guess you'd call it. But we grow, you know, and two people can't grow in tandem, so inevitably you grow differently, and you both know that, and perhaps it is good, perhaps it is not. So, one weighs the, what would one call it, the pluses and minuses, I suppose, not that one does that calculatedly, consciously even. But the reality sets in, and then, when one discounts the dissatisfactions because one knows the value of the satisfactions, inevitably one faults the other for the things missing. Does that make sense?"

Anne paused. Daniel remained silent. They held hands, looking into the darkening distance. "This must sound terrible to you, darlin'. Like I'm complaining, and I don't mean to.

"I seemed to want more than Micah could give, even comprehend. It was like I was a schoolgirl wanting a lifelong crush, and Micah was playing Love or Consequences—first you have a love affair, then the rest of your life you pay the consequences, working for your family, caring for your invalid wife, nursing the world's wounds. How naïve I was. How unfair to Micah, who I knew never loved another woman, never asked for more than I could give. I loved him, yes, but I know I let him know I felt disappointments."

"I understand. This is uncanny," Daniel finally answered. "Our image of one's friend's lives is so superficial. And I know Micah was always—your servant, really. Adored you. Yet, later on I did have the sense in some of the things he said, things I'd never question. Men don't do that, do they? About you. He seemed perplexed, baffled, about what he thought you wanted. I had the sense he felt you were not unhappy, perhaps unsatisfied, about something he could never understand, and so couldn't provide."

"Yes, some book I read said that in marriage couples move from biology to history. And that's okay. But I think we went too quickly. Because of me, really. I think Micah fixated on me being an invalid. He was careful and thoughtful, and delicate, and solicitous. And sometimes I wanted to be passionately overwhelmed. See what you've found yourself with, an overheated old lady." Anne smiled, squeezing Daniel's hand.

"So interesting. And for me it was the reverse. One passionate, short-lived affair after another—not that there were so many, my dear; don't misunderstand—but my life probably seemed ideal to my married friends. Yet for me, looking in on, say, your marriage with Micah, made me feel as if I was leading a superficial life. Animals cohabit, for goodness sake; human beings aspire for more."

"So what's different with us, with me?"

Daniel was silent for a moment, then answered. "Flaws, my darling. You don't have them. There, I'll regret saying that when we have our first quarrel."

"What do you mean? I'm full of flaws."

"Of course. We all are, really. But I've been so impossibly fickle. Something about every woman would, would seem to spoil it for me. Something they'd say, or do—little things, really. But they would have a crushing impact on me."

"Like what?"

"It might have been anything. Things that seem unimportant in hindsight. Something she would say about a subject under discussion. An observation about events. A revealing personal moment, a look, a private act observed."

"Sounds like you were a demanding critic."

"For a long time I thought I was hypercritical, to a fault. That my critical faculty was too sensitive. Then, there has been you."

Anne held Daniel's hand tightly, saying nothing.

"I'll make a confession to you. I idolized you, from afar, always. Thought I should find a woman who was what you seemed to be. Not that I was jealous of Micah, or coveted my friend's wife—it was different. You are the model I reached for, never found. Until now."

Anne listened, not wanting to interrupt, curious to know more, to know everything she had wondered about Daniel. She rose and brought them sweaters to deflect the early evening chill, not wanting to break the mood of privacy, of intimacy, of complete candor, by stopping to move inside and end their shared disclosures. Dinner could wait. It was as if the darkness made opening up to each other easier, more natural.

Daniel continued. "When all *this* happened, it was an epiphany for me. I still feel young, though I know I'm not. And I want desperately to have everything I care about now. To savor. For as long as I have." Anne stared at Daniel as she listened, deep in her own thoughts about all that he was saying.

"I know I, we, can never have what you were describing. First love, it's magic. But I don't regret for a minute what we *do* have. Precise love. Known love. You are, my darling, exactly what I want for the rest of my days. I know that I adore watching you in every aspect: gardening, walking away, in your shower, the way you smell, your sweet look after we make love, everything. That is my dividend for all that came before. All I missed. All I wanted. Want."

"Did you ever think of me that way when Micah was alive?"

"Yes, I confess, though I suppressed it, made certain not to show it."

"You never did. I wondered, though."

"I do feel that a man and a woman cannot be friends forever. It has to lead to romance, or to backing away."

"But if Micah had lived . . . ."

"I'd have backed away, faded into some kind of distant old age. We'd have corresponded on birthdays."

Anne laughed.

"You know, my darling, my life as a successful barrister would have been so incomplete. So privately empty. As I look back on my life, I regret only the things I did not do—never the things I did do. Being in love with you, this is so much more life-sustaining for me than any of my professional accomplishments. I only want to be with you for the rest of my life."

Anne smiled, holding Daniel's hand. Both of them stared silently at the vast starred sky, at peace, in love, in awe of their good fortune. The past was past. Their wonder was what their future would bring.

"Do you ever wonder whether winter love can be as wonderful as a spring or summer love, my darling?"

"It isn't whether it is *as* wonderful, dear one; late love is simply different, wonderful in its own way."

"It isn't fair to question that, is it?"

"But you've had both. I've only had one. You shall be the expert," Daniel whispered.

"I suppose one's needs and opportunities change. But the quality of our feelings does not."

"It isn't a question of better or lesser. Both are wonders. Your time with Micah evolved from young and passionate love to dutiful partnership, not out of intent, but out of need. Your first love was special, and while it was cut short, it never ended. Never will."

Anne listened quietly, thoughtfully.

"Ours," Daniel continued, "may be less intense than first love is . . . maybe not always," he added, smiling. A twinkle showed in Anne's eyes and a half smile showed on her face.

Daniel continued, "But our love is sure, planned, and totally indulgent. That's what late life gives us as we get older. Our time together will be total—uninterrupted by work, by family, by anything. I intend to hoard you." Anne's smile widened at this.

Looking deeply into Anne's eyes, Daniel quoted lines of Robert Browning, from a poem, he told Anne, that he always liked but didn't fully understand when he read it as a young man. The lines so clearly captured their lives now.

Grow old along with me!
The best is yet to be,
The last of life, for which the first was made.

"How lucky I am," Anne responded. "To have had such first *and* last loves of my life."

"Comparisons are for the novelists, I suppose," Daniel mused. "For us, for lovers, the only time is now. For me, the only one is you."

They clinked glasses. "St. Augustine's words," Daniel toasted Anne: "Late have I loved you, O Beauty." Anne smiled, nodded. Daniel added, "To which I add my own: And long and forever may it be."

Epilogue

She did it so well, my C. K., now such a fine and wise young woman, such a sensitive author, no less. It truly happened just as she wrote it. C. K. portrayed my story, gave my life a coherence I never would have seen. What a fine artist this child is. How blessed I am. In these final years, I will reread her story, my story, again and again.

Little time is left. After Daniel died—we had ten wonderful years together in New York City—the children persuaded me to return to California. Our New York years were wonderful—rich filet mignon years, Daniel once remarked. We lived so well. Had so much of each other—more personal, intentional time, strangely, than Micah and I had in 40 years, because it was so centered, so indulgent. We had many pleasant acquaintances in New York, but no true deep friends there. "You can make new friends," Daniel toasted to our dear visiting London friends, "but you cannot make old friends."

So when he left me, two hearts broken, I moved to the wonderful new retirement facility our UCLA center created. They pamper me, and all the newest possible medical facilities are right there when I need them. The children and my grandchildren are a joy. Josh's are even nearby.

Only my young Dan, not so young now, never married. He is so caring with me that I see him more than the others. I think he's still making up with Micah through me.

All the things written about Micah when he died, and Daniel, in many countries where he is remembered, do not equal in pure joy what my dear young C. K. wrote about them in this, my old-fashioned love story.

Acknowledgments

My boundless gratitude is owed to my very thoughtful, helpful editor Jon Malysiak, and my friend and colleague Gerrie Sturman. Thanks also to Max for the drawing and Jody for suggesting the title.